MARGARET O'DONNELL was born in 1932 in Merthyr Tydil in Wales and was brought up in England by her grandmother and aunt after her mother died when she was three. She married twice and moved to Ireland in 1968 with her second husband and her three sons. After a number of difficult years for the family when her husband went back to England in 1972, leaving her liable for his debts, she got a job with Family Planning Services, which provided free contraception at a time when women couldn't access it through their GPs. At this time she became involved with the campaign to legalize contraception for all (contraception being illegal in Ireland from 1935 to 1980 as a result of Catholic teachings on sexual morality.)

She moved to Kildare with her partner in the late seventies and threw herself into the renovation and expansion of an old thatched cottage. Being a highly talented and creative person she was equally at home wielding a large power saw or drill as she was weaving ornate tapestries and making batik paintings. Also an accomplished and passionate gardener, she created a stunning garden in the grounds of the cottage.

During these years, she found time to write *The Beehive*, drawing inspiration from her earlier struggles and later activism in the misogynistic Ireland of the time. While she started on a second book, she was not engaged by it, and did not write anything else after *The Beehive*.

Her relationship broke down in 1990 and the cottage had to be sold. She moved to an old farmhouse in Wicklow, which she also imaginatively renovated. She moved to Kerry in 2002 to help care for her granddaughters, and imported a Swedish timber home, which she lived in until her death on New Year's Day, 2019.

MARGARET O'DONNELL

THE BEEHIVE

VALANCOURT BOOKS

The Beehive by Margaret O'Donnell
Originally published in Great Britain by Eyre Methuen in 1980
First Valancourt Books edition 2024

Published by Valancourt Books, Richmond, Virginia
http://www.valancourtbooks.com

ISBN 978-1-960241-20-7 (paperback)
Also available as an electronic book.

Set in Dante MT

One

Sarah was insistent. 'Are you sure you weren't followed?'

'Of course I am. If any of the guards had seen me, they would have taken me in.'

'For God's sake, Steph, have some sense. They know our organization exists now—they're not going to pick you up if they think you will lead them to the rest of us.'

Stephanie's mind flickered urgently over the short journey from the hostel to the derelict building they were now in. 'No. I wasn't. I'm sure.'

Sarah relaxed slightly, wondering if the others had noticed how tightly her nerves were stretched. She had thought that the start of positive action would have released some of the tension inside her; but it had not. It had grown each day since they had made the first move that had committed them, and all the other women, to the Rising. This was no longer the intellectual exercise that they had amused themselves with for so long: it was now an independent thing, with its own momentum and irreversible course, that would either achieve their aims, or destroy them all. She looked around the small group, waiting silently for her to begin, and wondered how they would react if they knew about her fears and doubts. To them, she was a cool, clear mind that had worked and planned to the smallest detail; a mind that had no room for fears and uncertainties. She pushed the thoughts away from her and quietly assumed the role allotted to her. She turned to Joan first, knowing that the efficiency of the woman would calm her. 'Did we manage full distribution?'

Joan unconsciously hitched her glasses on her nose as she unfolded the sheet of paper and prepared to give her brief report.

Sarah's tension relaxed even more, Joan's routine preparations telling her of the success of the operation even before she spoke. She had spent so much time working and planning with these women that their automatic gestures conveyed as much as their spoken words.

'We completed the full print run of fifty thousand on time and without incident. Our arrangements for getting the papers out of the printing place worked beautifully and the runners got their quota for distribution by just after nine-thirty. Distribution was started at midnight and finished by five-thirty.' Joan glanced at the attentive women. 'As you know, this was the part of the operation we were most worried about, because of the number of women involved and the difficulty in co-ordinating them all. The whole thing went very smoothly, with the exception of one incident, and all the papers were distributed as planned.'

Joan sat back and waited for the inevitable questions as Sarah's mind raced. They could not afford any unplanned incidents at this stage, however small. 'What was the "incident", Joan?' she asked.

'It was in area eight. We were given incorrect information about the movements of the guards. The runner was outside the gates when spotted but she was lucky, as she had finished distribution.'

'Was she caught?' The question came, simultaneously, from two women.

'Yes.' Joan's voice was carefully emotionless. 'She was fortunate that she had nothing incriminating on her, and the guard was alone and bored. He beat her up rather badly.'

Sarah's voice cut across the silence, dragging the women away from their private thoughts. 'Who was responsible for charting section eight?'

'I was.' Eli withstood the looks of the women; self-confident, assured. 'It was researched thoroughly and all information double-checked. If the report back is accurate, then the guards' schedule was altered on the night.' She sat back in the chair; a big woman, physical and aggressive.

Sarah probed. 'Could they have known that you were monitoring the guards?'

Eli was reluctant to concede the possibility of any flaw in her work. 'Well, yes I suppose so, but it's very unlikely. And, surely, if the guards had been alerted in any way, that one wouldn't have risked what he did. He would have arrested her.'

It was a valid point and one that Sarah was prepared to accept.

'But even if he didn't suspect anything at the time,' commented another voice, 'he would have known later that she must have been responsible for the newspaper.'

Sarah controlled her impatience. It was Stephanie who had asked the question and she felt a special responsibility for her, for she was completely unequipped for all this cloak and dagger stuff. Sarah kept her voice casual. 'He wouldn't have been able to do anything then, without compromising himself.' She looked around at her companions, seeing a mirror of her own fears in each face, and pushed the meeting into movement again. 'I think we can assume that there won't be any repercussions from that incident. Joan, are you geared for the next edition?'

'Yes. The paper's in. We just need to go over a couple of the articles you want carried.'

'Ann, how's the strike register coming along?'

'At the present time, we can be sure of a complete shutdown in eighty-one per cent of Government offices, with severe disruption in the remainder. Fifty-three per cent of businesses will be unable to operate at all, and there will be considerable disruption in a further twenty-seven per cent. Sixty-two per cent of all shops will close; all domestic services will be severely disrupted. We'll be able to cut out all overseas and long-distance calls, but not all the automatic exchanges.'

Sarah hid a smile. Ann was incredible. Her world was peopled almost entirely by statistics. She had rattled off the figures from memory and she had worked out the odds in favour, or otherwise, of her own survival over the next few weeks. It would be interesting, Sarah thought with rather grim humour, to know what odds Ann would be prepared to give her.

'Do you need any help? Any extra women?' she asked.

Ann dismissed the suggestion with a small gesture. 'We still have the problem of the television and radio stations. We just haven't enough women in any of them to have any effect at all.'

'I still say we should add them to the bombing list.' Eli was sitting forward in her chair, challenging Sarah to reject the suggestion. Sarah hid her impatience. Eli was important to the whole operation and had to be handled carefully. Her problems were always black or white, as were her solutions to them. Her solutions were also, invariably, violent ones. Her hatred engulfed her, and over-spilt around her, until it became a tangible thing.

'I would prefer not to destroy the stations if at all possible,' Sarah answered. 'Ideally, we need the use of them. If we can't disrupt them internally, we'll have to find a way of jamming them. Surely, Eli, with the women you have in your section, you can come up with an efficient jamming device? If we could black them out when we need to and then come in with our own station, it would be far more effective.' She turned towards Eli, determinedly ignoring the aggression. 'Work on it, Eli. You've only got two weeks. If you can't come up with the answer, we'll have to add it to your bombing list.' The big woman was still trying to identify her dissatisfaction with this concession when Sarah continued, 'How are you progressing with supplies?'

Eli was diverted. 'We've enough explosive. The cleaners at the Ordnance Depot have had five years to get the obsolete stuff out. The problem has been the materials for the detonators, but we've almost solved that. We'll be ready in time, but I still think we should try and get into the ammunition dump.'

Sarah ignored the fresh challenge and accepted Eli's claim of readiness. She knew she could rely on her completely to be fully organized in her own area. The problem would be containing her once the operation started. A clash between them was inevitable and Sarah constantly looked inside herself to see if there was sufficient strength there. Doubts, however, were useless. Whatever happened, she knew that she would have to find the strength to control Eli's need to destroy. She turned to the gentleness of Stephanie.

'How are the medical facilities coming along?'

Stephanie moved restlessly on the wooden box she was using as a seat and shrugged. 'They are going to be very primitive. We can't get sufficient drugs or anaesthetics, and our level of medical skill is so limited. I just pray we can cope.'

Sarah tried to reassure her. 'If our plans work out, we won't need any medical services. You will just be sitting there all day with nothing to do. If not, I know you'll cope. You underestimate yourself, Steph.' She deliberately left unsaid that if their plans were not successful, no amount of medical supplies or degree of medical skill would help them. They would be wiped out.

Sarah looked around at the women. The cold, damp air of the derelict basement had eaten into them, taking away all colour from their faces and making them appear the same lifeless grey as their hair and the shapeless clothes they wore. The light from the small, naked bulb threw hard shadows, accentuating the bone structure, adding to the illusion of the walking dead. She wondered at the strength of these women who grew and developed behind the masks, who played the role of mindless zombies without ever mistaking the mask for the reality. Sarah felt a surge of her old sureness. These women were strong, as were all the others who had combined to put her plans into action. Their struggle to find their own identity and then to retain it, carefully hidden and guarded behind their anonymous exterior, had given them the strength to follow the plans through to the bitter end, if need be. And theirs was no blind emotional commitment. They had all calmly considered the situation and had arrived at the same decision. Gorston had sown the seeds of his own destruction when he had devised the Selection. What else would have banded together, so effectively, some of the best brains in the country? It was fitting, she thought, that one of Gorston's most vicious pieces of legislation would, in the end, destroy him.

'It's getting late,' she said. 'We'd better be getting back. I don't think we should risk another meeting until the Sunday before the Rising unless some emergency crops up. In that case we will use the usual method of contacting each other. Joan, we can get together on Monday to finalize the next edition.'

The women were already moving the broken chairs and wooden boxes that served as seating, and scattering them haphazardly among the debris and dirt of the partially demolished building. They all turned to look at Ann, partially hidden by the shadows as she gave a sudden small chuckle.

'Do you all realize that, with a bit of luck, we can all say farewell to this dirt and the rats after only one more meeting?' She gave a small grimace of disgust. 'I seem to smell of this dank decay for days after we meet here.' She turned to the door, which hung drunkenly from one hinge, where Eli was already waiting for her. 'Did I tell you that my birthday is the day after the Rising? I'll be twenty-nine then.'

The others hurried through the doorway after Ann, knowing what was in her mind but not commenting, leaving Sarah alone in the bleak room with an elderly woman who had not spoken throughout the meeting. Mary was a generation older than the rest of them and, while always ready with genuine kindness, she managed to maintain a subtle barrier between herself and the others. With the exception of Sarah. Sarah often wondered what made her unique, but accepted the fact gratefully. She found the older woman's company comforting and reassuring, as if there was no need to hide her doubts and uncertainties, no need to always project competence and sureness.

'What are you going to do about the runner who was caught?' Mary asked.

Sarah looked blank.

'The one who was beaten up. I'm sure Joan's women have taken care of her but—'

Sarah flushed at the rebuke. 'You feel I should contact her?'

Mary's hand brushed her arm. 'No. You're too busy using your head to know what to say to her. I'll go and see her.' She looked into Sarah's face as she sat directly under the harsh light and her voice was gentle. 'You should go home. You look very tired. And don't get offended by what I just said. The women need you as you are, with your head firmly in control. That's your strength.'

Sarah returned the look, sensing again the strong links between them. It puzzled her. She did not understand them; she only knew that they existed.

She turned and left.

The short journey back to the hostel was uneventful and Sarah entered the dark room gratefully. Mary was right, she was exhausted. She undressed quickly and felt a small satisfaction at leaving the heap of grey clothes on the floor as they fell. The dim light from the street lamp shone feebly on to the mirror and she crossed the room and stared at her reflection. It had been a long time since she had looked in the mirror and she experienced a shock as the grey face stared back at her—as grey as the faces in the basement. She unloosed the tight knot of hair and let it fall around her face. Grey hair to match the grey face. She always felt this shock when she caught sight of her reflection. She felt no grey inside her; she saw no grey in her thoughts. Her mind was full of colours, shades, varying moods. She bent forward, closer to the mirror, trying to utilize fully the fitful light, trying to catch a glimpse of the colours she knew were inside her. But the wide grey eyes looked back blankly, revealing nothing. Would she always look like this? A grey deception. She tried to imagine her hair as it used to be before she was eighteen and had to dye it. It had been blond, very blond, almost white. If they were successful, she would never have to dye it again. She turned away and climbed slowly into the narrow bed. Maybe it was naturally grey by now.

Two

Sarah placed the folder precisely in the middle of Nesbitt's desk, catching as she did so a faint smell of scented soap and whisky. He seemed to be drinking earlier and earlier in the day.

She crossed over to the tall windows, adjusting the shades to shield the bright glare of the early morning sun, and glanced into the busy street. The morning traffic was thinning as the cars filled up the parking places around the square, the odd car cruising slowly in the ritualistic search for an empty space. She looked back towards the heavily-built man lounging behind the desk. Drinking was only one of the signs of stress that he was showing lately, but she felt no curiosity about its cause. He touched her life lightly during the working day and dropped from her consciousness each evening as she put on her coat; and she knew that she existed in his mind only as an efficient machine.

She walked across to the desk, standing slightly to one side of it. 'There are seven letters for your signature and you have a meeting with Mr Hawkins this afternoon at four.' She understood the slight movement of his head and continued. 'You accepted the tender for the Government job that was submitted by Hawkins & Company. You're meeting Mr Hawkins this afternoon to give him the final specifications. A list of them, together with the time schedule, is in the folder.' She paused to see if he was listening to her. He was still sprawled in the chair in his customary pose, head tilted back, studying the ceiling, gently swivelling from side to side. As if in response to her silence, he pulled a pen from his top pocket and opened the folder she had placed in front of him.

'Do I have to read these?' he asked. She shook her head. 'And what damned Government job are you talking about?'

Sarah's voice was low and monotonous. 'You did discuss it fully with me three weeks ago. It's to arrange the public opening of the new People's Hall. Hawkins are the printers who will be printing the publicity material—all details are in the file.'

His attention had already wandered away from her as he finished scrawling his signature on the letters.

'You are also interviewing three men this afternoon—immediately after lunch—for a replacement for Mr Hollman. He's leaving in three weeks' time.'

'Hollman?'

Her face stayed expressionless. 'Yes, he gave in his notice last week. You'll find a résumé of the three applicants in the file.' She turned to the door and then hesitated. 'The first man you are interviewing is the artist who has just finished the commission for the large murals at the People's Hall. It may be politic to offer him the position.'

Nesbitt looked at her with a flicker of interest and then continued his study of the ceiling. He placed his feet, slowly and deliberately, on the desk top and settled down further into the chair. 'You haven't brought the coffee in yet.'

'I'll get it.'

He waited until she reached the door before he spoke. 'Hillard. Those murals—the ones at the People's Hall. Have you seen them yet?'

'No. I was down there last week discussing the seating requirements but the canvases were still covering them.'

'It would be worth your while going down again,' he suggested. 'See if you can get a look at them.'

'So that you'll know what they are like before this afternoon's interview?'

Nesbitt looked hard at her, searching for some sign of the sarcasm her words implied. She returned the look coolly and turned back to the door.

'I'll get your coffee.'

'No, leave it. I don't want it now.'

Sarah turned and left the room, quietly, glanced at the clock and decided to go to the People's Hall immediately. Allowing half an hour to view the murals and another half an hour to type up the report that would enable Nesbitt to air his artistic knowledge at the interview, she would still have an hour to loiter along the canal banks. At this time of the day, the wide grassy verges were deserted and the still water gave her an illusion of peace and solitude.

The sun had disappeared when Sarah walked down the steps from the office, the sky was threatening with a sudden summer shower and casual walkers hurried their pace as the first, large, lazy drops started to fall. She was still thinking about the conversation with Nesbitt. Did he always have to play that game about the coffee? He did not even like coffee, but they always went through the same ritual every morning; as if he needed continually to remind her of her position; or, maybe, he needed to reassure himself of his. Both of them knew that it was she who ran the firm. He had gradually become content to fill the chair, confident in the security of his position, atrophying with boredom.

Someone jostled her arm, jerking her back to the reality of her surroundings. The rain was heavier, giving a false sparkle to the streets, and she looked at her fellow pedestrians—nearly all women. They clustered in small groups, or walked in pairs, sheltering from the rain underneath umbrellas and turned up collars. How odd—they never seemed to walk alone; always the need for a companion. Sarah vaguely wondered why. And the prams—everywhere prams, babies, toddlers. Toddlers clutching at skirts, demanding attention, jealous of the adults who monopolized their mothers' attention. And colours—strange she had never registered them before. Maybe the wetness of the rain accentuated them. She crossed the street, pausing to avoid the clusters of women and children half sheltering in the brightly-lit shop doorways. She looked at the coloured clothes of the women, savouring the distinctions between the reds and the greens, the blues and the yellows. And their hair, half hidden under headscarves and umbrellas but still with the differing colours showing clearly—brown hair, black hair, copper. Her eyes caught sight of blond hair and her pace unconsciously slowed as she stared at the woman, bending over a small boy, dabbing at his face ineffectually with her handkerchief to remove the traces of some bribe. The woman became aware of the intrusion by a stranger and looked across the street into Sarah's eyes. The stare held for a moment, an anonymous chance contact, and then the woman's eyes roamed over Sarah's hair and clothes before sliding away in embarrassment. She turned back to the child, her scolding now a shade too vehement.

Sarah turned away from the encounter and hurried up the wide steps of the People's Hall, Gorston's latest gift to the nation. She paused at the massive doors, steeling herself for the immensity that lay beyond, remembering the dismay she had felt last week when visiting the monstrous building with a group of officials. Even with the hall full of irreverent workmen, the floor still scattered with the clutter of debris, she had felt dwarfed by the size of the place.

She pushed open the heavy door and stepped into the coldness of the entrance hall. It was empty, the workmen had gone, leaving no trace of their recent occupation. Sarah stopped, unprepared for the desolation that swept over her as she looked around the granite vastness, at the towering colonnades of sombre grey, their bases firmly earthbound in the equally sombre floor. She was dwarfed, exposed, a solitary figure crushed by these monstrous pillars that lumbered blindly into the shadows far above her head. She could dimly see the long gallery that ran the length of the hall, high up in the shadows; could see the balustrade where casual visitors could lean and watch the view below. How small it seemed and yet it was tall enough for people to lean on. The grey stones seemed to bear down on her, impressing her with their weight and indestructability. She must hide, find some corner, some shadow, where she could shield her own vulnerability.

She slipped into one of the alcoves, the granite striking cold against her shoulders, and she turned her face towards the towering column, her arms partially embracing it, as if, for a moment, she could be at one with this hateful, immutable personification of life. The cold bit into her cheek as she pressed closer against the hardness and all her reality ceased outside her weakness and desolation. It was unthinkable that she could pit her strength against this rock; better, far better, to embrace it, yield to it and relinquish all hope. The cold struck deeper into her body as she clung to the stone until, slowly, it came to her that there was warmth on her face. She drew away from the pillar, fingers touching her cheeks, tears trickling between them, bringing back warmth. She waited passively, patiently, for the wave of helplessness to pass. A small grey figure merging into the massive stone. She could not give up hope. No matter how powerful and immutable this society was, no matter how small her significance, she could not give up hope. She would continue to try and destroy it.

Hands rammed hard into her pockets, Sarah walked into the centre of the hall. 'Is anyone there?' she shouted.

'There, there.' The echo came back from the empty vastness.

She waited. Maybe the workmen were at lunch.

'Anyone there?'

'There, there.'

She looked around her, head tilted back to look into the dark recesses of the roof. Suddenly she spun on her heel, a look of delight on her face. She threw her arms wide, encompassing the whole vastness. 'You are nothing.'

'Nothing, nothing.'

This towering edifice that had dwarfed and terrified her was blind, unfeeling, unthinking. Its weakness was built in, an integral flaw, hidden from itself, but not from her, and not from the women. They would destroy it because it was blind. She stood there and looked again at the distant, high, gallery, her hands back in her pockets, her stance upright, defiant.

'You will fall.'

'Fall, fall.'

'I thought I heard someone.' The workman eyed her with resentment, a half-eaten sandwich in his hand.

Sarah turned, her face expressionless. 'The murals, I've come to see the murals.' She offered her authorization card but he had already turned away.

'Through there.' He hooked his thumb in the direction of the Inner Hall.

It was almost a replica of the entrance hall but on an even greater scale. She walked through the archway with confidence, prepared for its size.

Colours sang at her from all sides; strong, vibrant, alive. She stopped abruptly, then slowly turned, looking at each wall. It was real. There on the granite walls, obliterating them, transforming them; colours, movement, emotions, hopes and fears; aspirations soaring upwards; people alive and living, fulfilled and striving. It was all there, throbbing with vitality and sweeping her up into its being. She looked, in wonderment, at the captured elements: the woman's hair echoing the supple resilience of the trees, bent by the wind in the high places; the broad shimmering expanse of the powerful sea; the evening sun reflecting off the silver striations, evidence of many births, still, strong, fertile; and the brown, warm earth, responding to the labours of the people, abundant, rich, generous. And there were the people, loving and laughing, striving and assisting, in harmony with the elements and with each other. Unison and balance, the unit combining and blending, becoming the whole.

How did this happen here? In this place? And who?

She walked around the walls, touched with wonder at the joy on the faces of a young couple, climbing the wind-swept slopes of a stony mountain, looking closely into the face of an old man, lined and wrinkled from life but with contentment in his pose as he watched the children roll and tussle on the cushioning grass. She moved back towards the centre of the hall to see the full sweep of grandeur of the rolling browns and yellows of the undulating hills, deepening to blue as the eye was carried further, upwards, blending, confusing, no clear delineation, with the vastness of sky, encompassing all.

How could one man's vision of life echo her secret dreams so closely? How could he portray, on these barren walls, her convictions that life strove for a balance, an equilibrium; where the weakest combined with the strongest; the smallest with the greatest; so all developed to their full potential, filling their allocated space in the whole.

She moved back to one of the walls, her fingers tracing the foam where water and stones met. She must meet this man, talk to him, question him. Were these his private visions, or had he experienced these vivid representations? The questions tripped over themselves in her mind. She sank to the floor, emotions drained. She had touched the depths and the heights in a few short minutes and now she was numb. She sat still, staring at the walls but unable to absorb any more, unable to react to the depicted dreams.

Gradually, she became aware of the coldness closing in on her from the grey granite, and pulled herself slowly to her feet. She could not bear to look on those murals again and kept her head lowered, eyes focused carefully on her shoes, standing on the granite slabs. She needed to tear herself away from the visions on the walls, back to the reality of her existence. She started to move slowly across the floor; black, shiny shoes; careful steps; two steps to one slab; rain splatters spoiling the shine; walking across the anonymous floor; through the archway and through the emptiness of the entrance hall; out into the city streets. She paused at the top of the steps, looking at the hurrying pedestrians, the rain forming puddles on the uneven road, and remembered the blond woman's eyes slide away from her, rejecting contact, embarrassed by her chance invasion. She walked quickly down the steps and joined the oblivious people, matching her pace to theirs. She was late. There would be barely enough time to type the report before the interviews. What would she put in it? She rejected the rhetorical question as she turned into the square. She would fill it with meaningless jargon and pseudo-intellectual phrases that passed as artistic appreciation, and Nesbitt would be satisfied.

It was already written by the time Sarah heard his step on the stairs.

'Hillard, did you see the murals?'

'Yes. The report is on your desk.'

'Waste of time, waste of time.'

She waited patiently for the explanation, idly noting the pink flush that spread across his face, disappearing beneath his shirt collar.

'You slipped up badly, telling me to appoint that fellow who painted the murals.' She breathed carefully, her face expressionless as he continued. 'He's a foreigner. Damn silly suggestion of yours. You know the official attitude to employing foreigners.'

Her voice was calm. 'He was born here in the city. I saw his papers.'

'I know, I know.' He waved her objections aside, impatiently. 'But he has spent most of his life abroad. Amounts to the same thing. Spends most of his time outside the country and then comes back full of crack-brained ideas.' He looked hard into Sarah's face, as if hoping to see some sign of discomfiture. He tried harder. 'I gather there's some fuss about those paintings of his that you went to see.' He turned to the door. 'Anyway, when he comes this afternoon, tell him the position is filled.' He stood there for a moment, his hand on the door handle, his decision made and issued, before going into his office, closing the door behind him. She stared at the closed door. He had needed to overrule her and some chance lunchtime gossip had given him the ammunition. There was no time left for her to change his mind.

The intercom on her desk buzzed. 'Yes, Mr Nesbitt.'

'When you speak to the fellow, be tactful about it.'

Sarah replaced the receiver, remembering the impact of the murals. She needed to talk to the man who painted them, and now her only chance of real contact was gone. She absently picked up the phone again as it rang briefly. Joan's voice sounded in her ear. 'There's a Mr Carl Tolland in reception. He has a two-thirty appointment with Mr Nesbitt.'

'I'll be right down.'

She continued to sit. 'I'm sorry Mr Tolland, but we cannot offer you the position. I know that you paint murals that perform miracles but you have spent too much time out of the country. You have returned full of dangerous ideas about life and freedom, and that cannot be tolerated. You do understand, don't you?'

What could she do? Her reaction to the murals still carried an immediacy and her need to discuss them was almost unbearable.

She found herself walking down the stairs and into reception, her mind still in a turmoil.

Three

Carl straightened his tie and grinned at the unfamiliar figure in the mirror. He looked like a tailor's dummy. He posed in front of his reflection, arms sticking out stiffly, head bent to one side. 'Certainly, Mr Nesbitt, I can start on Monday.' He turned away impatiently. He hated wearing a suit and a tie; come to that, he hated the thought of having to take a job. But the murals were finished and he wanted to stay in this cottage a bit longer. He knew that he would do good work here. Ridiculous law, not being allowed to stay in the country if he was not employed. And it was not as if he was a foreigner, although all the forms he had had to fill in before they let him into the country made him think that they considered him to be a Martian or something. They were keen enough to cash in on his international reputation, however. God knows how he would have managed if he had not had the official commission for the murals in his pocket. He was not even sure why he had wanted to come back. He had never thought very much about the country while his mother was alive, and after her death he had been too occupied with his work and with living to spare a thought for the little country he had left as a small boy, although sometimes he wished he had been able to get his mother to talk more freely about the peculiar society she had run away from. He glanced at his watch and closed the cottage door behind him. Must get there on time—make a good impression!—although he was sure his murals had not gone down very well with the Arts Government Department. Maybe they would black him. He grinned to himself as he swung the car onto the road, seeing again the look of dawning horror on their faces as he had pulled the canvases from the paintings. He could not really understand their reaction as he knew the murals were the best work he had ever done. But they obviously did not like them. Maybe they did not like to be reminded about life in this country. He certainly had not seen much sign of it on his brief trips to and from that monstrosity they called the People's Hall.

He turned the car onto the main road into the city. He would stay on after the interview, look around the place. He had worked obsessively on the murals for the last eight months, only stopping to drive home after the light had gone, to eat, sleep and return to his work. Since finishing the large paintings, a few days ago, he had been feeling the familiar emptiness that always came after an intensive period of work. He needed to relax and find enjoyment in the company of others before another idea drove him back to a hermit-like existence.

He remembered, with gentle nostalgia, the company he had relaxed in after his last exhibition in Paris. She had been very beautiful—large green eyes, that any man would be willing to drown in; hair, thick and shining, glinting copper as it swayed in rhythm to her walk. He smiled at the memory of the few tumultuous months they had spent together. God, she was beautiful when she was angry. He remembered the last row they had had. He still did not really understand why it had broken up the relationship. She had been waiting for him one evening, full of excitement about getting a job in one of the art galleries. All right, so he could have been more tactful about it, but it really was ridiculous, someone like that talking about building a career for herself. It was not as if she needed the money, and besides, what sort of a relationship would it have been with her working during the day? She knew he was expected to socialize in the evenings during an exhibition. They would never have seen each other.

Still, it had been a good time. He sighed contentedly at his memories. Come to think of it, he had not met any women since he had arrived in this country. The only ones he had seen were a few early-morning shoppers with their customary cluster of children, and some elderly grey-haired women. Maybe this ridiculous law applied to everyone—it certainly looked as if the younger women had a full-time job with their children. Maybe they had to go back to work when their families grew up. The economy seemed to have improved considerably since his mother's day. One of the few comments she had ever made about the country had been about the poor state of the economy.

He stopped at the traffic lights and glanced around at the neighbouring cars. They all seemed to be quite new, but they were all of the same type. How peculiar. And all the drivers were men. He glanced at each car as he passed them. Yes, he was right. All the cars were driven by men; there were not even any women passengers. He tried to remember what he had heard about the country before his arrival. Burdett was certainly amazed when he had told him about accepting the commission; in fact he had tried to persuade him against it. But what the hell was it he had said about the place? Unions were illegal, he could remember that. And something about the women. He shook his head in a small gesture of self-exasperation. He just could not remember.

Carl saw the bulk of the People's Hall ahead of him and knew his destination was the next on the right. He circled the square slowly, looking for number forty-three, and also for a space to park the car.

Once inside the building he hesitated slightly, looking for the receptionist, before walking over to a grey-haired woman sitting at a switchboard.

'Excuse me, my name is Tolland. Carl Tolland. I have an appointment with Mr Nesbitt at two-thirty.'

The woman turned her head and looked at him over the top of her glasses. 'Yes, Mr Tolland. He is expecting you. I'll let his office know you've arrived.' Her hands busied over the switchboard and he noticed the slender fingers of a young woman. He looked at her face, puzzled, and saw the firm jaw-line, smooth skin. From a distance he had thought she was one of the elderly women he had seen in the early mornings. Why on earth did she dye her hair that terrible colour? Did she think it was attractive?

'Mr Nesbitt's secretary will be right down.'

He dismissed her from his mind and thought about the interview. He wondered if Nesbitt realized his luck in getting him as his chief designer for this tin-pot little publicity firm. The joke was he may not be given the job if those Art Commission fellows had anything to do with it. Still, it would be something to laugh over with his friends when he did decide to go home.

'Mr Tolland.' A calm voice was addressing him. 'I'm Hillard—Mr Nesbitt's secretary. Maybe we could talk here.' She was leading him to a small table at the far end of the room. Grey hair, shapeless grey dress, flat black shoes—the clothes all these elder women wore. But she was young, the same as the woman on the switchboard. What the hell sort of place was this?

He took the seat she offered him automatically, all his concentration on her face. Smooth pale skin, with minute creases at the corner of the eyes; but the eyes—grey, pale grey and large, yet with no expression in them. Thirty—she must be about thirty, but those eyes were looking at him as if he did not exist.

'—our present chief designer is considering staying on—'

He listened to her voice without taking in the words. It flowed around him, cool, melodious, but remote. He forced himself to concentrate on what she was telling him.

'—so, of course, Mr Nesbitt cannot consider a replacement until Mr Hollman's plans are more definite.'

So, they were blocking him. He was not surprised. 'You are very kind.' His trite phrase covered the silence as he tried to come to terms with the effect this woman was having on him. He searched his mind to think of something to say that would make her register him, but she seemed content to sit in silence. Then she looked directly into his face and he felt a small fear, an unsureness inside himself that he had never experienced before.

'I've seen your murals,' she said.

He experienced a shock of surprise. That was the normal opening gambit of all the transitory women in his life—attracted by his fame and the mystique of his occupation. Was her strangeness just in his imagination, and strengthened by her weird dress and weirder hair?

'What do you think of them?' he answered, intrigued.

The face opposite him remained passive and blank. 'I'm afraid I know very little about art, Mr Tolland, but I found them interesting.'

He leant forward, feeling the familiar excitement about his latest work. 'It's the best work I've ever done. I've tried the same idea before but it never quite came off. But down there in that tomb, it worked. I could feel it growing, coming alive.'

There was no responding echo to his enthusiasm and he sat back, suddenly deflated. Her lack of response annoyed him and he wanted to knock down the barrier of passivity she had wrapped around herself.

He grinned at her, a boyish, conspiratorial grin. 'You've been very kind. Have coffee with me after work and you can commiserate with me that I'm not up to your Mr Nesbitt's standards.'

She sat looking at him for a long moment with those large, grey eyes. 'I'm sorry Mr Tolland,' she replied finally, 'but it's quite impossible. As you know, I'm restricted to certain eating places, and men are not very welcome there, I'm afraid.'

She stood up, forcing him to follow her to the door. What the hell was she talking about? He felt as if he had slipped sideways into another reality and he did not know any of the rules.

'I will contact you, Mr Tolland, if Mr Hollman decides to leave. Maybe you would still be interested in the position.'

She was forcing him to play her game. He tried to think of something to say that would break that calm gaze but there was nothing.

He walked down the steps, feeling her eyes still on him, and a rebellion against her disinterest flared up in him. He turned and looked up at her and raised his hand in a small parting gesture. 'I'll see you,' he said.

Carl sat in the car, trying to understand what had happened, trying to analyse the difference between that woman and all the others he had known. What was it she had called herself— Hillard? Was that her Christian name? If it was a surname, was it Miss or Mrs? No, she would not be Mrs; she was not married. It was not just her disinterest in him; he felt she was not interested in any man sexually. She proclaimed it in her dress, in her actions. But that was not quite right either. He stirred restlessly as he worried at the thoughts at the back of his mind. It was as if she did not know that she was a woman. That was it, or was it? He thought about the lesbians he had met. No, that definitely did not fit. He returned to his last idea and tried to remember how girl children behaved before they became sexually aware. That seemed closer, but . . . his thoughts petered out. What was it she had said about being restricted to certain eating places? Was she serious, or was it some peculiar put-down that he did not understand?

He turned the key in the ignition and reversed, at speed, out of the parking space. He would find out. He would go around this city and find out what was so damn peculiar about it. He drove the short distance to the main shopping centre and parked the car. He stood there, looking at the shoppers, the shops, the passing cars, and felt a bit foolish. It all seemed so normal. Where would he start? He wandered into a large store and found himself looking at an over-sized poster of a heavily-built, middle-aged man, with silver-grey hair, heavy jowls, proclaiming the slogan 'Gorston, the people's friend'. So that was what he looked like.

The display counters spread out before him, stretching the length of the store, artificial lights sparkling off the usual selection of goods. There was a scattering of women shoppers with their mandatory brood of children, but all the shop assistants had grey hair and grey clothes. He looked carefully at all the counters. They varied in age, he could see that now, but their hair was uniformly grey. He glanced back at the shoppers. They were wearing varied colours and their hair was of varying shades. It was only the shop assistants who were grey. For some reason, then, all the women who worked dyed their hair grey. He thought back to his meeting with Hillard. What had she said about having to eat in special eating places? He walked across to one of the assistants, seeing immediately he came near her that she was a young girl of about eighteen.

'Excuse me, could you tell me where the restaurants are?'

The girl turned towards him, her face blank. 'Fourth floor, sir. The lifts are to the right.'

She had looked at him in the same way Hillard had. He turned away, puzzled, and made his way to the bank of lifts, reaching them slightly ahead of a heavily pregnant woman struggling with bulky packages and complaining toddlers.

'Here, let me help,' he offered. He reached towards her, keeping the lift door open with his foot, and then drew back, uncertainly, as he saw the expression on her face. She was frightened.

'Do you want the lift?' he asked gently.

She shook her head. He stared at her for a moment before stepping into the lift and pressing the button for the fourth floor. Why on earth had she reacted to him in that way? The lift stopped and he added the new puzzle to the others in his mind as he stepped

out into the carpeted hall. The restaurant was large and indistin-
guishable from any store restaurant he had seen. They all seemed
to achieve the same subtle degree of planned anachronism and
he turned to look for another eating place. This could hardly be
the place Hillard had spoken of.

He walked down the wide corridor, past the euphemistic
Powder Room and the rather more stark Gents, and stopped at a
door simply stating Women Workers. Was it some kind of apart-
heid? He argued silently with himself. It was most probably for
the female staff in the store. As he hesitated, the door opened and
a grey-haired woman walked out, and Carl hurriedly walked on,
annoyed with himself. He was behaving like an idiot. A woman
looked at him with complete disinterest and he had to dream up
some bizarre reason for it, just to soothe his confounded male
ego. For all he knew, the stupid women were following the latest
fashion craze and thought that grey hair was the greatest turn-on
since hot-pants and boots. And it was not as if she was a raving
beauty. He could see her face again with his artist's eye; the plane
of the cheek and the sweep of the high, clearly-defined cheek
bones, carrying the eye towards the wide, grey eyes that looked
at the world through some invisible film. No, she was not beautiful, at least not according to the requirements of contemporary
beauty. He could not imagine her in the trappings of modern
fashion, but there was a depth to her that he felt had never been
revealed. He tried to imagine her still features mobile with emotion, but he could progress no further than her eyes. He shook
himself in exasperation; he was mooning like some schoolboy
who was experiencing the first, unrecognized stirrings in his
loins. He needed a drink. He headed back for the lift, lengthening
his stride as if to outpace his thoughts, when he caught sight of
the arrow. He must have walked straight past it as he came out
of the lift. 'Women Workers' Restaurant.' Was this what she had
meant? Each time he succeeded in pushing away his bizarre suspicions, something happened to make them surge up again. He
turned and strode in the direction of the arrow.

It was a small, drab room. Everything was brown, even the
sections of the gloss-painted walls, that had started life as a sickly
cream, were now streaked with the evidence of rust-stained riv-

ulets of condensation trickling down for countless years. A long brown counter stretched the length of one side of the room and the small brown wooden tables sat empty and repellent on the drab brown lino. He thought the place was empty until an old, grey-haired woman hurried painfully across to him from behind the high counter. She wore the same shapeless clothes as Hillard, except for the shoes; her swollen, deformed feet were encased in frayed carpet slippers; and her grey hair held no deception as the thin wisps broke free from the tight knot and clung to the sunken cheeks.

'The restaurant is up there, sir,' she whispered. Her eyes looked at his chin, but he felt that she was not seeing him.

'I'd rather have my coffee here, if I may.'

She turned submissively, and shuffled back to the counter on those painful feet, picking up a thick white mug. 'The restaurant coffee is much better, sir.'

She was trying to get rid of him. That was what Hillard had said. Men would not be very welcome. But he could not feel any resentment from the old woman, just a passive defeat.

'You don't want me here.' It was a statement, not a question.

She poured the brown liquid into the cup, hands trembling slightly. 'It's not for me to say, sir. You can drink your coffee where you please.'

Carl took a step towards her, impatience surging. He wanted a reaction from her. 'And you? Can you have your coffee where you please?'

Her hands spilt coffee from the cup as she instinctively pressed back against the wall with closed eyes. He could see her lips quivering, the small facial muscles twitching as she stood there. Her voice was low, monotonous, almost a chant. 'Gorston is the people's friend. Gorston loves me. I am nothing. I contrib—'

'Don't.'

His voice cut across the mindless words, needing to still this parody of a human being. He stared at her as she stood in the same stiff pose, eyes closed, hands trembling on the scratched, stained counter-top. She was sick. She should not be working. For heaven's sake, the woman ought to be in a home where she could be looked after. He needed that drink. She was not his problem.

He took the shallow stairs two at a time, too impatient for the lift, needing to feel the easy movements of his body and the co-ordination of his eye as he wove his way through the small groups of shoppers on the stairs. He hesitated, briefly, at the kerb, unsure of his direction, and then aimed for a small semi-basement bar he spotted across the road.

'Whisky, please. Straight.' Carl heard his voice quiver slightly.

The room was intimate, soft lights reflecting off the glasses, thick carpet absorbing any noise. Not that there was any. The bar was empty except for himself and the barman. He needed to think. Stupid of him to react like that to the poor, harmless old woman. He had been overreacting all afternoon—ever since he had met that woman at Nesbitt's.

He downed the drink in a single swallow and pushed the empty glass back towards the hovering barman with a nod.

He grinned at himself. He definitely needed a bit of relaxation. It must be all those months he had spent in that mausoleum working on the murals. The drink had done him good and he sipped the refilled glass and looked around the room. Not a bad little place to have stumbled on by chance.

'You visiting the country, then, sir?' The barman was anxious to talk, in these empty, quiet hours of the late afternoon.

'Yes,' Carl answered. 'How did you know?'

'Oh, you can always tell, sir. Different things, you know. Some-times it's the clothes, sometimes the accent. Now with you, sir, it's your tan. Great tan you've got there, if I may say so. Much too good for this old climate. Though I must say, we're not doing too badly so far this year. Fair bit of sun we've been having the last few days.'

'You're very observant.' Carl smiled at the thought of the sun lamp at the cottage. Locked away in the People's Hall all those months, the deep tan built up over a long succession of lazy, hot summers had started to turn to a sickly yellow. Not at all his image for when he returned to his old crowd.

'I've just been looking around your city,' Carl went on. 'First real chance I've had.'

'Oh, there's a fair bit to see now, no mistake. Have you seen the new People's Hall? 'Course, it's not quite finished yet, but it'll be a fine place when it is. The President will be opening it himself, y'know. In another couple of weeks or so.'

'Yes, it's very impressive. I tell you what struck me as rather funny, though.' Carl pitched his voice to match the casual bonhomie of his new friend. 'A lot of women seem to dye their hair grey. Is it some fashion craze I've missed out on?'

The man threw his head back, delighted at the innocent joke, and chuckled merrily at the ceiling. 'Lord love us, no, sir.' His mirth broke out again as he leant towards Carl. 'They are just the women workers. Fashion? There's no fashion there.'

'Then why do they dye their hair?'

The man paused in his chuckling. 'Because they're women workers.' His tone was the one used to explain the obvious to a child.

'I'm sorry—' Carl shook his head in bewilderment. The man just was not making any sense.

The barman leant closer, preparing to explain patiently to an unusually stupid customer. 'You see, sir, all the women workers have grey hair because—well, because, they'd look like proper women if they didn't.'

'But aren't they proper women?'

'Good heavens, no, sir. They're just the workers.'

Carl groped for a question that would make some sense of the man's words. 'So, when they get married, they stop dyeing their hair?'

The man looked at him with concern. 'They don't get married, sir. I told you, they're not proper women.' Another customer entered the bar. 'Excuse me a moment, sir.'

The man was an idiot, Carl decided; he was not talking sense. And what was worse, he was treating Carl as if *he* was the idiot. He finished his drink in a swallow and walked out to the street.

Maybe the man was partly right; he had been behaving foolishly. He had definitely over-reacted to Hillard and he had been letting his imagination run away with him. After all, this country was a dictatorship. If there was some stupid law about women workers wearing some sort of a uniform, it was not his concern how bizarre that uniform was. Anyway, he had had enough of this nonsense about the grey women. He had come into the city to relax, and the whole evening was ahead of him. First he would find a sauna bath, then have a few drinks before a first-class meal and finally visit a few nightclubs. He nodded in satisfaction at his plans as he got into the car.

Carl sat back, content. The barman had been absolutely right when he had recommended this restaurant. He smiled at the memory of the man's face when he had gone back to the bar and asked him to recommend a good place to eat. The poor fellow had thought that he was going to start asking about the women again. That really had been an excellent meal, though, and the service was first class. He gestured to a hovering waiter to refill his brandy glass and, stretching his legs luxuriously, looked around the room. The décor had seemed a bit overpowering when he had first entered, with all that deep red velvet and matching carpet, but now it seemed perfectly to match his feeling of well-being. He would linger over his brandy and cigar and then head on to the nightclubs. How peculiar, there still were no women here. When he first came in, he had thought it too early for many diners to be out, but the restaurant was now quite busy and all the customers were men.

The waiter hovered again, this time with the coffee pot.

'Waiter, do you always have this few women in?'

'This is a man's restaurant, sir,' came the reply.

Carl grinned at the little irony. Just his luck. The whole purpose of the evening was to find some pleasant female company and he had ended up in a 'Men only' place. He thought they had all disappeared with ankle-length skirts. He hesitated, wondering whether to ask the waiter to recommend a nightclub. He really was an excellent waiter, unobtrusively attentive throughout the meal, but he did seem a bit slow-witted. Even the question about the women customers had seemed to confuse him slightly. He would ask the head waiter, later.

He watched the smoke from his cigar curl slowly upwards before dissipating into the air. This was just the sort of evening he needed after all those months of continuous work. His mind wandered idly back to the décor of the room. That's what was lacking—they should have some paintings on the walls, luscious, over-developed nudes, perfect with the heavy opulence of the place. He imagined the walls peopled with voluptuous Goya females. The whole atmosphere demanded them. Whoever had designed the room should have realized it. He finished his brandy and prepared to leave, the head waiter solicitously inquiring about his meal.

'Excellent. It couldn't be faulted.' Carl was effusive. 'Except, perhaps in its absence of female company.' He looked at the man who was returning his look blankly. Oh, God, was he as slow-witted as the waiter? Nearly everyone he had spoken to in this city seemed to be stupid. He put on his coat. 'Could you suggest somewhere I could remedy that?' he persevered.

'Sir is a stranger in town?'

'That's right. The first night out I've allowed myself for a long time. It's much too early to finish it yet. I thought, maybe, somewhere where there were some bright lights and music.'

'Of course, sir. If you will wait a moment, I will get you a visitor's ticket for the Opera House.' He returned almost immediately and handed Carl a small card. 'It isn't very far from here but the roads are rather confusing.' He walked to the doors, explaining the route.

Carl pulled the car into the stream of traffic. The fellow had not been slow witted after all. The directions were a bit complicated but he had been very precise, although it seemed a peculiar way of arranging things—needing a pass before you were allowed in. It must be a very popular place. Carl wound down the window of the car as he crawled up to a busy intersection. The rain of the early afternoon had given way to sunshine and the warmth still lingered in the late evening air. He would meet Hillard as she came out of work tomorrow night and dispel the slight feeling of pique he still felt when he remembered the complete lack of interest in her eyes. He grinned to himself, his sense of well-being still strong. With a bit of luck, he would not be so susceptible to those large grey eyes the next time he saw them. He would turn up with a flask of coffee so that she would know he had called her bluff and they could drink it down by the river.

He suddenly realized that he was no longer driving through the bright street lights of the city centre. He was in a much narrower road of small houses, each one a replica of all the others, each postage-stamp of a front garden the echo of its neighbours, all silent testimony to the stultification of suburban life. Maybe that was what he would try and paint next. Suburbia, the phenomenon that cut across national boundaries, eliminated racial characteristics and reduced man to a grey, concrete anonymity. Come and live in a progressive society and become a suburbanite. He drove slowly down the road, his eyes caught by the parallel angles of the roofs, silhouetted against the soft, dark blue of the summer night sky; the faint after-glow of the city lights formed a subtle halo around the monotonous chimneys. The road seemed endless, sending out branches in all directions, all replicas of the parent trunk. He was lost.

He glanced around for a sign of life. Everyone seemed to go to bed ridiculously early here. He eventually stopped outside the only house in the long row that still had lights on. He would knock and ask for directions.

The front door flew open as he paused with his hand on the neatly painted gate. The harsh glare of the light streaming onto the narrow concrete path illuminated the pathetic blooms of struggling flowers, as a figure stumbled, in a flurry of limbs, to crash at his feet on the hard concrete. He stood in the sudden darkness as the door slammed shut, stunned by the sudden eruption of violence in the silent street. It was a woman, moaning in the monotony of pain. He touched her uncertainly as he fumbled for his cigarette lighter, and the moans turned to incoherent babblings at the touch. She was bleeding, the blood forming an indistinct shape on the concrete as the small flame flickered on the white face. Angry red weals stretched across the cheek, purple red marks on the jaw line, a thin trickle of blood oozing between the swollen lips. Anger flared in him as he bent to gather her in his arms. The woman needed to get to a hospital. He would get the police later and bring them back to deal with the animal who had done this thing. A woman joined him from a neighbouring house.

'It's all right. I'll see to her.' The woman leant over the prostrate figure, hands expertly probing for broken bones.

'Are you a doctor?' Carl asked.

'No. She'll be all right. I'll take her next door with me.'

His anger found an outlet against this woman who showed no emotion at the sight of such pain and suffering. 'What the hell is wrong with you? Can't you see she is badly hurt. She needs a doctor—X-rays.'

The woman looked up at him, a mixture of fear and bewilderment in her eyes. 'No. No doctor. I can take care of her.' She slipped her arm round the moaning woman and tried to lift her to her feet. 'Please go now. I can manage.' The fear showed more strongly in her voice as Carl stood looking at her. 'Please go!'

She was terrified. He looked from her to the semi-conscious woman, struggling weakly to get to her feet, and sensed a bond between them. He glanced at the house, now in darkness, and back into the pleading eyes of the woman. 'Please!'

He started to protest but stopped as the pleading flared to panic. He did not understand this. He felt a clumsy stranger who had stumbled into someone's private hell. He looked at the two women a moment longer and then turned and got into the car, grating the gears in his haste to get away from the hidden horror that surrounded him; driving back along the road in an effort to reach the lights of the city; a blind, primitive need to get out of the darkness.

Four

'How do you think he has taken the news?'

The two men sat in the back of the long limousine as it made its way through the park that led to the Presidential Palace.

Marsham, immaculate in his pin-striped suit, stared idly out of the window at the avenues of trees in full blossom. 'Well, of course, he can't admit to himself that the women were responsible; so, I assume, he will be ranting about foreign infiltrators trying to undermine the country. It's the usual sort of stand-by.'

'Do you really think that he can fool himself when the evidence is so strong?'

Marsham turned to look at his younger, dark-haired companion. 'He has got to, Martin. If he admitted even to himself that the women were responsible for the newspaper, he'd have to accept the fact that all his years of brainwashing and repression were unsuccessful. He couldn't stand that.'

'But surely,' Martin went on, 'that's overstating it slightly. How many women workers are there—about two hundred thousand? It would only take a handful to produce a paper like this. He can't believe that his whole programme is a failure because of a few that have somehow resisted the programming.'

'Well, I estimate that we are dealing with a group of about forty to fifty women.'

'As many as that?'

Marsham smiled briefly at the note of shock in Martin's voice. 'Yes, it surprised me too. But when you start working out how they distributed as well as printed it, forty to fifty is a conservative estimate.'

Martin persisted in his point. 'Well, even if we're dealing with that number of women, it doesn't invalidate the whole pro-gramme.'

Marsham leant across, his silver-grey hair briefly catching the light, touched his companion on the shoulder. 'My dear Martin, you are forgetting that we are not talking about a rational man. I agree with you, completely. The fact that forty or fifty women have got together and produced a newspaper like this doesn't mean that all the women are suddenly capable of independent and rational thought. But Gorston will be threatened by the fact that any of them can think for themselves, so he will have to believe that they are not responsible.'

The two men lapsed into silence as they followed their own thoughts. Martin, sitting upright in his corner of the spacious car, was serious and reflective; Marsham, lounging, was completely at ease, as his eyes still wandered over the rolling greens and well-spaced trees of the large park.

'How serious do you think this business is?' the younger man insisted. Martin was obviously still engrossed in the problem that had arisen the day before, when all the businesses in the city had received a copy of an underground newspaper, giving the first hint that there was some type of subversive group at work.

Marsham's manner remained casual. 'Not at all. I was surprised, of course. I still am. I can't understand how any of them could have retained enough personality and independence to have conceived such an idea, let alone implement it.' He turned to his companion again, with a slightly amused air. 'But what can they do? They have surprised us all by printing their claims, but they can't take them any further. They won't get support from anywhere, and without support, what can they do?' He shrugged expressively and returned to his apparent enjoyment of the scene. 'The interesting aspect of this whole thing is the fact that it may bring our plans that much closer to implementation.'

Martin glanced at him sharply, before smiling with a hint of amused exasperation. 'You old fox. I knew you'd be thinking along those lines, but you certainly played it close to the chest all morning.' His face resumed its habitual serious air. 'How do you think it will help? My immediate thought was Gorston's health, too, but if he refuses even to consider the possibility that the women are responsible, I can't see that any of the alternatives would put sufficient strain on his heart.'

Marsham gave up his pretense of looking at the scenery and turned to face his friend. 'Well to begin with,' he explained, 'it puts pressure on Steiner. He will have to pretend to Gorston that he believes in this foreign infiltrators nonsense and put up a show of tracking them down. He will also have to make sure that he finds the women responsible and eliminates them. Don't forget, the paper claims that they will print again in two weeks time. Steiner can't allow that to happen. He will have to find them before then. He may not be quite so interested in us with his hands full in those directions. If he can't prevent the women printing again, then we are really into an interesting situation. Steiner would have great difficulty in keeping Gorston calm under those conditions.' Marsham smiled a wide, ingenuous smile. 'How do you think Gorston would react if he found out that his Commissioner of Police was spending most of his time tracking down women because he still thought they were responsible for the paper?'

Martin stared at the older man for a moment as he worked out the possible implications. 'Well,' he began slowly, 'depending on how serious this heart condition of his is, it could result in a severe attack; if not, it would certainly put Steiner's position in jeopardy. Is that how you intend to play it?'

Marsham was now very thoughtful. 'I'm not sure yet. I'll need to consider it more fully. As you know, I've always been against the cold-blooded killing of Gorston—not for any moral reason, just that it seems an unnecessarily complicated way of doing things. It would cause too many problems immediately afterwards. But now that we are sure that he has a bad heart condition, we could consider using this move by the women to speed up our plans slightly.'

The car drew up to the flight of stone steps leading up to the main doorway of the Presidential Palace and stopped. Two armed guards sprang smartly to attention as the uniformed driver opened the door for the ministers.

Marsham walked up the stairs slowly, waiting for Martin to catch up with him, then they entered the large hall and walked briskly down a long, deeply-carpeted corridor. 'There are still too many unknowns,' Marsham continued, quietly. 'We need to find out exactly how serious his heart condition is and we also need to watch Steiner's progress with the investigation very carefully indeed. Do you think your man could get himself on to the assignment?'

Martin's voice was low, almost a whisper. 'I doubt it—he is in the administration division. But I'll have a talk with him.'

Marsham glanced briefly at his watch as he saw an old, white-haired man in the corridor ahead of them. 'You go on to the cabinet room, Martin. I want to have a word with Werner.'

'You'll never get anything out of him. He's too attached to Gorston.'

Marsham watched the old man as he drew nearer to them. 'No,' he said. 'I don't think it's affection that keeps him at Gorston's side; it's something else. God knows what. I've never been able to figure that old man out.' His manner became more casual as they neared the old man, his face assuming its customary friendliness. 'Werner, the very man. Can I trade on our friendship for a few moments and ask some professional advice?' He turned to Martin. 'You go ahead. I'll be with you shortly.' Martin nodded and walked on.

'I was hoping to catch you before the meeting,' the old man said, looked at Marsham intently but with tiredness in the eyes. 'The cabinet will be discussing the illegal newspaper, won't they?'

Marsham nodded in surprise. Werner never expressed any interest in politics even though Gorston had insisted over the past few years that he attend the cabinet meetings. It had just been assumed that Gorston had wanted his doctor near him at all times, and Werner had never before shown the slightest interest in the proceedings. Marsham adjusted his pace now as the old man led the way towards his suite of rooms.

'I wanted to see you because you're the most outspoken of all the ministers,' Werner said. He lapsed back into silence as they walked along the empty corridor, leaving Marsham to wonder at the cryptic comment. What could the old man want with him? He had tried to form a relationship for several years—ever since he had decided that he would become Gorston's successor—but the old doctor had resisted all his well known charm and had managed to keep him, though courteously, at a distance. He followed him into a small, cluttered room. Werner gestured towards a comfortable-looking armchair and Marsham sat, relaxed and at ease, waiting for the old man to explain his comment.

'Gorston mustn't be upset.'

Marsham trod warily. The old man must be particularly worried about Gorston's reaction to the paper for him to have come out so abruptly with his reason for wanting to see him.

'He isn't a well man,' the doctor continued.

Marsham fished his pipe out of his pocket and absently filled it, his manner remaining carefully casual. 'Nothing serious, I hope.'

The old man looked at him for a long moment. 'Yes, it's serious, Alan. It has been for some time. That's why I wanted to see you before the meeting. This newspaper business has upset him greatly. He found it hard to believe that there were any malcontents in the country. He has spent his life working for the people's good, as you know, and now he finds that foreign influences have been at work trying to disrupt everything he's worked so hard to build up.'

Marsham looked at him sharply. 'Is that what you believe? That the paper is the work of foreign infiltrators?'

The old man sat down heavily opposite him. 'That's what the President believes,' he said. He leant forward towards Marsham, his face earnest and intense. 'Alan, he must be allowed to continue thinking that. You're the only one likely to contradict him and I'm asking you not to.'

'But I don't believe this foreign nonsense,' Marsham replied. 'I believe that the paper is obviously the work of a small group of women. You are asking me to sit idly by when Gorston instructs Steiner to look for these subversives in the wrong areas. I'd be failing in my duty to my country and to Gorston.' He felt a brief twinge of conscience as he saw the indecision on the tired old face.

Werner got up and wandered aimlessly around the room before eventually standing in front of him, a new determination in his expression. 'Don't play politics with me, Alan.' His voice was low and tired but there was a strength there too. 'I said you were the only minister that would contradict Gorston. The others are too frightened of him—with the exception of Steiner, and he is too clever to oppose him. He is also too clever to believe anything other than that the women are responsible. So, whatever Gorston believes, Steiner will still track down the women responsible. You'll gain nothing by arguing with the President, except, possibly, endanger his life.'

Marsham's face abruptly adopted an expression of shocked surprise. 'Are you telling me his health is that bad?'

Werner sat back in the chair. 'Yes. It's that bad.'

'Heart?'

'Yes. I've been trying to persuade him to let someone else take over some of his responsibilities—to relax more. But, the more I try to persuade him, the more he throws himself into planning new legislation, meeting with heads of departments, poring over statistics—work his ministers should be doing.' Marsham sat silently. 'I've told him,' the doctor went on. 'If he doesn't relax, I cannot be responsible for the result. And this women's thing—' He ran his hands through his hair in a gesture of desperation. 'I had to sedate him completely last night. That is why I am asking you not to contradict him at the meeting this afternoon. Anything could bring on a fatal attack at this stage.'

'I didn't realize that you thought it was that serious,' Marsham said with concern. 'Of course, I'll do whatever I can to help.' He leant forward, earnestly, but the old man was lost in his thoughts. Marsham knew there was something else besides Werner's concern about Gorston's heart, but he still could not bring himself to say it aloud.

'Do you think he will implement his educational programme?' Werner said suddenly.

The abrupt change of subject caught Marsham by surprise. What was the linking thought process? 'Yes,' he answered, 'I think it will be passed this afternoon. It's only a formality. And then it will be implemented very rapidly.'

Werner closed his eyes and leant back in the chair. He looked very old, the lines etched deep in his face, the pale lips set in defeat. What else was it that was causing him so much worry?

Marsham got quietly to his feet. Werner would not say any more now. He glanced again at the old man still sitting with his eyes closed and felt he was watching a man who had fought a battle that had gone on for too long and had not the strength for the final effort.

Five

Sarah put on her coat and hurried to the main door, saying a brief farewell to Joan as she passed her in reception. The rain had stopped and the early evening sun slanted down, golden and warm. She looked up at the newly-washed blue of the sky and was glad the day was nearly over. The tiredness in her resented the elation she still felt about the murals and she could only focus on getting back to her room, lying on the bed and letting her jumbled thoughts sort themselves out without any conscious effort on her part. She paused at the kerb, waiting for a break in the commuter traffic. She would get home, shower and rest. She did not have to go out again until about eight when she would go to her usual eating place in case any of the women wanted to contact her. She found that the detailing of her actions for the evening soothed her, as did her expectation that none of the women would need to contact her so soon after their meeting. With luck she would be alone all evening.

She walked against the stream of commuters hurrying home and turned on to the concrete yard that surrounded the hostel, walking through the doors and into the drab hall, still lost in her thoughts.

'There's Sarah. She'll know.'

A small group of girls stood in the doorway leading to the communal kitchen, their faces alive with an amusement that belied their whispers and cautious glances towards the stairs. A dark-eyed girl in her late teens beckoned to her impatiently as the others went into the large, sparsely-furnished room.

'Sarah, you know all about the People's Hall. Settle an argument for us.'

Sarah closed the door carefully behind them and joined her friends at the bare, scrubbed table. She watched them silently, disturbed by their mood. There was a recklessness in them; a false bravado in their merriment. This was a danger she knew would arise as soon as a date was set for the Rising. These three obviously belonged to the organization, and although only the six main leaders knew the actual date, all the other members had been told that the operation would soon be entering its final stages.

'Marie, here, says the National Theatre is going to be moved to the People's Hall. Is that right?'

'Yes, it is,' Sarah answered. She turned to leave, adding coldly, 'Is it wise to make so much noise? You know friendships are discouraged and—' She shrugged expressively, and they knew she was referring to the insidious spy system that had been set up among the women.

'Oh, that's all right,' one of them said. 'We've checked. The place is almost empty except for the three of us and yourself.'

Sarah turned to face the girl who had called her into the kitchen, sickening apprehension starting in her stomach at the dangerously casual manner of them all. Her voice was hard. 'Val, I know you are young and have only recently started work, but, believe me, it would be better for you if you didn't flout the laws so blatantly.' She looked around at the three young faces. 'How do you know that I'm not prepared to report your behaviour in exchange for an extra late pass, or perhaps a new record player?' She watched the faces turn solemn, the previous light deadened, and hated herself for being responsible, as she hated being forced into the role of the older, caring woman.

Val twiddled her fingers, part woman, part still child. 'We're sorry, Sarah. You're right. It's just that Joanna has told us the most fantastic news.'

Sarah stopped breathing, asking the question, but not wanting to hear the answer. 'What news is that?'

The three younger women exchanged conspiratorial glances, hesitating to answer, until Joanna turned to her, a chuckle breaking through. 'You're not going to approve.'

Sarah felt old and tired. 'Marie wrote a play,' Joanna went on. 'Not a long one. More a one act playlet really. And—' She paused for effect. 'The National Theatre have accepted it.'

Sarah stared at them, incredulous but infinitely relieved. 'But they can't have,' she said.

Marie looked at her uncertainly, wishing they had never started this conversation. 'Well, I knew I couldn't send it in with my name on it; so I made up a man's name and put the University address on it. I work in the post room so I see all the mail that comes in, and the acceptance came through this morning.'

Sarah sat down at the bare table as the others looked at each other nervously. 'And what do you intend to do now?' she asked.

'Well, nothing.'

Joanna broke in. 'Marie is going to write back as Mr Whatever-he-is and say she's changed her mind about wanting the play performed.'

Sarah looked at the young faces around her and resented the responsibility they unknowingly placed on her. She did not want to carry the responsibility for all the women; she did not have the strength. She slowly got to her feet, looking into their faces, willing them to pay heed. 'Please, please, take care.'

The stairs to her room seemed endless. She hung up her coat and opened the window in the distracted manner of routine movements, then sat on the bed, staring unseeingly at the cream wall opposite her. Had she been right? Now that the date was set, she seemed to be asking herself that question all the time. A long time ago she had had a dream. How long? Six, seven years? No, seven years ago it was not a dream—it was a game. They all had different, private ways of surviving in this crushing, destroying society. Stephanie spent all her spare time turning bits of material and silk threads into breathtakingly beautiful tapestries; Ann played with figures—she knew their laws and their secrets so that the most impossible calculations just unravelled themselves in her head; but Sarah's way of surviving was to pretend to overthrow the dictatorship. She planned it in meticulous detail, working out moves and counter-moves. She recruited her armies, won her battle, and led everyone into Utopia. She tried to remember when the game had turned into a dream, but she could not.

Her eyes still stared unseeingly at the blank wall as she thought of the young women in the kitchen. She knew Marie wrote. She had carefully investigated everyone in the hostel, and in the previous one, and in the one before that. Her life seemed an endless, careful investigation of her fellow women until she was sure that none of them were Steiner's pathetic little spies. Writing was Marie's way of survival. But if Sarah had not influenced her, albeit by proxy, would she have been content to have spent the rest of her life as a post-room worker, writing in her spare time and piling up the dusty manuscripts because she was not allowed to have them published? And if she would have been content, had Sarah the right to cut through the years of careful brainwashing and show her the falseness of it and sow the seeds of discontent?

She kicked off her shoes in a sudden gesture of impatience. She was indulging herself. She had argued this point with herself many times and knew that the conclusion was always the same. Marie would write and have her work published; Ann would get away from the factory floor where she watched the milk bottles fill themselves endlessly and automatically while she idly calculated the annual gallonage each machine was capable of; and Stephanie would be able to take all her beautiful tapestries out of hiding and hang them on the walls where all could enjoy their perfection; and she—? Sarah turned abruptly away from her thoughts, unwilling to look into her future. Her future had always been the Rising; there had never been anything after that.

She undressed quickly, wrapping the grey, coarse dressing-gown around herself and hurried to the shower block. She stood under the water, willing herself to stand the heat until her body was adjusted to it. She had committed herself, and the women who thought the same way as she, to the Rising. The time for doubt was past; the only doubt that could remain now was whether they would succeed. She let the water run down her body and give the illusion of washing away the tiredness and fear along with the dust of the day.

She walked back along the bleak brown and cream corridor towards her room wondering if it was time to go to the coffee bar. She would be able to get the time from the large clock on top of the town hall.

One of the doors on her right opened and Stephanie beckoned to her. 'I want to talk to you,' she said, 'after you come back from Mason's. It's all right, this floor is empty.'

Sarah nodded briefly, wondering what Steph wanted her for. 'What time is it?' she asked.

'Half past seven,' Steph answered.

Sarah nodded again and hurried back to her room. She dressed quickly and efficiently; fingers twisting her thick hair expertly into a tight knot at the back of her neck, not glancing once in the direction of the small mirror over the shabby dressing table. She looked briefly around the small room, smoothing the slight creases on the bed cover where she had sat earlier; straightening the wooden chair that was set crookedly at the bare table; carefully removing all evidence of her existence in the room, as if the anonymity of her home would add to her protective mask. She walked over to the two shelves filled with books, the only sign of identity in the bleak room, and selected one quickly before hurrying out. All the floors were quiet as she walked down the stairs, but she could hear the faint hum of the washing machines from the communal wash-room and the sound of the National Anthem prefacing the television news.

The café was small and drab, painted in the same colours as the hostel. A few women were sitting separately at the dark brown tables but none of them looked up as Sarah walked across to the long, high counter.

'Just a coffee, please.'

'That won't do you much good, dear. You don't eat enough to keep a sparrow going.' The elderly woman behind the counter treated her with the casual familiarity that grows from numerous anonymous meetings. Sarah smiled briefly with her lips and shrugged slightly, knowing that no answer was expected. She watched the older woman pour the brown-grey liquid into the thick cup and noticed the puffy red hands on the handle—the result of endless hours spent washing thick, cracked cups. She looked again at the woman's face, knowing that she had been a biochemist with a significant future before Gorston had transformed her into one of the faceless grey ones. Was there any part of that earlier woman left behind the lined, grey face and shrouded eyes?

Sarah took the coffee and sat at a table facing the window. If any of the women wanted to contact her they would walk past between eight and eight-thirty and then would meet her later at the derelict building they were now using as their meeting place.

She opened her book on Leonardo da Vinci and, skipping the sections dealing with his art, turned to the chapters on his scientific achievements. The man intrigued her. A man capable of being part of, and apart from, his society; capable of dreams that became realities long after his death. He was a superb artist who went to bizarre lengths to represent the human body accurately. Why did he turn away from creating mankind on canvas to contemplating the creation of machines? He had even dabbled with the creation of robots. She skimmed the book, glancing constantly out of the window to the empty road. She turned a page and read da Vinci's thoughts on robots. Ideally there would be three types of robots. She skimmed the page until a line near the bottom caught her eye. The third type of robot would 'perform the duties of a loving wife while remaining a source of conjugal bliss'. She closed the book. Was Gorston's reality just a slightly distorted view of the male dream? Without Gorston and his army of civil servants would the women still find that men saw them as robots to perform the functions men wanted them to perform? Was it some basic flaw in men's make-up, some buried fear, that prevented them from realizing that women were people as they themselves were?

The sight of Mary walking past the window brought her abruptly out of her thoughts. The middle-aged woman had gone past without a glance towards the small women's café; her pace had been slow but sure and purposeful; an anonymous grey one going about her unimportant business. Sarah finished her coffee slowly and thoughtfully. Both Stephanie and Mary wanted to see her. What had been happening during the day? She remembered Mary's concern about the runner who had been caught by the guard. She had intended to go to see her sometime today. Maybe she was more seriously injured than they had thought. She got up from the table. No more women would pass now—it was gone eight-thirty. She nodded briefly to the woman behind the counter. The other women still sat at their solitary tables and ignored her departure.

She went straight to Stephanie's room, making sure the corridor was empty before walking in quickly without waiting to knock. The small brown table, a replica of the one in her own room, was laid for two, the chipped brown paint hidden beneath one of Stephanie's intricate and delicate embroideries.

'Is that wise?' Sarah asked.

Stephanie followed her look and gestured her to a chair at the table. 'I'll take it off again as soon as we've eaten. I thought it would be nice to use one this evening.' She turned towards the small two-ringed gas burner in the corner of the room, calling over her shoulder to Sarah, 'You haven't eaten, have you? I knew you wouldn't have, so I've prepared enough for the two of us. It's all ready.'

Sarah looked at Steph fondly, relaxing in the warmth of the welcome. There were times when Stephanie's fussing exasperated her beyond measure, but tonight she needed her affection and care. The plump little woman placed a plate in front of her and stood back waiting for a reaction. 'Steph, this smells great. What's in it?'

The other woman's eyes beamed with pleasure. 'Wine,' she admitted. 'Mr Sanson was discharged today. He's the one that was in for the gall bladder operation. And he left nearly a full bottle of wine in his locker. He asked me to get rid of it for him, so I didn't really steal it or anything. I smuggled it out under my coat.'

Sarah felt a surge of warmth for her friend. She leant forward impulsively and pressed her cheek against Stephanie's in an untypical display of emotion. 'Oh, Steph. You having to persuade yourself that you weren't stealing; after all they have stolen from us.' She drew back, suddenly embarrassed by her action. 'Come on, let's eat before it gets cold.'

'You never cook for yourself, do you, Sarah?'

Both women were eating with obvious enjoyment.

'If my efforts turned out like this, I might try more often.' Sarah parried the question with her usual adroitness.

'I've been thinking.' Stephanie was in her element. 'I've just finished one of my pieces and I was wondering what to make next.' She wiped her mouth with a napkin and set her elbows on the table. 'I want to make the next one for you.' Sarah glanced up from her plate, prepared to casually protest at this display of friendship. 'No, I'm quite determined,' Steph said. 'The trouble is—do you know, I don't know what sort of things you like? I've thought about it a lot. I like flowers and things, with lots of detail and soft colours, but I couldn't imagine what you would like. Isn't that funny? And I've known you for over three years. I know you like going out into the countryside a lot but that doesn't necessarily mean that you like pictures of birds and things, does it?'

She picked up her fork and started to eat, watching Sarah's face, waiting for her answer. Sarah's mind flew back to the murals, vibrating, alive, inspiring, until she realized that Stephanie was still waiting quietly.

'Oh, I like anything. I think all your pieces are beautiful.' Sarah did not want anyone to know the colours and forms that filled her mind. 'Why don't you surprise me?' she offered. 'After all, you are creating it, so it should be a bit of you, not a bit of me.'

'Mmm, that's true. I hadn't thought of it that way before.' Stephanie looked at Sarah with transparent affection. 'It'll be the best piece I've ever done—and it will be ready for you on the Day.'

She stood up and bustled around clearing the now empty plates, and pouring coffee. As she came back to the table, Sarah saw that her face was solemn; the escapism of the last half-hour was over. She stirred her coffee thoughtfully as Sarah waited to hear the real reason for this evening's meeting. Eventually Stephanie looked into Sarah's face, her hand still stirring the greyish liquid automatically. 'There's unrest among the men, as well,' she said. She continued as Sarah sat silently, making no response. 'I overheard it when I was clearing a patient's meal away. They forget I'm there most of the time. He was talking to a visitor.'

Sarah felt a stillness inside herself. 'What were they saying?'

'The patient is an elderly man. He obviously remembers what it used to be like. He was talking about the unions they used to have before Gorston made them illegal, and how the workers used to have a say in the working conditions and how they could force the employers to increase their wages by going on strike.'

Sarah interrupted impatiently. 'I know how the unions used to work. Did they say anything of significance?'

'Yes. They were talking as if they had formed a union. They were talking about members and recruiting new ones.'

Sarah got to her feet and walked over to the window. It was almost dark and the city looked less harsh in the dark blue light. It gave its usual illusion of emptiness, and thinking of the hundreds of thousands of people hidden from view among its countless concrete compartments, she felt the overwhelming isolation and loneliness that always swept over her when she looked at the sleeping city.

'Damn them. Damn them,' Sarah muttered. The words were low and charged with feeling. She turned back to Stephanie who was looking at her confusedly. 'Did you get any idea of how many men were involved? How long they have been planning this?' Her voice was hard and there was no gentleness in her eyes as she looked at the puzzled woman opposite her.

'Well, no,' Steph answered, hesitantly. 'I had the feeling that their numbers were quite small, but I don't really know why I thought that.'

'So, really, you don't know?'

'But, Sarah why are you like this?' Stephanie raised her hands in a small gesture of helplessness. 'I thought you'd be pleased. I thought, if the men were prepared to organize themselves like this, maybe we could join forces.'

Sarah sat down at the table and buried her face in her arms for a short moment before lifting her head to look hard into

Stephanie's face. 'Did you ever wonder how Gorston came to power?' she asked. 'Don't you ever think about how this country was turned from a democracy that had lasted for centuries into a dictatorship?'

Stephanie shook her head mutely, unable to speak against the force of suppressed feelings that trembled at the edge of Sarah's voice.

'Well I have,' Sarah went on. 'It was important to find out why the people welcomed this man—because they did welcome him. He didn't have to fight for power—the people forced it on him.' She sat back in the chair, pausing, searching for the words that would make this woman understand. 'For about eight years before Gorston came to power, the economy of this country was deteriorating. It had never been very strong, for various reasons. But there was a world-wide recession and it affected a weak economy very badly. Prices were spiralling, wages were frozen and unemployment kept climbing. The men started to protest against the women workers. They claimed that married women should not be allowed to work as they were taking jobs away from men. They also claimed that women were unreliable workers, and untrustworthy, and only fit for unskilled work. They marched in the streets and demanded legislation; they manned the factory gates and prevented women from entering. And all the time, the unions were agitating for higher wages for the men, calling them out on strike, crippling the economy even more. The government of the day had brought in partial legislation regarding the women's wages. It stated that women should be paid the same rate as men for the same work. The employers reacted by placing women in categories that could not be compared to men, starting the segregation we have today. And then Gorston came on the scene. He asked the people to put him into power and promised that he would make it illegal for married women to work. He also promised that no woman would ever deprive a man of a job or of promotion. And the people put him into power. Even the married women who didn't work voted for him because they believed their husbands when they told them that their jobs were in jeopardy because of women working.'

The two women looked at each other in silence, Sarah trying

to control the anger that fought for expression. She relaxed slightly as she brought the emotion under control. 'Like all good dramas,' she continued, 'it had its irony. The second piece of legislation that Gorston brought in made all the unions illegal.' She smiled wryly in an attempt to lift the oppressive atmosphere her feelings had created. 'So you see, Steph, unrest among the men can't help us. They are only thinking of themselves, the same as they did before. They saw no injustice in their attitudes to women then, and I don't suppose for one minute that they see any injustice now.' She rubbed her hand across her forehead as she tried to work out the implications of Stephanie's news. 'If only we knew how organized they are, what action they plan to take.' She looked sharply at her companion. 'They could ruin our plans if they intend to move in the near future.'

She stood up suddenly, needing to be alone. 'I'd better go, Steph. Find out as much as you can.' She touched the woman's arm in an unspoken apology for the tension she had created in her. 'The meal was delicious. The best I've tasted for a long while.'

Steph's face was immediately full of concern. 'Do you have to go out?' she asked.

'Don't worry. It's best you don't know.'

Sarah returned to her room, switched off the light and sat in the darkness thinking about the men's unrest. She felt no sympathy for them. They had brought their present position on themselves by their own arrogance and prejudice. Their present discontent was as self-centered as it had been over thirty years ago and their prejudice was even stronger now than it was then. It had been carefully cultivated over the long years that Gorston had been in power. She was quite sure that the men saw themselves as the only oppressed group in the society. As she sat in the darkness, waiting for the time to pass, she knew that the men's belief was even more dangerous than that. They saw themselves as the only group in the society—all others existed for their service and amusement. She lay back on the bed, staring blindly at the ceiling. There was another group of men—the intellectuals. They caused some minor protests at times, but their concern was not for the injustices of the society, only for the inefficient use of the country's brain-power and the long-term effects on the average intelligence of the population. It was an intellectual exercise that sometimes grew too loud. Then there would be a small flurry of arrests and a dozen or so would disappear into the work camps.

She got up from the bed and walked across to the window, drawing back the curtains, carefully scanning the silent expanse of concrete and deserted road beyond, before glancing at the distant illuminated face of the large clock. It was time to go. She smoothly and deftly climbed over the sill on to the narrow ledge that ran the width of the building, inching her way along it with the sureness of long practice. She swung precariously around the corner of the building, reaching for the half-rusted support of a disused fire escape and rapidly climbed down, her feet close to the uprights where the metal was strongest. She skirted the looming building, keeping in the darkest shadows, and made her way silently and quickly through the maze of narrow lanes that led to the derelict basement where Mary would be waiting for her.

The small naked lamp was already lit, the small pool of light throwing Mary's face up in contrast to the remaining dark shadows. Sarah stopped in the broken doorway, shocked by the paleness of the woman's face; but most of all by the tormented anguish that lay in the still darkness in her eyes.

'What is it?' Sarah asked.

Mary stared at her in silence, her hands fluttering slightly as they lay in her lap. Sarah could see her tongue flickering over the dry lips as the older woman tried to regain sufficient control to tell her what was wrong.

'They've been arresting students and lecturers from the university,' she finally said, her voice heavy and lifeless, all energy being used to feed the inner torment.

Sarah stepped across the debris on the floor and walked up to the woman, tensely sitting on the wooden crate. 'But that's nothing new,' she said. They've nearly always got a few in there.'

Mary stared at her, slowly shaking her head from side to side, her face immobile except for the shadows that swung across as she moved her head, probing and finding the hollows. 'No, this is different.' Her voice was so low that Sarah had to step still closer to catch the almost whispered words. 'The detention cells are full—twenty, maybe more—and the noise. Oh, God, the noise.'

'But why?' Sarah knelt at the woman's feet so that she could look into her face.

'They can't think that they published the paper?'

'I don't know what they think.' She was close to breaking-point, her eyes looking down at Sarah but not seeing her, seeing only the pictures in her head. 'They had started when I got there this morning.' Her hands made vague gestures in the dank air. 'Cars, vans, men everywhere; hurrying, silent. Then I went to get my brushes and I could—hear.' Her eyes suddenly focused on the grey one looking up into her face and she leant forward slightly as if trying to make the grey eyes see what her own could not blot out. 'Screams, Sarah. High strangled screams that went on and on, until you thought they would never stop. And then, when they did, the silence was even worse than the screaming. All day, Sarah, all day, it went on and on as if it would never stop. And then this afternoon, I was supposed to clean C block. That's where they are keeping the men—before they interrogate them—and I didn't know what to do. No one had told me not to clean there and that meant I was still supposed to do it. There wasn't anyone I could ask, so I went there—'

Sarah put her hand urgently on Mary's arm, trying to pull her back from her inner hell but the words kept coming, broken, disjointed, needing to be said. '—and I turned the corner into the main corridor, with the cells all down one side, and I saw the men, silent, huddled. And on the floor, in front of me, where all the men could see—bodies. Bodies there, just lying in front of me. And I could see their faces, and their hands, and the wire around their throats. Oh, God.'

The cry came from her depths, strangled, tormented, forcing itself past her throat, out into the bleakness of the derelict base-ment; and she started to rock back and forward, moaning and whimpering like some sick animal.

Sarah was still, unable to cope with the woman's grief. Des-perately she searched inside herself for some help she could give but there was nothing there.

The climax of emotion passed and Mary sat more upright on the wooden crate, exhausted but calm. 'I can't be responsible for any more misery,' she said seemingly to herself, appearing to have forgotten the presence of Sarah still kneeling among the scattered rubble at her feet.

Sarah reacted to the implied threat to all her plans. 'Mary, listen to me,' she said firmly. 'Today's experience was something that should never exist. It can only happen when human beings are considered to be less than human; when a part of society can proclaim their superiority and degrade, humiliate and destroy their fellow humans in their efforts to prove it; when a section of mankind tries to lay exclusive claims to those aspects of human nature that we all aspire to. It will go on happening, Mary, until we stop it.'

Mary continued looking at her hands as they lay limp in her lap, giving no reaction to Sarah's words.

'They won't go on torturing them now,' Sarah persevered. 'Don't you see? They must have thought the university people were responsible for the paper so they arrested them and tortured them to make them talk. But they didn't talk; they had nothing to say; so they died. And still the others didn't talk. The police will realize that they have the wrong people.' She looked intently into the still face, searching for a sign that her words were getting through the blankness. 'Mary, I know that men died there today in a horrible, brutal way. But how many others have died like that in the past? How many women have died in the detention centre? And will continue to die if Gorston isn't stopped?'

Mary looked at the intense face looking up into hers and gave a small, tired smile of affection. 'Child, child—it is so easy for you. Your head talks sense, but your heart—'

Sarah got abruptly to her feet and looked around the dirty rubble, hearing the scuttling of the rats in the dark places, smelling the dank, rotten smell of filth that hung in the air, and anger rose hard and demanding inside her. She turned back to the exhausted, defeated woman. 'You are wrong, Mary.' Her voice was quiet, but the anger made it hard and the hardness showed through the softly spoken words. 'You talk as if I have no feelings, no emotions; as if I'm nothing except an empty shell housing a cold calculator for a brain. And you are wrong. It is because I have feelings that I am determined to destroy Gorston and all he stands for. He killed some men today, but how many women has he destroyed? We hide in filthy holes like this one so that we can drop the pretence of being mindless zombies and can search to find what parts of us still remain after his indoctrination and education. How many of us are whole people, Mary? How much of us has been destroyed without our even knowing it? You told me once that Gorston had destroyed a part of me that I didn't even know existed. I didn't understand you then, and I don't understand you now, but I'm going to get the chance to find out what you meant.' She walked back to the silent woman and dropped back down on to her knees, her hand covering the still hands that lay in the lap. 'My head does rule me, Mary. It's the way I survive. It doesn't mean that I have no feelings; but emotions are dangerous things and I can't afford them now.'

Mary looked into the serious grey eyes and shook her head slightly. 'You're right, Sarah. Emotions are very dangerous things, but sometimes they cannot be denied. Sometimes the heart speaks so loudly that one cannot hear the head.'

Sarah searched her face, trying to understand her words. She felt that Mary was no longer talking about what had happened at the detention centre but about some other tragedy that she knew nothing about. 'And yours,' she asked 'does your heart speak louder than your head?' Sarah's voice was tight as she felt the threat to her plans closing around her.

Mary looked at her calmly, emotions drained, but with her inner strength reasserting itself. 'Sarah, child,' she said, 'I would never do anything to hurt you. After all these years, I can stand it a short time more.'

Six

The early morning sun held the promise of another fine day but Sarah was oblivious to the gentle warmth as she hurried along the dusty pavement. Her thoughts still turned on the meeting with Mary the night before. She could not shake the picture of Mary's face, pale and distraught, in the harsh glare of the naked bulb. Sarah absently fumbled in her pocket for the office keys as she walked up the small flight of stone steps to the front door.

'Hillard.'

A short, burly man stepped out in front of her; broad, muscular shoulders; dark, swarthy skin; eyebrows that met at the bridge of the nose; a faint hint of stubble on his chin; and wearing the brown of the State Police uniform. The impressions flashed through her mind in the endless moment she took to push the climbing fear back into the controlled recesses of her being.

'Yes,' she replied, her voice expressionless. She looked directly into his face—dark eyes, no emotion, but a trace of boredom. It would be a routine questioning. She had warned the women to prepare themselves for such interviews and had urged them to remember that they had left no trace of their activities. 'Answer all their questions clearly and calmly,' she had told them. 'There will be no need for you to get tense, or nervous—they will be asking the wrong questions.'

'Just a few questions,' the man said. 'Shall we go inside?'

She turned the key in the lock and opened the door, aware of his gaze on her hands as she did so. Her hands were steady.

She gestured towards the chair she had sat in when talking to Carl Tolland. The man ignored the silent invitation and took a step nearer to her.

'You open up the premises every morning?' he began.

'Yes.'

'Do you always arrive alone?'

Sarah nodded, forcing herself to withstand the man's nearness.

'So you would be in a position to place something in the mail without being noticed?'

The man's voice had turned belligerent and Sarah relaxed fully, knowing she had nothing to fear.

'Yes, I could,' she answered, 'but so could anyone else who walked past the front door.' Her tone was low, monotonous.

'What do you do with the mail when you arrive?'

'Nothing. Mr Nesbitt has the only key to the mail box. He opens it as soon as he arrives and it's then distributed to the various offices.' She waited impassively for him to continue his fruitless questioning.

'What time does this Mr Nesbitt arrive?'

'He won't be here for another hour.'

The man turned away abruptly and sat in the chair, ignoring her completely.

Sarah took the dismissal and turned, catching Joan's eye as she walked through the door. She gave her a quick half-smile of re-assurance before climbing the stairs to her own office. She closed the door quickly behind her and leant back against it in relief. It was an insignificant encounter with Steiner's man, but the experi-ence with Mary the night before had unnerved her, however well she had hidden it. She stood there a moment longer, glad of the emptiness of the room, before she took off her coat and busied herself with the routine tasks of another working day, no sign of tension evident in her brisk, business-like movements. As she sat at the typewriter, she felt a satisfaction that Steiner's inquiries were going as she had predicted, although she was surprised that she had not been interviewed yesterday. Maybe she was towards the end of the list. Steiner would also be checking the source of their paper supply and ink; his men would be checking every letterpress machine in the city and any factory that made any sig-nificant amount of noise and worked a night shift. She estimated that it would take him about five days to exhaust all those lines of inquiry. That was why she had planned to print the second edition in three days' time. It was safer to store the printed sheets than delay using the printing press.

She wondered if she would at last meet the man she had studied at a distance for so long. Nesbitt had a final meeting this morning with Steiner to discuss security arrangements for the official opening. He had insisted that she went to all the other meetings. Would he take her to this one? She wanted to meet the man. All his press photographs showed a slim, well-groomed figure, always at the back of the scene. All her knowledge of him had been obtained by carefully studying his methods over the years; the thoroughness with which he implemented Gor-ston's laws; the painstaking way he had built up his spy system throughout the women workers, rewarding any little piece of gossip with minor easing of the restrictions; his ruthlessness in carrying out investigations. He was a man who dealt in details, with slow, relentless determination. The fear he generated—and he created it all around him—was the fear of never being able to escape from him. Was there a greater breadth to the man, a vision, an imagination that she had missed? She had of necessity studied the actions and not the man. If she had missed something in the way he worked, it could put all her plans in jeopardy.

'I knew that there would be trouble about that wretched news-sheet.' Nesbitt was flustered. 'I told you, didn't I? Who on earth was mad enough to produce such a thing? And for what?' He glared at Sarah as if expecting answers to his questions. He had asked the same questions in the same blustering manner when he had first shown her the copy he had found among the mail. But he had read it, secretly, in his room. She could tell from the way he looked at her at odd moments. As if, for the first time, it had occurred to him that she might be something other than an efficient robot, constructed to run his business.

Her face was expressionless as she commented. 'He thought I put it in the letter box.'

'I know, I know. Ridiculous. I told him—it was right at the bottom of the pile of mail. It obviously came before the letters.' He turned towards the door of his office. 'They won't rest, you know, until they find them. Why should anyone want to stir up that kind of trouble?' He was still muttering about the stupidity of the whole thing as he opened the door.

'You have an appointment with Commissioner Steiner at ten-thirty, to finalize the seating arrangements for the opening. Will you want me to come?'

The bluster disappeared. 'Yes,' he answered, hesitating slightly. 'Yes, I'll want you there. I shall need you to take notes.'

Steiner stood at the window, looking across the expanse of lawn and the profusion of flowers. He had turned the whole roof of police headquarters into his own exclusive garden, spending hours each day tending the banks and swathes of roses that bloomed from early May until late Autumn—a magical oasis of colour and exquisite beauty, amongst the city's roof tops. In contrast, his office was barren; a desk and two chairs standing in an expanse of carpet; no pictures; no ornaments; just a vase of his beautiful roses sitting on the bleak desk.

He walked across to the desk and, gently stroking a velvet petal, spoke into the intercom. 'Progress reports, Erling.'

The door opened almost immediately and a young blond man came in carrying several files. Steiner did not bother to glance in his direction as he seated himself at the desk. 'We'll start with the interviews,' he said.

Erling hesitated, still standing near the vacant chair, unable to sit in the presence of this man until specifically requested. 'Yes, sir.' He tried to open the folders efficiently, unwilling even to place them on the desk until Steiner briefly indicated the empty chair.

Erling began. 'A total of twenty-three students and five university lect ...' His voice petered out as Steiner raised his hand slightly.

'No, no,' came the calm voice. 'The women interviews.'

Erling hastily selected another file and cleared his throat, nervously. 'There are eighty-three women workers who are the first to arrive at their places of employment in the mornings. Sixty of these were interviewed yesterday; the rest are being interviewed this morning. Of the sixty already interviewed, seventeen were in the company of other people who are prepared to state that the women were not carrying anything. None of the remainder could prove their claims that they did not deliver any paper to their place of work, but neither could our interviewers break their stories.' He paused and looked anxiously at the quiet man opposite him. 'I'm afraid that line of questioning wasn't very fruitful,' he apologized.

Steiner dismissed it. 'It wasn't to be expected. These women are too well organized to be broken that easily. It was just a clearing operation.' He leant forward slightly and looked directly at the young man for the first time. 'Remember, Erling, the first rule of any investigation is "Clear the undergrowth". You investigate all the possibilities, however obvious, however remote, however absurd. Then you eliminate one possibility after another and the truth blossoms.'

He sat back and resumed his previous position, hands steepled in front of his face, eyes on the beauty of the vase of roses, and Erling recognized the signal to continue. 'Er, apparently different types of paper were used in the printing. There are insufficient amounts of any one type to enable us to determine the source. However, all women workers at firms using any of these papers are under surveillance.'

Steiner nodded absently.

'The printing method used was letterpress,' Erling went on. 'There are several hundred of these presses to be checked—men are working on it. We had the ink analysed but I'm afraid that it's a similar situation to the paper. A house to house inquiry has been started, regarding any unusual noise.' He glanced up at Steiner, trying to gauge his reaction to the report, but the man's face was impassive, as if he was not even listening to the young man's words. 'I, personally, followed up your suggestion about the electricity consumption in the women worker hostels, but there's been no increase of usage in any of them.'

Steiner nodded slowly, lips slightly pursed. 'Right, right. We are clearing the ground nicely—very nicely.' He stood up and walked back to the window. Hands clasped behind his back, rocking gently to and fro on his toes. He was a man lost in his thoughts, oblivious of the uneasy young captain at his desk. He spoke almost to himself. 'They would have printed where there was already noise—and at night—and with a power source. They're careful, very careful. Paper from different sources, and they would have built their own press.' He turned sharply. 'Check them all anyway.' He turned back and studied his small well-manicured hands—fingers spread wide, as the silence in the room lengthened. 'Right, Erling.' He walked back to the desk, hands clasped together at his chin in a peculiarly affected pose. 'We will now check all factories that run a night shift. Put surveillance on all women employees and examine their persons and their belongings for traces of printer's ink.'

He looked steadily at Erling and the young man shifted uncomfortably under his gaze, nervously fingering the papers in front of him, his eyes firmly fixed on the shining wood of the desk top.

Steiner's eyes were unfocused as he examined his private thoughts. 'Yes, yes, they're very clever but overconfident,' he said. 'Claiming that they will publish again in two weeks. Foolish, very foolish. But there's been a depth of planning that is interesting. I look forward to meeting them.' His eyes refocused on Erling and he smiled at him bleakly. 'That will be an interesting meeting.'

He pointed to an unopened file. 'And that one?'

'Surveillance reports on Marsham, sir,' Erling said. 'I knew you'd want to see them.'

'Ah, yes, Mr Marsham. Anything I should know immediately?'

'No, sir. The only contact he had with James Foster and Brian Martin yesterday was at the cabinet meeting, although he did travel to the meeting in the same car as Martin.'

'And the driver?'

'No, I'm afraid not. He insists on always using his private chauffeur. He never uses an official car.'

'Then why haven't we bugged his car?' Steiner's voice was still soft but Erling was aware of the coldness that lay beneath.

'You ordered a second grade surveillance, sir,' he answered. 'That doesn't include the planting of listening devices.'

'All right. Leave that with me and upgrade the surveillance on him.'

Erling recognized the dismissal and rose, hesitantly, to his feet. 'The students, sir. The arrests that were made yesterday . . .'

Steiner had cupped a rosebud in his hands and was fastidiously smelling the perfume. 'What about them?' he inquired.

'You gave instructions, sir, that they be made to talk.' Erling wiped his hands across his mouth, hesitating to continue. Steiner waited impassively and he plunged recklessly on. 'Well, they didn't talk, sir. It's just—well what do you want done with the remainder?'

Steiner thought for an instant. 'Keep them in one of the work camps—away from the other prisoners. We will need them later.' He opened Marsham's file and started to read.

'You have an appointment, sir—the seating arrangements for the official opening of the People's Hall.'

Steiner glanced up at him. 'I know, Erling. What's the man's name?'

'Nesbitt, sir. And he usually brings his secretary with him.'

'And his name?'

'It's a woman worker, sir.'

Steiner sat back in his chair. 'How nice, how very nice. Do you
know her name?'

'Hillard, sir,' came the answer.

'Hillard. I must remember that. Show them in as soon as they
arrive. And Erling, we won't need another chair.'

Sarah could see the tension in Nesbitt as they waited in the glass
reception area of Police Headquarters, for clearance to the upper
floors. He had started by blustering, voice pitched slightly too
loud when telling the wooden-faced policeman that he had an
appointment with Commissioner Steiner. As the waiting lengthened, Nesbitt's pretence at self-confidence had evaporated, until
now he just stood and fidgeted with his brief case.

His nervousness comforted her. As she followed him past the
armed guards into this vast, glass space, with no shadows and no
hiding places, she had felt a crescendo of fear surge up inside her
as if all her hidden fears and forgotten nightmares had lain in wait
until this single moment. Her face felt stiff and alien in its mask
of blankness and she kept her eyes lowered so that no one could
see past them. Her intellect struggled to regain control. Nesbitt
was nervous—irrationally so. This was the effect Steiner had on
all who came in contact with him. Steiner knew nothing about
her, nothing of the knowledge inside her head. Only her own
weakness could betray her.

But in her mind, she saw the pictures that Mary had painted for
her in that desolate basement. Pictures of broken bodies and stilled
minds that had spent their last conscious moments in a blackness
of terror and pain. She tried to banish them. She must see Steiner
as he was. She must separate him from his power, his ruthlessness,
his armed assassins. She must see past all those things and learn
what sort of an adversary he really was. She must strip him of all
the accoutrements of terror and try to see the man beneath. She
must not project her terror-stricken fantasy on to the reality.

'This lift, if you please, sir. Top floor. You will be met.'

She moved after Nesbitt automatically, still striving for control,
but her mind kept slipping into irrelevancies. The lift was fast,
smooth, efficient; eighteen floors in silence, Nesbitt grasping the
handle of his briefcase too tightly.

'Good morning, Mr Nesbitt.' A man met them at the lift. 'Commissioner Steiner is expecting you.'

Deep-pile carpet; no noise; no screams; endless corridors; follow that blond head.

Then they were with a slim man, well-groomed, self-contained. Steiner.

'Mr Nesbitt. Just a few final details to discuss,' he said.

Steiner ignored her. She didn't exist, and slowly the panic subsided. She stood near the door, notebook in hand. There was nowhere for her to sit, and the conversation of the two men washed over her. 'At two forty-five, the official party will arrive in the order given on page three,' Nesbitt was saying.

She looked around the room, still unable to bring herself to look at the man who instilled such fear. There was nothing to see except bare walls and a glimpse of an incongruously beautiful roof garden through the window. She steadied herself and glanced across at the two men looking at the seating-plan. The height and bulk of Nesbitt dwarfed the man by his side, but his nervousness had evaporated before the urbane affability of the slight, precise figure. She could recognize the Commissioner's known characteristics; attention to detail, preciseness, thoroughness. But what else? Suddenly she saw the rose and the sight riveted her attention. They must be from the garden outside—his garden? She tried to imagine him tending them, nurturing them, and as she looked directly at him at last, she could imagine it. But how? How could lifeless bodies keep company in the same mind with living roses?

'Your firm always handles these affairs beautifully—fine attention to detail,' Steiner was saying smoothly. 'It will be a magnificent occasion.' The voice was seductive as it sounded the conventional phrases.

Nesbitt grasped at the trite praise. 'Very kind of you, very kind. We try to do our best.'

'Nesbitt, do you always take a woman worker around with you?' The words cut through the room; the cold, chilling tones hanging in the bewildered silence.

'I'm afraid—I—' Nesbitt was bewildered.

Steiner looked at the stammering man, no expression on his

face, no movement in his body. The tension increased as Nesbitt lapsed into a despairing silence.

'Hillard, isn't it? How remiss of me.' He was standing by her side, hand under her arm. 'And standing all the time.'

He led her across to the chair that Nesbitt had been sitting in and gestured her to sit. She could still feel the touch of his hand and the nearness of him. Panic started to rise again.

'Do you like flowers, Hillard?' he asked. 'I saw you admiring my garden.'

So he had been watching her, yet she had been sure that he had not looked in her direction. Her mind raced while still clinging to the word, Hillard. It was a technique. His switch of mood; his pretence at omniscience; even the absence of a chair; planned, carefully planned. But he had called her Hillard and Hillard could still call on the years of carefully programmed responses if Sarah allowed her to.

She looked up at him, eyes expressionless. 'They are very beautiful,' she said quietly.

'And, of course, you are not allowed to grow flowers in the gardens of your hostels.'

He was playing with her. 'The gardens have been concreted,' she replied, tonelessly. 'It is more practical that way.'

'Still, it's a pity. There is something very satisfying about planning a creation and then seeing the living result.'

His eyes were fixed on her hair as he pulled a rose from the vase in front of him and lifted it slowly to his face. His eyes slid down over her body and then up, abruptly, to look hard into her eyes. 'You may be right. Concrete is more practical.' Then he leant towards her, hand outstretched, holding the rose. 'For you Hillard. To remind you of your visit here this morning.'

Seven

They drove back to the office in silence, each wrapped in private thoughts. She had met the man who stood between her and Gorston, who could destroy all her plans, who would not hesitate to kill her friends.

Nesbitt parked the car, swinging it too tightly into the kerb, reversing it with mutterings of annoyance and slamming the door shut behind him before striding up the steps of the office block without a glance in Sarah's direction.

By the time she reached her room, he was already in his office, the door firmly shut. She filled a glass with water and carefully placed the rose in it. She looked at its beauty as she hung up her coat and then walked across to her desk, sitting down to study it more closely. It was as if the secret that was Steiner was locked in its fragility. She realized that her blind fear of him had gone. It had disappeared the moment she had found the courage to look into his face with the blank eyes of Hillard. She had clearly seen his eyes lingering on her hair and wandering over her body, but when he looked directly into her eyes, she had known he was not seeing her. He saw only what he projected there, an image created in his own mind. She was still afraid of his power and what would happen if he defeated her, but now it would be a personal conflict of minds; move and counter-move; her small band of women against all his resources; a game of chess where all his pawns would readily be sacrificed, and all hers had to be cherished and protected.

'You can get me at home if you need me.' Nesbitt had come into her office, his face flushed. They both knew she would not need him, and that he would not be at home. He would be in the nearest bar, finishing the drinking session he had obviously started in his office. He was still frightened by the meeting with Steiner, still puzzling over the humiliation of being forced to stand while she sat in his chair. She wondered, briefly, what his wife was like. She had met her once at some publicity function, but it had been impossible to get to know her at that brief meeting. The woman had displayed the usual discomfort all wives felt when confronted by one of the 'grey ones'. She had inquired about Sarah's job and, to save her boredom, Sarah had kept her reply short. After that, there was no further point of contact and the encounter had petered out into embarrassment. Exchanges like that saddened Sarah far more than did the unseeing arrogance of the men. She picked up the sheaf of papers Nesbitt had placed on her desk as he was leaving and saw they were the final draft of the seating plans. She carefully worked out the time schedules and settled down to type the detailed instructions for all the personnel concerned.

She worked steadily for several hours, the typed pages growing, the various folders filling as she planned the day of the official opening in the greatest detail, until she finally sat back and buzzed reception.

'Joan, would you send the messenger girl up. I want some reports distributed.'

'They won't be delivered until tomorrow,' Joan replied. 'It's quite late.'

'Yes, I know,' Sarah said. 'I just want them out first thing in the morning so everyone has them on Monday morning.'

'Sarah,' Joan's voice sounded strained. 'Are you leaving soon? I'd like to talk to you.'

'I'll meet you in the cloak room in a few minutes,' Sarah answered immediately.

She looked thoughtfully at the telephone after she had rung off. Why was Joan so tense? Maybe Steiner's man had questioned her before he had left this morning, although there was no real need for him to do so. Joan was never the first one in the office and she did not hold any keys. No, it had to be something else that she wanted to talk about.

Joan's body was stiff with tension as she watched Sarah come into the small cloakroom. Immediately she asked, 'Is it true what's going round about the raid on the university yesterday?'

So that was it. Sarah nodded tightly. 'Mary saw the result of the questioning.'

'But why?' Joan demanded. 'They can't think they published the paper.'

'No. They don't. They know it's us, and I can't work out why they should arrest the students and pretend they think they're responsible.' As Sarah spoke, she remembered again Steiner's face as he had looked at her hair, as he had admired the rose, and knew that the answer was in understanding his twisted mind. 'I need to think about it,' she said. 'We can discuss it tomorrow. Can you make it? I want to finalize the contents for the next edition.'

Joan nodded, her thoughts still on the arrests. 'Yes,' she

promised. 'I'll be there at the usual time.' She stood up, but her expression was still tense and withdrawn. There was obviously something more she wanted to say. Sarah took her coat down from the hook and started to put it on, watching as Joan fiddled with her glasses.

'Sarah.' Joan's face was set as she brushed her hand across her eyes. 'I've been thinking a lot about it since I first heard the rumours.' Sarah waited quietly for her to continue. 'I couldn't stand it if I was caught, Sarah.' She looked directly into Sarah's face and Sarah could see the fear in her eyes.

'Don't think about it, Joan,' she said quietly. 'You won't get caught. If we start thinking about it, we won't be able to do anything.'

'No. Listen to me.' The fear was still there but she was determined to talk about it. 'I've got to think about it. I know I wouldn't be strong enough to cope if I was caught. It's the feeling of helplessness that frightens me the most. They could do whatever they wanted and I couldn't do anything to stop them.' Joan turned away as if to hide from Sarah's gaze, but her voice was firm and steady. 'If I was caught, I would want to kill myself immediately—before they could do anything to me. I want you to ask Stephanie if she can get me something from the hospital. Something I could carry around with me in case they ever arrested me.' She turned back abruptly and looked directly at Sarah. 'It's the only safe way. I know I'm not strong enough to withstand them. I could destroy all our hopes if I talked.'

Joan was echoing Sarah's own thoughts and fears and had come to the same conclusion. Sarah's voice was gentle as she reached out to touch the tense woman. 'You're right, Joan. I feel the same. I'll talk to Stephanie tonight. If she can get enough, I suggest we make it available to any woman who wants it.'

Joan nodded silently and the two women looked at each other for a long moment. Sarah broke the tension as she turned towards the door. 'Come on, Joan. I'll make the arrangements tonight, but we won't have to use the stuff. We're going to succeed.'

She locked the main door behind her and walked out into the warm evening with the feeling of death and horror still around her. She had to shut it out of her mind or the fear would paralyze her thoughts. Tomorrow, she would go over the final contents of the second edition, and, as soon as it was printed, they could destroy the press. She thought of the long hours Eli had spent in building it up from the discarded parts they had all collected so painstakingly over the months. Watching it take shape was the first experience of the reality of their plans and it had assumed a significance that far exceeded its true importance. It was the first step after more than two years of planning, carefully recruiting women, dreaming of life after Gorston had gone. It would be a shame to break it up.

She paused at the kerb, waiting for a break in the rush-hour traffic. One car was travelling much slower than the main stream, hugging the kerb to let the other cars overtake. She watched carefully, waiting to see the driver clearly enough to identify him as one of Steiner's men, a knot of tension forming inside.

The car stopped as it drew level and Carl Tolland got out. She stared at him, the memory of the murals suddenly coming back to her.

'I was very clumsy yesterday,' he said. 'I didn't know.'

The meeting with Steiner had pushed her back into the world where the things shown in his paintings did not exist. Her meeting with Mary in the ruined building had blotted any joyous thoughts of life from her mind. She looked at the blue eyes that were regarding her so seriously and wished she could share his vision of life for just a moment. He was still watching her, obviously waiting for her to say something. But why had he come here?

'There's no need for you to explain your actions,' she said stiffly.

He reached into the car. 'I've solved the problem of the coffee.' He held a flask out towards her, a mischievous grin on his face. 'I thought maybe we could drink it down by the canal. Parts of it are very beautiful.' He paused for a moment trying to find a reaction in her face. 'As a sign that you've accepted my apology?'

He confused her. Why had he waited outside the office to speak to her? Did he think she had enough influence to get him the job of chief designer? Sarah's face was blank as she answered him. 'Mr Tolland, there's no need for you to apologize to me.

And we shouldn't be talking here like this.' She glanced around the street to see if anyone was interested in their meeting.

He insisted. 'But I offended you yesterday. I didn't know the laws and what I said was clumsy.'

She looked into the blue eyes and could not really believe that the job was so important to him. He had obviously been making inquiries about this society since she had seen him yesterday. Maybe he wanted to ask her to explain more about it. Suddenly she could remember vividly her reaction to the murals as she had walked out of the towering, oppressive entrance hall and into the colour and vitality of his work; and her need to be able to discuss them with him came back as strongly as before. She wanted to talk to him, to hear him speak about life, to hear him confirm all her own ideas of what it should be like. She heard her voice, cool and remote. 'I'm sorry Mr Tolland, I'm not allowed to meet with you.'

The blue eyes now showed disappointment, and something else—stubbornness. He was talking about driving along the canal to where it was quiet. He still did not know what it was like to live in this country. Suddenly she realized that she wanted him to remain unaware of the repression and fear that formed her environment. She wanted him to keep his vision of life intact. But she also wanted to hear from him what his concept of life was like. 'I can't get into the car with you, Mr Tolland,' she said. 'But I will meet you somewhere, tomorrow.'

He smiled, relaxed. 'Great. Where?'

'There's a spot by the river, about ten miles out from town. Follow this road for about nine miles, until you come to a humped bridge. Take a small lane on your left, just past the bridge and it will lead you down to the river.'

'I'll find it,' he said. 'But how will you get there? Have you a car?'

He had an innocence about him that she found painful; an innocence and a feeling for life. It would be worth the risks to be able to talk to him, and there was little risk in meeting him at that spot. 'No, Mr Tolland,' she answered. 'I can take a bus.'

'But I can pick you up somewhere,' he assured her. 'Somewhere quiet. There's no need for you to go by bus.'

Sarah looked at him slowly; then at the car; then back into his face. She suddenly felt he was vulnerable and she could not understand it. She could not hurt him. 'You don't understand,' she said quietly. 'I couldn't get into an enclosed space with you.' Shock flitted across his face, and anger, and—she could not read it. 'I couldn't get into an enclosed space with any man.'

She saw his eyes run briefly over her hair and clothes and look for a long time at her shoes. Then he looked into her face. 'I don't understand you,' he said.

The words surprised her. Why should he want to? And how could he expect to if he did not know her? He was trying to see past the blankness in her face. Did that mean he expected to find something behind it? She looked intently into his eyes, trying to read what was in his mind. He was a man. Was he actually trying to see if there was anything behind the mask? 'There's nothing to understand, Mr Tolland,' she said finally. 'I'm used to segregation, that's all.'

He stood there, staring at the car for a long time as she watched the emotions flickering over his face. Eventually he turned back to her. 'You must hate men.'

She felt the link between them; a slight brush of understanding. 'No. Not now. For a long time I did.' The contact hung in the silence.

'You didn't say what time tomorrow,' he said, smiling at her.

'I will be there at three o'clock.'

He got back into the car and looked up at her. 'I'll see you then. And I'll bring some more coffee.'

Eight

The street was deserted, with the stillness that descends on the office ghettos of all cities when the workers have gone back to their suburban boxes for the weekend. Sarah waited for a solitary car to pass before crossing to the empty bus-stop.

The meeting with Joan had gone well. Sarah had given her all the information she had gathered about Gorston's rise to power: the economic reasons; the blind prejudices; and then had listed the erosion of personal liberties. Joan had taken the scanty notes and her stumbling attempts at explaining her beliefs about mankind and had turned them into an article that seemed to blaze with honesty and perception. She had read it with a growing excitement, unable to make any comment except, 'That's right, that's right,' until Joan's laughter had broken the spell.

Sarah remembered the closeness between them; Joan's eyes gently mocking her from behind her glasses, hands making exaggerated gestures of exasperation as she leant forward to touch her arm. 'You are impossible, Sarah,' she had said. 'I've only written what you told me, what you have told all of us.'

Sarah re-read the article and realized that Joan was right. The difference was her inner fears and doubts were not expressed. Was this how the women saw her—clear in her thinking, her understanding, her emotions? But most of all, absolutely sure of herself and their success?

The half-empty bus rumbled to a halt and she waited to see if the conductor would let her on.

'All right,' he said, grudgingly.

She walked to the small compartment at the back and, looping her hand through the leather strap, adjusted her balance to the bumping and swaying. The few other passengers were sitting in the main body. She was the only grey one on board so she had the small, dirty compartment to herself. She watched two women, deep in conversation, making the occasional absent-minded gesture towards controlling the motley collection of children that swarmed over the empty seats.

'Well he's very good really,' one was saying. 'Now that he has the car, he takes the oldest boy to the football match every Saturday. Of course, he didn't do it before. Before he got the car, that is. Well, you couldn't expect him to, could you? Kids are such little devils on the bus.' She hoisted a whimpering toddler on to her knee, making perfunctory noises of affection before rounding on a small girl sitting quietly in the seat behind. 'What do you think you're doing there, girl?' she snapped. 'Didn't I tell you to look after Eamon? And look at Jimmy's face—he's got it filthy.'

Sarah winced as the woman's hand came down across the child's head. The other children fell silent, stopping their horse play to watch with looks of eager anticipation on their faces. Sarah closed her eyes to shut out their twisted pleasure. It all started so young.

She forced herself to think of something else, her meeting with Carl. She wanted to talk to him about his paintings, to ask if he portrayed his experience or his dream, but she also wanted to know much more than that. She could see him as he had stood on the pavement, looking at her intently: blue eyes that showed an awareness, a questioning; tiny laughter lines that formed creases as he talked; lips that smiled readily, with no need for hiding. That was it. She wanted to know why he trusted people enough to let them see him.

The bus had left the outskirts of the city behind and was now empty except for the two women and their children. Sarah shifted her grip on the hanging strap and wished that it was time to get off. Her muscles ached from trying to keep her balance as the bus swayed and jolted over the bumpy road, and her hand had become numb. She wanted to get out of this dirty, stuffy compartment, with its slatted half-partition that obscured her yet displayed her—a creature apart.

She sensed someone near her and glanced down to see the small girl looking up into her face, dried tears staining the plump cheeks, eyes round with fear and wonder. Sarah looked at her for a long moment, seeing the beginning of the pattern that would change the childish stare into the blank, defensive gaze.

'Can you talk?' the girl asked.

'Yes, but you had better go back to your mother.'

The child stood there gazing up at her as if at some alien being. 'Can you feel?'

Sarah caught her breath, held in time by those wide eyes waiting for the answer, then nodded her head. 'Yes,' she whispered, 'I can feel.'

The child stood back, still looking into her face.

'Susan, what are you doing?' The mother's voice shrilled into the silence of the little compartment. The child threw a frightened look down the bus and then, stepping closer to Sarah, kicked her viciously on the shin before running headlong back to her seat. Sarah winced with pain as the raucous laughter of the small boys rang around the metal walls. Everyone needed a victim.

She waited at the side of the road until the bus was out of sight and then turned into the small lane closed in with hawthorn and wild briar, the grass reclaiming the broken asphalt surface. She stopped as soon as the curve of the lane hid the road from sight and felt the stillness around her. The air cleared her throat of the diesel fumes and the cloying smell of stale sweat. The gentle rustles in the hedges and the beautiful extrovert squabblings of the birds made her forget the squalor of the city, the ugliness of the bus. She spent all her spare time enduring unpleasant bus journeys, to come to the peace and freedom of spots like this. She stood and looked up at the clear blue sky and the fear inside her fell away. Maybe that was what she would do when the nightmare was over. She could never envisage her life when they had won their struggle and she had nothing more to contribute. Maybe she would do nothing, just live in a spot like this and let its peace wipe away all the horrors she had lived through. She felt a surge of well-being at the thought and threw her arms wide to embrace the dream.

The lane stopped abruptly at a wide grass clearing, sheltered by tall trees, the river flowing and rippling in a wide sweep between intermittent clumps of waving reeds. The quiet beauty of the place caught her as it had done every time she came.

His car was pulled in under a tree but there was no sign of him. She walked to the water's edge, pleased to savour the continuing silence.

'I was watching you coming.' His voice was close by.

She watched him as he climbed down from the tree, pulling small twigs from his hair and sweater, and still watched him as he walked towards her smiling. 'I'm glad you came.' He seemed relieved to see her, as if he had not really expected her.

'But I said I would come,' she answered. 'Am I late?'

He shook his head, still smiling, and pointed to a picnic basket at the river's edge. 'I thought you might be hungry. I am—I didn't bother with lunch.'

She looked at the hamper but made no move towards it. Was he going to ask her about the society she lived in? She knew now that his life was very different from those men she met at work or observed around her. She remembered the shock she had felt when he had asked her to have coffee and she had tried to find a sign of cruelty in his face. She had not been able to accept the fact that he did not know about the laws.

'It's a beautiful spot,' he said, throwing his arms wide, embracing the whole scene. 'Do you see the sun making patterns through the trees? And the birds, do you hear them?' He turned back to her with a slight mocking shake of the head. 'But of course you do. You come here quite a lot, don't you?'

'Quite often,' she admitted.

He tried to recapture the brief contact of the previous evening. 'Shall we have some coffee? I can bring the basket into the clearing here.'

She recognized his attempt at understanding and walked over to the hamper, sitting with her fingers in the rippling water. It was the first time she had not been alone here, but he did not intrude. In some peculiar way, he blended with the atmosphere. Her mind wandered over the events of the last few days: the feeling she had thought was fear when Steiner's man had stepped out in front of her; the blind, overwhelming emotion that was the true fear when she walked through the doors of police headquarters; her sense of helplessness and insignificance when she felt Steiner's hand on her arm and the horror of his nearness. And all the time, Mary's face in the harsh light, as if she was already sitting in the interrogation room. She closed her eyes, seeing the tortured body, but with Joan's calm, reasoning face, asking her for something to stop the pain. How could she talk to this man about his vision of life when the reality was ugliness and death?

She glanced across at him and looked directly into the blue eyes watching her closely. 'Why did you come this afternoon?' she asked.

His voice was gentle, but his eyes were puzzled, looking into hers. He sat forward, hands clasped around his knees, intense. 'You must know that I'm a stranger here. I was born in the country but I know nothing about it, or about the society.' She watched him as he shifted and sat staring at his hands. He looked up into her face again, seeking some sign of encouragement, but she still could not give it.

'When you told me yesterday that you were restricted to certain eating places,' he went on, 'I didn't believe you. I thought—oh, I don't know what I thought. And then I decided to find out if what you said was true.' He was still watching her, still looking for a reaction to his words. 'I found out some things—but I don't understand them.'

He did want her to tell him about the society. He wanted her to tell him of the emptiness and the isolation and the fear, of the small cage she was packed into, of all the small cages that all the women were packed into. Why did he want to let that horror into his view of life? It had no place in those singing murals.

He leant forward towards her, exasperated, demanding. 'I want to know. Why do you wear those clothes? Why do you hide the colour of your hair? Why do you sit there looking at me as if I don't exist?'

She watched the anger rising in him but it did not threaten her. He needed to know: as she needed to know about his paintings. But why? Did he only want to know about the society that had formed her—an idle curiosity aroused by her lack of reaction to him? She knew he could not understand her blankness and lack of response. It irritated him, she could see it in his eyes, feel it in the tension of his body. But why should he expect a reaction from her? No one else expected reactions. She had been taught to have none. So she wore the mask society had placed on her and lived secretly, and safely, behind it. Except when she was with the women. There was no need for the mask then. They knew and accepted the different moulds that lay beneath the similar masks.

Could he be trying to do just that? Was it something more than just idle curiosity that made him pull at her blankness, trying to see beyond it? Did he know that, under the male body he wore, he was a human-being the same as she? Or was he, in his awareness of his own being, trying to find out if she existed? She looked at him closely as he leant against the tree, his eyes still intent upon her face. Could he have painted those murals if he were unaware of the people beneath the bodies? She remembered their beauty and the balance. Finally she said, 'You didn't put any death in your paintings.'

Her words confused him. 'Yes. There was death there,' he answered.

'I didn't see it. I didn't see any ugliness.'

He was puzzled. 'But death doesn't have to be ugly.'

She looked at him, seeing the broken bodies that Mary had painted for her in the desolate basement. And then she saw again the soaring sweep of the murals reaching up into the darkness of the vaulted ceiling. 'Can life be that beautiful?'

She saw him staring at her, making some sense, at last, of her thoughts. His eyes wandered over her face and hair, her shapeless grey clothes, the thick grey stockings that blunted any identity in her legs and ankles, the flat-heeled black shoes that weighted her firmly to the void of anonymity, and he dropped his head on to his chest, his fingers idly plucking at the blades of grass between his feet. He turned to her, at last, and his face looked empty, the face of a man who had the courage to look at his thoughts and did not like what they showed him. 'So it's true,' he said softly. 'All the things I saw and heard yesterday, they're true. I tried to ignore them. I didn't want them to be real.'

She heard the slight tinge of pain around the edges of his voice and wondered if the pain was for himself or for the society in which he found himself. She sat forward suddenly, looking hard at him as another thought came into her mind. Could the pain be for her?

He ran his hands over his hair in an unconscious gesture of concentration. 'You dye your hair and wear those clothes because you're a woman worker. You eat in separate restaurants, squalid, horrible restaurants. And you're not allowed to talk to me because you're a woman worker. And you look at me as if I don't exist because . . .' The confusion showed on his face as he tried to form a conclusion from his thoughts. He shook his head slowly. 'I don't know.' He looked at her and raised his hands in a small gesture of defeat. 'I don't know. It's something to do with all the rest.'

Sarah watched the conflict in him and suddenly, surprisingly, she wanted to help. But she needed reassurance first. She leant towards him, surprising him with her action. 'Tell me,' she whispered. 'Can life be that beautiful?'

He nodded, not understanding. 'Yes. Life can be very beautiful. More beautiful than I can show.'

She believed him. She had not led the women into this uprising on the strength of fantasies. All she believed, deep down inside herself, was right. 'All my life,' she said, 'I have been taught that I don't exist.' He stared at her in a frozen stillness. She went on in the same calm voice, watching his eyes. 'I have been taught that I have a body, arms, legs that can work at a humble level for the good of the state, and that I have no function outside of that. I have no intelligence, no reasoning, no emotions and no needs.'

She saw fear in his eyes as he stared silently at her. Why, fear? Was he afraid of her? Or was he afraid for her? Did he see her as a person who had been bent and moulded beyond recognition? Or did he see the mould as a reality?

She saw the questions beginning to form in his eyes and felt she was suspended in space and time as she watched him. Would he be able to accept that she could still exist under this mask? Would he have the courage, the interest to ask? She sat and looked at him, her eyes blank, her face expressionless.

He got to his feet and strode across to the large tree. He stood looking up into the high branches where he had sat as he waited for her to come, then turned abruptly and looked back across the grassy space that separated them. 'I saw you,' he shouted defiantly, his arms pointing up into the height of the tree. 'Do you hear me? I saw you.'

He walked back to her, hands half-clenched, looking down into the grey eyes. He bent slightly towards her, holding her gaze, body tense. 'You don't believe any of it.'

Sarah closed her eyes. This stranger, this human being who wore the body of a man, had reached out and touched her. He had seen that she existed, he had not doubted, he had not questioned. He had *known* that she existed. She felt a gentleness inside her towards this stranger, a gentleness that she had only felt for the women. 'No,' she smiled, 'I don't believe any of it.'

He looked at her for a long time as the tension gradually drained from his muscles and she let him see the happiness in her eyes. He threw himself full length on the grass, hands behind his head, looking up at the blue sky and drifting clouds before turning to look at her again, emotions bubbling inside him and chasing each other across his face; happiness, discovery, curiosity.

He sat up urgently and leant towards her. 'But why do they do it?' he demanded. 'Do you mean that they really teach you all that stuff? And the clothes and . . .' The gesture of his hands encompassed her whole body. 'Are there laws? I mean, do you really break the law if you don't wear those clothes?'

Sarah smiled at the impatience, the need to know. She knew that she would have to tell him, would answer all his questions. She would eventually tell him about the destruction and humiliation, because he did not see her in a cage. She was also sure that there was plenty of time for the telling. She did not know why, but she felt the links already between them would strengthen into something that was, at the moment, beyond her comprehension.

She looked around her, absorbing the beauty of the spot; the shining water with the small moorhens bobbing their busy way against the current; the faint scent of wild briar and woodbine; the sense of stillness that hid the teeming life in the hedgerows. And suddenly she did not want to bring in the ugliness of her society—not yet. She wanted to savour the unexpected contact with another human being—no conflict, no deception, no fear.

She looked at the forgotten coffee flasks, still unopened, and at the hamper, still full of packages. 'I'll tell you—but later.' She looked at him questioningly. If he insisted, she would tell him now. But he seemed to sense her mood, following her gaze across the water and the trees.

He grinned across at her. 'I'm starving. Let's eat.'

He had gone to considerable trouble with the picnic—chicken, salads, crisp rolls, cheeses. Sarah stared at the abundance of food, protesting at the amount he tried to persuade her to eat, covering her plate with her hands in mock desperation as he slipped extra pieces on to it. She sat back and watched him eating with relish, marvelling at the contact between them.

'You don't eat enough,' he said.

'I'm not used to so much food.'

She remembered the woman behind the counter of the café, where she sat each evening. She too had said she did not eat enough.

'You're hiding again.' His voice broke in on her thoughts, but gently, the smile in his eyes taking away any possibility of offence. She looked at him, puzzled. 'Your eyes,' he went on. 'You were looking through me again, as if I didn't exist.'

'No.' She smiled at him. 'I was only thinking. About a woman I know. She was a bio-chemist when Gorston came to power—married, with a child. When the new laws came in she was sent to one of the rehabilitation centres. She works in a small café now. I don't know what happened to the child.'

'But, how can these things happen? And why?'

He had not tried to ask her any questions while they were eating, but had gently teased her about the food she would not eat, boasting, in a self-mocking way, about his prowess as a cook and assuring her that he had cooked the chicken and prepared the various salads himself. But, she knew the questions were still racing through his mind.

She looked down at her hands, trying to sort out the words, to tell him of the full horror. 'How?' she began. 'Because the people voted him in as dictator. The powers he didn't have in the beginning, he took. Why . . . ?' She looked up at him and gave a small shrug. 'I don't know if I have the full answer.' Her eyes slid past him, looking into the distance, as if trying to work out a familiar problem that still escaped her understanding. 'It was as if a concealed hysteria broke out. Gorston didn't create it. He only fed it and brought it out into the open.' She turned to look at him, the puzzlement clear in her eyes. 'It was like a wave of fear and hatred released against the women. There were injustices against women before Gorston. They were paid lower wages. There were certain jobs they couldn't hold. The social welfare benefits were unfairly distributed. Various things like that. But when Gorston started to speak and told the men that they were the only ones significant to the economy and the women were only fit to care for men and give them children, it was as if he were verbalizing all the feelings that had lain hidden. Gorston didn't make the situation—the situation made him. And when the Church backed him and said the woman's place was in the home producing children, that put the religious seal on it as well.'

He was listening attentively, trying to understand, his face serious, frowning with concentration. 'But, surely, preventing married women from working during an economic recession is a long way from what you have now?'

She looked at him in dismay. Was he blind after all? Was he like all men, with one set of values and justice for themselves and a different set for women? She looked directly into his eyes and her voice was low. 'Is it?'

He saw her reaction and hurried on. 'I mean—how did that turn into this present society?'

'Very easily. The economy couldn't balance without the women working. So, to maintain the position that only men were important, women were only allowed menial jobs. The number of women needed by the economy was calculated and this percentage was extracted from the female population. The rest had to marry.'

'But, why didn't he let the women who wanted to work, work?' He suddenly picked up a word she had used. 'What do you mean "they were extracted"?'

Sarah closed her eyes. She had said she would answer his questions and she would keep to her word. But she could not watch his face when she told him.

'At the age of ten—' Her voice trailed off as the buried memories re-emerged. Her childhood; the special school; the regimentation; the enforced anonymity; the erosion of personality; the school books; the teachers; the catechism class. God, God, God, the catechism class! 'Repeat it, Hillard! Repeat it, Hillard! Again Hillard!' She stopped, dragging away from the memories, opening her eyes to tell herself she was here, at the river, under the open sky.

'Don't.'

She felt a soft touch on her arm and looked into blue eyes full of concern. She shook her head, mutely, unable to control her voice, her hands fluttering uncontrollably, her breath sucked in.

'I'm sorry,' he said. 'There's plenty of time. You can tell me another day.'

She still could not speak but her thoughts screamed at him. 'No, now.' She had to control her voice, her body. What was wrong with her? She had felt strong emotions before but she had always been able to bury them deep in the dark places were no one could see them. She had to push them down. Now, now. She felt fear as she looked at him. Did it mean that once you let someone see past the mask, you could never wear it again? Was it a step you could only take once? If you reached out and touched another human being did the touch prevent you from ever turning away?

She looked up at the sky, willing her body to stop trembling. She leant forward, putting her hand into the running water, watching it trickle through her fingers, cool, clear. She wiped her fingers in her sleeve and got to her feet. Her voice was calm again and her eyes were cool as she looked at him.

'I must go. It's getting late.'

Nine

'He's a sick man, a very sick man.'

Marsham sat back in his comfortable armchair, sucking at his pipe. He always felt good in this room, with its book-lined walls and soft sheens of polished wood and old leather.

'But we know that,' the other man answered. 'His laws have got madder and madder over the years. His solutions to the problems of the economy are more extreme. And those changes of mood—well . . .'

Marsham looked across at his friend. Strange, the affinity between them. There must be—what?—about twenty years' difference in their ages. But Martin was one of the few men he could communicate with as an equal without tediously having to explain his thought processes. He'd caught him with this one, though. He felt an impish pleasure at the thought. 'No. I don't mean that,' he said. 'I mean his physical health.'

Brian Martin looked at him, suddenly alert. 'You got something out of Werner.'

Marsham waved his pipe in the air, a gentle, innocent smile on his face. 'Now you have it, Brian. Straight from the horse's mouth, so to speak.'

'Well, go on.' Martin was in no mood for intellectual guessing games, and Marsham could see the suppressed excitement in him.

'Apparently Gorston could have the fatal attack at any time,' Marsham explained. 'That's what Werner wanted to see me about. He wanted to ask me not to suggest the women were responsible for the paper. He had to sedate Gorston heavily the night before and he was pretty worried about the cabinet meeting.' He absently picked up his pipe again, toying with it in his hands. 'Funny thing was, I got the feeling that he was trying to say more than he actually did. He's a tired old man, with something on his mind he can't handle any more.'

'Any idea what?'

'No.' Marsham was pensive, remembering the exhausted face, eyes closed in defeat. 'No, but he seemed concerned about the new educational programme. He jumped straight to that after telling me how ill Gorston is.'

'If he's that ill, we can move straight away.' The third man who, until now, had sat silently listening, jumped to his feet impatiently. 'Well, doesn't it?' he demanded. 'If he's as ill as you say, his death can easily be made to look natural. We are organized. You know that. We could take over tomorrow.' He turned to face the two men, looking challengingly first at Marsham and then at Martin. 'Well couldn't we?' he persisted.

'Not so fast, James. Not so fast.' Marsham got up and patted his shoulder. 'There are other things to consider.'

'Such as what?' James Foster's tone was truculent.

'Such as the women's business.' Brian's cool, incisive voice cut across the display of impatience, as Marsham nodded in silent agreement.

Foster looked from one man to the other, not understanding. 'But the more unrest, the better,' he said.

'James.' Marsham pushed him gently into the chair. 'Listen. When that paper came out, we were all surprised—shocked even. I still can't understand how they managed to break through their conditioning and achieve such a thing. But they did. That means there's now another force to be considered. They're not very strong. They have no power to do anything. But they are a united group, however small. If Gorston dies, they might respond. Obviously, they see him as the personification of all their grievances. With him dead, they might be foolish enough to do something rash. I don't know quite what, but it could lead to open unrest. That's the last thing we want when we take over.'

Brian cut in with less patience than Marsham. 'The takeover has got to be smooth—no outward signs of violence, no outward signs of change. This country is a powder keg and doesn't even know it. Take off the lid too fast, or let it appear to be slipping, and the whole lot will explode in our faces.'

Foster, young and inexperienced, still was not satisfied. 'But we plan to use the unrest among the men,' he said. 'You've culti-vated it.'

Brian stirred in his chair, exasperation clear on his face, but Marsham stilled him with a small gesture. He could hear an echo of his own youthful impatience in the earnest young man and he wanted to overlay that remembered impatience with his experi-ence over the years. 'The men's unrest is controlled,' he said care-fully. 'We instigated it, selecting the men and only involving those who were in the right places. When we take over, these men will openly support us, giving the lead to those around them, reassur-ing them, promising them reforms. And there will be reforms. Small ones at first, then gradually more, until we get this country functioning properly again.'

James was restless under the lecture. 'I know all that. What I can't see is why we can't do the same thing with the women. I know you haven't been involved with organizing them, but they *are* organized—you said it yourself. So why can't we approach them and offer them reforms, the same as the men?'

'For heaven's sake, James.' Brian's suppressed irritation finally broke out. 'What's wrong with you? I know you're not interested in women, but I would have thought even you would see the dif-ference between the two situations.'

The young man started to his feet, an angry flush sweep-ing across his face, until Marsham interrupted smoothly, 'It's a difference I didn't see for a long time.' He lied glibly, giving the young man his dignity back. 'But when you think about it, it's a very important one. As I see it, we would have great difficulty in contacting them. Do you fancy your chances in talking to one of those women and getting through to her? All right, we know that there must be some of them who are using that blankness as a cover, some of them must be thinking behind that mask. But who? How many? And how do you find out?' He shrugged expressively, continuing his pretence of identification. 'I wouldn't know where to start. And I think there's an even greater problem. Supposing you did manage to meet one of the thinking ones—one who has somehow managed to shake off Gorston's brainwashing. You're still dealing with a woman, someone who reacts emotionally, who's unable to see the wider implications in a situation, who reasons with instinct and not with logic. How would you explain the importance of a cool, calm approach to someone like that?'

The silence extended as the two friends watched James for his reaction. Finally he spoke. 'So, if what you are saying is correct, the women will react in some way, as soon as Gorston is dead, and that reaction could trigger an explosion in Brian's powder keg?'

Marsham nodded, the benign professor with his favourite pupil. 'That's right. And it needn't be a very dramatic reaction. Cheering in the streets could do it.' He smiled at the ludicrous picture he had painted.

'There's another point,' Brian said, relaxed now, glad that Marsham had taken responsibility for the tedious explanations. He cocked his head sideways at James. 'Did you read that paper of theirs?' James nodded. 'Well, you'll know that they were talking about all humans being equal? Equal opportunities for women— that sort of thing.'

'Yes.'

'Well, that's what they would want from us.' He waved his hand expansively. 'All right, that's no big deal. We could promise them equality and the chances are they would progress a bit further than where they are at the moment, but nothing dramatic.' He leant forward in the chair, tapping his knee with his finger, giving emphasis to the words. 'The point is, the people wouldn't see it that way. They would see it as a threat and, instead of supporting us, well—' He shrugged expressively.

James looked from one man to the other. 'Well, what do we do?' he asked.

'Nothing.' Marsham's voice was certain, brooking no argument. 'We wait. We wait until this women's business has died down. They've made their gesture. There's nothing more they can do. And no group can keep its solidarity when it's just kicking its heels. Besides, it won't take Steiner long to round them up.' He looked around the room, appreciating the colour the evening sun had brought to the mellow tones, and then smiled his innocent smile. 'We'll just have to hope that Gorston lives a bit longer. I rather like the irony of that.'

The two friends sat in companionable silence, relaxing in each others company after James had made his farewells.

'You shouldn't have said that to him, Brian,' Marsham chided. 'He's very vulnerable.'

'I know, but he's so exasperating sometimes.'

Marsham's voice was mild and affectionate as he went through the ritual movements with his pipe. 'He's young. You're too impatient with him. We need young men like him. They're our successors, y'know.'

'Any sign of a baby?' Martin replied.

Marsham moved into the change of topic with the ease of familiarity. 'No. And I don't think there will be.'

'How long has he been married now?' Brian stretched his legs out, settling deeper into the comfort of the leather armchair.

'Three years at Christmas, I think.'

'They'll be checking up on him soon.'

'Mmm, I know. They always check up early on the late marriages. He got a two year deferment, didn't he, on the grounds of extra study?' Marsham pulled himself lazily from his chair and walked over to the small drinks table, to pour out two liberal whiskies, adding ice to one and handing it silently to Brian. 'I tried to talk to him about it the other day. I told him that they would be around soon and that he should do something about it—have a chat to one of his friends who would oblige.' He looked across at the other man with a mischievous grin on his face. 'Told him I'd only be too pleased, but I didn't think I could get it up any more.'

Brian gave no sign of seeing the humour of the suggestion. 'Well, if he can't or won't do it, he'd better get someone who will, *before* they start checking. We don't want any of us being investigated by some tin-pot little official at this stage. It's stupid things like that that can wreck everything.'

'I think he's relying on the take-over coming before it happens.'

'I noticed you steered him away from asking what we'll do if Gorston dies before Steiner rounds up the women,' Brian said.

'Yes, well, I've been giving that a lot of thought.'

'I bet you have, you cunning old fox. And I'll lay odds I know what your solution is.'

'Done,' Marsham replied quickly, delighted at the prospect of his favourite game. 'Loser stands lunch tomorrow.'

'Right. If Gorston dies before Steiner rounds up the women—' Brian sat back in the chair, staring at the ceiling, trying to get into Marsham's head '—we will . . . we will replace all Gorston's key men with our own, as originally planned. But with the exception of Steiner. Steiner will be approached and persuaded that unless a strong man replaces Gorston immediately, etc etc etc. That his own position depends on it. He would buy that. Then we put a man to watch Steiner and wait for him to dispose of the women.'

'Well done,' Marsham laughed. 'You know me too well. And—?'

'And? Is there an and?'

'Of course. After Steiner cleans up the women, we have him killed and you take over his position as we agreed.'

Brian looked at Marsham sombrely, the amusement suddenly gone from the game. 'Of course,' he said. 'That is what you would do.'

'Right. I think we'll call that a draw. What do you think of the solution?'

'It has its dangers,' Martin said, after some thought. 'Do you think Steiner knows how ill Gorston is?'

'Oh, I think he's bound to. His men are everywhere.'

'Right, then if I were Steiner, I would watch anyone I thought might be interested in taking over from Gorston. And I would carefully groom my own man as the future president. We know Steiner isn't interested in the job himself. He likes to be the threat behind the throne. When Gorston dies, I—still being Steiner— would make pretty sure I moved first.'

'Excellent.' Marsham beamed across the room. 'You back up my interpretation exactly.'

Brian got up to refill his glass and walked over to his old friend. 'Come on,' he said. 'I know the signs. What are you waiting to spring on me?'

'Patience, patience.' Marsham's enjoyment of the intellectual guessing game was too great to allow it to be hurried. 'So—' He looked expectantly at Brian, waiting for him to make the next jump.

Brian stood pensively, twirling his glass slowly between his hands, watching the amber liquid swirl in gentle circles. Marsham observed him intently. Suddenly, the younger man threw his head back and gave a snort of laughter. 'You old fox! You know who Steiner's man is!'

Marsham was nodding, delightedly. 'Yes, yes,' he admitted. 'And that's the key to our solution! If Steiner's man dies just before, or immediately after Gorston, Steiner will have to accept our offer. Even if it's only to give himself time to think.'

Brian was impatient. 'Well, come on,' he demanded. 'Who is Steiner's man?'

Marsham lit his pipe slowly, carefully, as Brian shifted with exasperation. At last, he looked through the curling smoke and grinned his boyish grin. 'Blake.'

'Blake?' Brian looked at him in disbelief—much to the older man's satisfaction as he sat puffing vigorously at his pipe. 'But the man's a fool!' he declared.

'True.' Marsham nodded in thoughtful agreement. 'But isn't that exactly what Steiner needs? He wants a man who can be controlled easily, who the people associate strongly with Gorston, who subscribes to Gorston's beliefs. Blake fits the bill on all counts. He could sit on that chair for years with Steiner pulling the strings.'

'But only if there was no one else pushing for power,' Martin answered.

'Ah.' Marsham sat back, waving his pipe at the man who was standing tensely, looking at him. 'There you have it. As soon as Gorston dies, whether by fair means or foul, Steiner will have to move against anyone who might be interested in stepping into the dead man's shoes. But with Blake dead as well, he's checked. And—when he clears out the women—checkmate.'

Brian walked slowly back to his chair, going over in his mind Marsham's theories, probing for weak points. 'What happened about the new educational programme at yesterday's meeting?' he said finally.

Marsham looked at him sharply, wondering where his thoughts were going. 'It went just as expected. Gorston propounded his theories and the motion was carried. Implementation to be immediate. All the preliminary work has already been done. Yesterday's meeting was a mere formality.'

'I was trying to work out whether this new measure will stir the women up even more,' Martin explained.

'More likely they'll see it as a retaliatory measure,' Marsham replied. 'It may even quieten them a bit, although the chances are Steiner will have them before the programme actually starts. There are still some administrative details to implement.'

Brian wasn't satisfied. 'I don't know. I don't dismiss the women's significance the same way that you do. They've pulled one surprise on us so far.'

'Oh, really, Brian. What can they do? There's only about forty of them. Come on. We can discuss it again after dinner. You are staying, aren't you?' Marsham moved over to a small table with an unfinished chess game on it. 'Let's get a few moves in before we eat.'

Ten

Sarah turned into the door of the hostel, thankful for having the bus journey behind her. She needed the solitariness of her room to sort out the jumble of thoughts and feelings that her meeting with Carl had sent whirling through her mind. She was tired, her legs leaden as she walked slowly up the stairs. She did not even want to think. She just wanted to sleep.

The hostel had the strange emptiness that seemed to descend at weekends, the deception of a deserted building that is hiding its inmates behind locked doors. The faint strains of Chopin drifting from one of the rooms merely underlined the isolation.

'I've been watching for you,' a voice said close by. The panic was clear on Stephanie's face as she pulled Sarah into her room, leaning back against the closed door as if to keep out invisible dangers. 'I thought you'd never get back.'

'Steph, what is it?' Sarah demanded. She watched the frightened woman staring at her, trying to put into words the fears she had lived through during the long afternoon. 'At the beginning, Steph. Start at the beginning.' Sarah could feel the tension mounting in her as still she waited, restraining the need to shake the information from the staring, inarticulate woman.

Finally Steph spoke. 'Joan has been taken.'

Oh God, no. When? This afternoon? After their meeting? The articles. Was she still carrying the articles? She suddenly remembered Joan's face, calm, considered, telling her that she wanted to be able to kill herself if ever she was captured. And Sarah had not got her anything. She caught Stephanie by the arm, leading her to a chair, willing her to control her panic and tell her, in detail, what had happened. 'When did it happen? How do you know about it? Come on, Steph, you've got to tell me.'

'This afternoon,' Steph stuttered, 'about two o'clock.' She steadied herself, forcing the words to come out in sequence. 'I was coming home from work when one of my women contacted me. She lives in the same hostel as Joan and she saw two men drive up in a car, and then leave almost immediately with her. The peculiar thing was, the men weren't in police uniform.' She turned to Sarah with a pleading look on her face. 'I didn't know what to do. I knew you'd gone off on one of your trips to the country and—'

A picture of the river and the picnic and Carl came into Sarah's mind. This had all been happening when she was on her way to meet him. She should have been here.

The faintly breathless voice was still going on. 'So I contacted Ann and Eli. I took a chance. The woman at the local café is one of my group and we used the small room at the back. I had to do something, Sarah.'

'I know, I know. Go on.'

'Well, Eli said we needed to get in touch with Mary—to see if any of her women knew which Detention Centre Joan had been taken to. But we couldn't do that until four. And, then, Ann kept wondering why the men weren't in uniform—they weren't even using an official car.'

Yes, Sarah thought, Ann would spot that. It was the only hope she had. Why would Steiner send men out of uniform? Were they Steiner's men? If not, who were they?

Steph was still speaking. 'So then Ann said we may be jumping to conclusions. We had assumed that Joan had been arrested because of her part in the paper but, she said, we should consider what else might have happened.'

Sarah could almost hear Ann's logical voice, calming the panic in Stephanie, curbing the open aggression in Eli. 'So?'

'She suggested we contacted our groups and find out if any other women had been taken. And, Sarah, I don't understand it, but they have. Three women from my chain have gone, and one from Eli's. There may be more. We haven't got all the reports back yet. Eli has gone to try and see Mary so we should have some information about where they are by tonight.'

Sarah walked across to the window, staring out at the empty street. If they weren't Steiner's men, who were they? What was the connection between Joan and the other women? Had they found the articles? 'Steph,' she said quickly, 'listen.' She sat opposite the nervous woman, noticing that her tension was lessening slightly now that she was no longer responsible for organizing their actions. 'What work do the other women do? Do they live near Joan? We have got to think of something that connects them all.'

'The three in my chain all work in or around hospitals,' Steph replied. 'The one from Eli's chain works in a factory. They all live in different hostels.'

'The three who work in hospitals, what jobs have they got?'

'Two are cleaners, the other is a ward orderly, the same as me.'

Sarah persisted. 'Do we know yet if any are missing from Joan's chain?'

'No. We didn't know how to check that out. None of us knows how to contact Joan's group.'

Sarah's mind reacted as it always did in emergencies. All tiredness had gone, her thoughts now completely occupied with solving the problem. 'I'm going out,' she said. 'I can contact Joan's group.'

Stephanie sat huddled on the bed, dejected. She was not equipped to deal with situations like this. Sarah sat beside her on the bed, wanting to lift the weight of depression. 'I'm sorry I wasn't here, Steph, but you did everything that had to be done. Are the women going to the basement tonight?' Stephanie nodded. 'Well, try and rest. You're due back at work at six. You need to get some sleep before the meeting.' She left her, still huddled on the bed, knowing she would spend the next several hours imagining the horrors that Joan and the other women were suffering, waiting for more cars to arrive, more men pushing more of her friends into them, until it was her turn.

Sarah walked quickly towards the city centre. The shock of emotion she had felt on first hearing the news had gone. She was taking a chance by trying to contact the woman at the post office, but she was the only one in Joan's group whom she knew. Would the woman respond to her? How did Joan usually contact her?

She crossed the wide, busy bridge that led to the main street of the city, past the towering bronze of Gorston that overshadowed the other statues of the country's historical heroes, and through the large pillars that flanked the entrance to the main post office. The hall was busy with the last-minute rush of customers and Sarah looked anxiously for the face she had seen only once before. She spotted the woman standing at the telegram counter and Sarah, after a moment's hesitation, took down a form from the rack and scribbled a hasty message before joining the queue of waiting people. She studied the woman's face carefully as she made her slow way towards the counter. How would the woman react to a stranger? And, even if she accepted her, how could she communicate with her? She stepped up to the counter, handing the small form through the grill. 'I'd like to send this telegram, please.'

The woman's eyes flickered over her without interest and glanced down at the scrap of paper. 'I'm sorry. You have to get sanction to send this. Do you know where to go?'

Sarah followed the woman's lead and shook her head silently.

'If you'll follow me, I'll show you.' The woman turned, gesturing to a young girl to take her place at the counter, and joined Sarah in the body of the hall, walking briskly towards the stairway. Sarah followed her into a small empty room on the first floor and the woman turned to face her, making no attempt at communication.

'Joan has been taken,' Sarah said, without preamble. 'We don't know yet if it was by the police. Four other women are missing and I am trying to find out if there are more.' Her voice was sharp, incisive. She had to make this woman accept her fully. 'Can you contact the others in your group and find out if any are missing from your chain?'

The blankness stayed on the woman's face as she looked steadily at Sarah for a moment longer, then it gave way to concern. 'When did it happen?' she asked.

'This afternoon.' Sarah relaxed slightly.

'A woman was taken from the hostel I stay at—this morning, when I was coming to work.'

Sarah stepped towards her. Another piece of the puzzle? 'This woman, is she in your group?'

'No,' the woman answered. 'I wouldn't think she's in any group. She's a very quiet, timid sort of a woman. Terrified of everything. I don't think anyone would have approached her about the organization.'

'And the men—did you see them clearly?'

'Well, I didn't look at them for too long, but I saw them clearly enough. I felt there was something peculiar about them. They weren't in uniform, but there was something about the car that seemed familiar.' Sarah waited, tense, not daring to hope that the woman's passing glance at the car would give her the lead she was looking for. 'I couldn't make out what it was, at first,' she went on, 'and then, when I got to work, it dawned on me. It was the registration number of the car. We handle the government registrations here, and the number of the car was one of a block that was registered to the Department of Health about a month ago. I processed them and the numbers just stuck.'

Sarah remembered the blankness in the woman's eyes that, so effectively, hid the mind behind them. The Department of Health? A sickness gripped deep in her stomach as she fitted this new piece of information into the jigsaw. Gorston's education programme. They could not be starting it already. The women had carefully monitored its progress ever since they first found out about it. It would be another six weeks before it was ready for implementation. That is what had decided the date of the Rising. Sarah pushed the thoughts away for a moment. She had to arrange for this woman to take Joan's place as the head of her chain. A friend had gone and she had to plug the gap in the organization.

'Every necessary woman has been contacted, and that covers all the detention centres, men and women. They, definitely, have not been taken to any of them.'

'But they must be in one of them,' Eli challenged, pacing around the room, her anger burning. 'Your women must have missed something. They must have.'

Mary shook her head gently, her eyes clouded with a personal pain. 'No, Eli, they haven't. The women haven't been taken to any of the detention centres.'

Eli kicked aside a piece of debris, careless of the noise. 'Then they must have been taken straight to—that hell hole.' Even Eli, in all her rage, could not bring herself to say the name that spelt terror to them all.

'No,' Mary answered. 'Even if they were sent straight there, it would have shown up on records at the main centre. No one has been admitted for the past eleven days.'

Eli came to a halt at the edge of the pool of light. 'Headquarters,' she said through clenched teeth. 'Police headquarters.' She was striking her open hand with a tight fist in an unconscious gesture of anger and aggression. 'It's because of that damned newspaper. Steiner has them there, questioning them himself.' She rounded on Sarah, needing to spill her hate. 'I told you not to publish that paper. We should have attacked without giving them any warning that we existed. But, no. You, and your psychology rubbish about the women needing proof that they could challenge society before they would accept that they were strong enough to destroy it.' She took a step closer to Sarah who sat in silence, not responding to the threatening gesture. 'They've got Joan up there now—and the other women—and they are torturing all the information about the Rising out of them.'

'Eli, stop it.' Ann's voice cut across the torrent of words. 'Sarah was right about the paper. Before we published, the women didn't believe we had a chance of destroying Gorston and all he stood for. They thought the structure was too strong for us. But since the paper has been delivered, you can feel the difference in them. They have proved that Gorston's society isn't omnipotent, and now they believe, really believe, that we will win.' She talked smoothly, smothering Eli's attempts to interrupt. 'Anyway, Eli, that isn't what we should be discussing. Those women who have been taken are far more important than personal feelings at this time.' She met Eli's stare, calmly, for several moments, before gesturing to an empty chair. 'Come on. We've got to discuss what happened.'

The powerfully built woman moved across the cluttered floor, still dissatisfied, still turning her anger against Sarah who had said nothing throughout the tirade. 'Stephanie isn't here yet,' she said finally. 'Has she been taken, as well?'

'Stephanie will be a bit late.' It was the first time Sarah had spoken since she had walked into the basement and found the other women already there, discussing the happenings of the day. She had known what reactions to expect from all of them and Eli's outburst had not surprised her. She had waited for it to be over before telling them of her theories. 'I asked her to make some inquiries before coming here. She shouldn't be long.'

Ann picked up the implications of the words. 'You think you know where they are?'

Sarah looked at the strain showing on the three women's faces and knew her words would add to it. 'Yes, I think so.' Her voice was heavy. 'I don't understand the hows or whys yet, but I think I know who took them. I think the education programme has started.' Her words hung in the silence of the women's stares, in the moments it took for them to understand and react.

'No, Sarah. You must be wrong.' The pain in Mary's voice cut across the room.

'But they can't have. We know that they'll not be sufficiently organized for another six weeks.' Ann was pulling figures out of her head, proving Sarah wrong. 'They have only just got the first print-outs from the computer regarding genealogical suitability.

They still have to match blood groups, fertility factors, organize replacements. There's still three more weeks of computer work before they can start the actual setting up of the clinics.'

Sarah wished Ann's words could prove her wrong, but she knew that, somehow, they had left something out of their careful calculations. Somehow the authorities were ready to start now. 'I know all that, Ann. I told you I didn't understand how they've organized so quickly. But the cars that picked the women up weren't Steiner's cars. They belong to the Ministry of Health. The women who were picked up aren't connected in any way— one of them doesn't even belong to the organization. Mary's women say they have not been taken to any of the detention centres. I've asked Stephanie to contact her women to find out if there's been any unusual activity in any of the hospitals over the last couple of days.'

'All right, supposing you're right,' Eli said. 'What are we going to do about it? Just sit tight and let it happen?' She was sitting forward in her chair, pushing for action, challenging the other women. 'We set the date of the Rising for a month before the earliest date they could've organized this horror. It was the news of this latest piece of legislation that decided us to move. If Sarah is right, we've been badly out in our calculations, so we've got to move now. We've got to bring the date forward.'

Sarah watched Ann considering the suggestion and Eli trying to dominate her, putting the full weight of her forceful personality into the hard stare. Why did Eli have to choose to challenge her now? She always knew it would come, but had expected it nearer the time of the Rising.

'Well,' Ann said finally, 'apart from the fact that the earliest we can organize the Rising is forty-eight hours, I tend to agree with Eli. The final thing that bound all the women together was finding out what Gorston had planned in his education programme. It's what enabled us finally to break through the years of brain-washing that so many of the women still accepted. And now we've let them down. We've let it happen. I think we've got to bring the date forward before any more women are taken in.'

Sarah sat forward, her voice urgent. 'But, Ann, you're missing something. Only six women were taken in today. The first was picked up at about eight-thirty this morning. And none of them have come back. Why? Artificial insemination only takes a few minutes. And why only six? We know they were planning a throughput of three hundred per clinic session. These are the things that still don't make sense, which was why I asked Stephanie to make inquiries.'

She stopped as they heard slight sounds on the stairs, experiencing the usual tightening of muscles until Stephanie walked into the room. The women watched her, knowing from her face that what they feared was true, as Sarah felt herself cocooned in the silence. 'Go on, Steph,' someone said. 'Tell us.' Sarah's chest was tight.

'You were partly right,' Steph said. 'It *is* to do with the education programme, but it hasn't properly started.'

Sarah held up her hand to still Eli as she started to interrupt, impatient to understand what Stephanie meant.

'They are in my hospital,' Steph continued, 'all of them. They must have brought them in after I left. They're going to—' She stopped, staring at Sarah, unable to say the words. Her hands were held out in front of her in a gesture Sarah did not understand. Was she asking for help, or trying to give it?

Sarah stepped closer to her and took hold of the hands that expressed so much misery. 'What are they going to do, Steph?' she said gently.

'They're going to use them to train the technicians.'

Sarah felt sick. No one had spoken since Stephanie had told them the news and Sarah could feel the silence weighing on her, broken only by the harsh, rasping breathing. It seemed to come from a long way off, from another world, but she knew it was Mary, sitting stiff and tense a few feet away from her. She fought down the waves of nausea, breathing deeply to control her body and her mind. She must regain control. She must think. 'Have they started yet?' Her voice was cold, practical.

'No. They had them in for tests today. The training starts tomorrow morning.'

'Does Joan—do the women know why they're there?'

'No.'

'And they are all together? The women, are they all in the same room?'

'Yes.' It was barely a whisper.

'And you know exactly where that is?' Sarah persisted.

'Sarah, what are you thinking?' Ann said, looking at her intently, excitement, doubt and fear chasing themselves across her face.

'We're going to get them out,' Sarah said. 'Tonight.' She looked at the disbelief on their faces, even Eli's, and hurried on, determined to carry them with her, sure of her decision. 'Stephanie, I want you to draw a lay-out of the hospital—exits, entrances, where the women are, everything, in detail.'

'But, how? They're on the first floor. We can't just walk in and take them.' Stephanie was staring at her in disbelief.

'Yes, we can. That's exactly what we can do. Come on, Steph, there isn't much time. We need that sketch.' She turned to the others. 'They've made us grey and anonymous, so we'll use just that fact.'

The ground felt wet under their feet as they waited, quietly, in the thick shrubbery that bordered the car park. Sarah could smell the sweet, damp smell of the leaves. Strange, she would have thought the present heat wave would have dried out even the densest undergrowth. She could feel the tension in Ann as they stared intently at the small, green door that led to the hospital kitchens. It felt as if Stephanie had been gone an hour. Supposing she met someone who knew she was not on the night shift this week? She could have been seen going into the consultant's room.

Ann leant close to her, mouth near her ear. 'Look.' She pointed across the low roof to the large hospital clock illuminated high on the main block. 'She's only been gone seven minutes.'

Sarah felt a shock of surprise and kept her eyes fixed on the large, shining face, seeing the jerk of the hand writing off each minute, until Ann squeezed her arm. 'She's coming.'

'I've got everything,' Steph whispered. 'There's a panic in casualty—nobody even noticed me.'

Ann started to put on the unfamiliar nurse's head-dress, while Sarah hesitated slightly over the sheet of official paper Stephanie had given her. She leant close to Stephanie's ear. 'Are you sure this is the paper they use at St Mary's?'

'Yes. Browne is a consultant at both hospitals. He keeps both papers in his rooms.' She was busy pinning on the impedimenta of a nurse—watch, badges—then looked down to examine the effect. Sarah hastily scrawled a message on the paper, finishing it with an indecipherable signature and clipping it to the official-looking board that had been part of Stephanie's haul. The three women looked at each other for a brief moment.

'Right, Ann. Now.'

Sarah watched her step quickly into the open expanse of the car park and walk briskly down the side drive, giving a slight nod to the lounging guards at the gate, before turning down the street in the direction of the nurses' home.

'Three minutes,' Sarah whispered. 'Three minutes if Eli is there.'

'You'd better go.'

'I'll wait till they get here.'

They stood stiffly among the damp foliage, eyes fixed on the section of road. Sarah could hear the faint clatter of the hospital kitchens beginning the bustle of another day, the steady throb of the air-conditioning plant that seemed to keep in rhythm with the hard beat of her heart.

'She's got it!' Steph exclaimed.

They watched the ambulance drive down the road, indicators flashing, turning in through the main gates, past the uncaring guards, stopping at the wide, brightly-lit entrance. They watched as Ann got out, calm and unhurried, board in hand, looking strange in the unfamiliar dress, disappearing through the glass doors, swallowed up by the bright lights, Eli sitting far back in the shadows of the dark driver's cab.

'Here, they'll need food.' Sarah took the bag from Stephanie and nodded briefly before turning, crouching low to avoid the thicker branches, pushing her way uncaring through the dense bushes that caught at her body as she passed. She hugged the deep shadows of the small streets, past the darkened, silent houses, making for the bulk of the People's Hall.

She rested her head against the small side door that was still surrounded with builders' debris. She had seen no one in the empty streets and she was now safe in the shadows of the large building among the clutter of scaffolding and broken stones. If all went well, the ambulance should be here in fifteen minutes. She unpinned the key from inside the lining of her coat and gently turned it in the lock. It took a few seconds for her eyes to adjust to the deeper gloom, before she could make out the narrow stairs, curling up the stone wall to the smaller galleries in the roof. She knew the little room she would take the women to. There was no need for her to climb the stairs until they arrived. Her feet seemed to move of their own volition, carrying her up the winding stairs, the stone of the wall striking cold against her shoulder, the metal of the key getting warmer in her hand. Upwards, into the long gallery that overlooked the main hall.

They had started to build the ornate dais that would bear the official party at the opening. She could make out the dim outlines of the raised platform, the curving back supports that would carry the flags and the inevitable portrait of Gorston. Her mind threw up pictures of him standing there, arms thrown wide to his audience, the hall crowded with the invited guests, the obedient mob outside the building chanting his name. She could feel the weight of the gun in her hand as she waited for him to start his speech; could see the body falling; screams, consternation, panic. The silence of death settling over the man who had destroyed so many.

There could be no other way. Sarah knew that. When they had planned the Rising, everyone was determined there would be no bloodshed. How could they proclaim the value and dignity of life if they grasped it for themselves by taking it from others? She had spent months planning, studying schedules and movements, ensuring they could succeed without a bloody rebellion. But all the time, deep in her mind, she knew. Gorston would have to die. And she knew that she would have to take the responsibility herself. Could life only grow out of death? She thought of the murals, unseen, but only a short distance from her. Carl was wrong. Death was always ugly. As her death would be ugly. She had planned her escape route from this long, cold gallery, but she knew there was little chance that she would walk away from Gorston's body and out into the daylight. She would not live many minutes more than the man who had tried to destroy her.

She drove the future from her mind and made her way back

down the narrow stairs. Waiting for the ambulance, the women. Thinking, planning, where she could hide them from Steiner's men. They could stay here the night. It was the best place she could think of. But she would have to move them out before the workmen came on Monday. But they were late. How long had she been in the gallery? How long since she had stood in the bushes with Stephanie and watched the ambulance drive into the harsh glare of the hospital lights? She could see Ann, passive, blank-faced, waiting endlessly for the official release of the women on the strength of a worthless piece of paper. Would they query it? A brief phone call. Alarms, policemen. Were they already being taken to the detention centre? There had been so little time. She could have overlooked something, some minor regulation. She remembered Stephanie trying to answer all her questions, suddenly losing her sureness of knowledge because of the importance of her answers. Suddenly, the waiting was in the past. The ambulance turned slowly into the unfinished drive, the noise of its engine shattering the sleeping silence for endless moments before Eli stopped under the trees and the noise became an echo in the stillness.

Sarah stood rigid, looking at the door of the van, counting the shadowy figures as they emerged into the shadowy light. Three, four, five. They had got them. Her breath came out in a long sigh, her legs felt weak as she started towards the small group. 'This way,' she whispered.

'It was perfect,' Eli said jubilantly. 'Ann just stood there and they brought all the women down and just handed them over.' She grinned at Sarah, all memory of animosity washed away. 'Mind you, it was a bit hairy, sitting there in that damned ambulance, trying to think myself into looking like a man. And Ann, standing there in the bright lights of reception, people walking all around her. I don't know how she did it.' She climbed back into the now empty ambulance. 'I dropped Ann off on the corner. I'll give you a few minutes to get the women inside and then I'll dump this by the river.'

'Take care, Eli.' The dangers of the night were not over yet.

But Eli could not be repressed. 'Don't worry. They won't find it for hours. And look. I've been reading too many paperbacks.'

She held out her hands for inspection, the grin showing even more clearly. 'I made all the women do the same thing.'

Sarah looked at her hands, bound around with handkerchiefs, and broke into a quiet laugh. 'Eli, you idiot.'

She led the women through the small door and up the stone steps, passing the long gallery without hesitation, moving further up into the heights of the building—the silence only broken by the sobs of one of the women. 'Here.' She led them into a small empty room. 'You'll be quite safe here,' she said, trying to make her voice soothing and assured. She watched the shadowy outlines of the women as they sat on the bare floor, two of them trying to comfort the still sobbing woman.

Suddenly Sarah was tired. She let her back slide down the stone wall and sat on the floor with the others, leaning her head against the hardness of the stone. Had Eli told them why they had been taken? She was too tired to speak.

'Sarah, why did you do it? What did they want us for?' It was Joan, sitting in front of her, the dim, early light of dawn making her face a white blur against the surrounding darkness. Sarah looked at her in silence, glad that they had not known through the long day what was waiting for them in the morning.

'They did nothing to you?' Sarah asked, her voice flat and lethargic, as she tried to shake off the incipient tiredness.

'No. I thought they were Steiner's men at first, but then they just took me to the hospital and left me in a room with the others. They didn't even search me. We didn't see anyone all day except the nurse who came in to take blood pressure, and she didn't know what was happening either.'

Sarah still did not want to speak. She rested her head against the wall, hearing the quiet whispers of the other women, the first few calls of the city birds announcing another day, smelling the musty stone of Gorston's edifice. She stirred slightly, fighting the lethargy. 'It will be all right now, Joan,' she managed finally. 'Stephanie sent some food. You can stay here for the day and then we'll move you to a safer place.'

She felt Joan's hand on her arm, gently insistent. 'It was something to do with the education programme, wasn't it?'

Sarah pulled her reluctant body away from the supporting

wall, seeing the tension of the past day in Joan's face that had already formed shadows under the calm eyes. 'Yes. They were going to use the six of you for training. They were going to train the technicians on you—all of them.'

Eleven

Blake was content. He thrust his short legs out in front of him, noting the faint pink sunburn over the mildly swelling belly. It was a beautiful day and he had nothing to do except relax in the garden and maybe potter with the flowers later on. He looked across to the small bank of roses, frowning with a passing annoyance at the brown tinge on the slightly drooping petals. He could never get his flowers to blossom with the perfection of Steiner's. He did everything the gardening books suggested, but every time he saw the exquisite roses in Steiner's office, he realized again that he had only achieved the mediocre. He would have to ask Steiner's advice—he would be seeing him this evening. The man obviously liked him. Strange how he, Blake, had feared him all these years. Which just showed that one should never listen to gossip. All that talk about the terror Steiner instilled in everyone; the things he made his policemen do; the way he was supposed to walk around the women workers' hostels during the day when they were empty, not looking for anyone, or at anything, just being there. It was all rubbish. The man was a gentleman. Blake felt an inner warmth at the thought that he was friend to the most powerful man in the country—after the president, of course.

On the rare occasions he allowed himself a degree of self-honesty, Blake knew that he was still afraid of Steiner, that the friendly gestures hid a deeper motive than friendship. But these were unpleasant home truths that he pushed away from his conscious mind.

'You're wanted on the 'phone, dear,' his wife called.

Blake looked lazily at the middle-aged woman—hips widened through too many pregnancies, breasts heavy and pendulous through the sucking of too many infant mouths. She had been a good wife. True, she had objected at first to the Gorston rulings that demanded she gave birth every year, forcing her to give up that job she had when they were first married. But that was all a long time ago, and she had gradually slipped into the role of wife and mother, devoted to making his home life comfortable, cushioned by unobtrusive attention to his every whim. Yet she had had such life in her in those early days. He suddenly remembered with a shock her laughter when they had had their first holiday together—by the sea, where she had made mock complaints at the coldness of the water. He had forgotten that she had used to laugh like that. How strange he should remember it now.

He pulled himself out of the clinging deck-chair. 'Who is it?' he asked.

'Someone from your office. He said it was important.'

What on earth could they want on a Sunday? What was anyone doing at the office on a Sunday? The room felt cool as he picked up the phone, impatient to get back to the heat of the garden. 'Yes, Blake here. Who? Oh, Thorpe. Yes, what is it?'

He listened to the apologetic voice. Six women workers had disappeared. What workers? Hospital, ambulance? What was the man talking about? The guinea pigs—they had disappeared. He cut across the voluble explanations, his voice petulant. 'Listen, Thorpe, six workers can't disappear. They're not small objects that can be mislaid. There's been some sort of a mix-up between the hospitals. Sort it out and don't come running to me with every bit of departmental inefficiency.' Ridiculous man. Disturbing his Sunday with such nonsense. But he had told him what was what. He wouldn't disturb him again in a hurry. Blake walked back to the garden with an unconscious swagger in his rotund little body.

The warm evening air carried the perfume of roses as the two men lingered over their brandies, and Blake blossomed under the attentive ministrations of Steiner. He was the first man that he was aware of who had been invited into the solitary man's house, and the sense of being accepted by such a powerful man lulled his personal fears and inadequacies. It was a beautiful room, with its cool greens effectively displaying the carefully selected furniture—a showpiece of good taste, like the first exquisite wash of a watercolour that waited for the highlights of the artist to give it life. Because, for all its beauty, the room remained a dead thing, as anonymous and barren as the large office at headquarters, the walls bare of paintings, the gleaming wood, unadorned.

Blake accepted the proffered cigar, relishing the ritual, leaning back in the chair to watch the lazy curl of blue smoke. Steiner really was a charming man. Blake was suddenly discontented with the piecemeal clutter that defined his own home. It would be nice to throw it all out and start from scratch. He could afford it now. In fact, he could have afforded it some time ago. He should have thought of it sooner. He owed it to himself—a man in his position. He should have a home to match his level in society. He imagined the clutter transformed into a replica of this elegant room. Of course, the children would have to be kept out of it. He couldn't have them ruining the sophisticated emptiness with all their paraphernalia.

Blake idly wondered how many children Steiner had. Strange how little he knew about the man. Come to think of it, he had never seen his wife, and Steiner never mentioned her. Maybe she was dead. Blake made a mental note never to mention her. The poor man obviously missed her a great deal to so remove all traces of her.

'I'm very worried about Gorston,' Steiner said quietly, his voice shaded with concern and confidentiality. His pale face was emotionless, but Blake could see the worry in the dark eyes.

'Gorston? You worried? Why?'

Steiner carefully removed the accumulated ash from his cigar. 'I thought you'd have noticed it as well. His health is very bad at the moment. Very worrying.'

Blake leant forward slightly, eager for the confidences that strengthened the friendship between them. 'Well of course,' he agreed clumsily. 'I'd noticed that he was showing signs of illness lately, but I thought it was the usual problem of overwork. He really does work far too hard for his own good. I was saying to him only the other week that he should allow his ministers to relieve him of some of the burden. Not that any of us could, of course, not with the important matters, but the small routine things, y'understand?'

'You're very observant, Blake,' Steiner replied smoothly. 'He relies on you a great deal, you know.'

'Well.' Blake made a small deprecating gesture, the pleasure visible on his face. 'I do my best. He's a very great man. The wonders he's achieved with the country during the past thirty years—' He shook his head in admiration.

'That's true. He can never be replaced.'

'No. Absolutely not,' Blake answered quickly. 'Of course, we shall have to face that unpleasant fact one day—but not for some time, surely?'

'That's what is worrying me.' Steiner rose from the table, the perfect host considerate of his guest. 'Shall we take our drinks over to the fire? The evenings seem to get quite chill after the heat of the day.'

Blake settled rather self-consciously in the chair, avoiding contact with the unblemished shine of the polished arms.

'Yes,' Steiner continued, 'as I was saying, that is what's worrying me. I fear his health is cause for far greater concern than any of us have realized.' He tipped the golden liquid around the glass and looked at Blake, still perched on the edge of the chair. 'I fear we may have to consider the possibility that our great president may not be able to lead us for very much longer.'

'But that's terrible! Are you sure? I mean, could you possibly be mistaken?'

Steiner crossed one elegant leg over the other and considered the anxious face opposite him. 'No, I'm afraid not,' he said. 'It came as a great shock. As great a shock as it obviously has come to you. It's his heart, apparently. He's had two severe attacks already. And, as you say yourself, none of us seem to be able to persuade him to slacken his pace.'

The silence lengthened as Blake finished his brandy in a swallow and sat staring at the empty glass.

Finally Steiner spoke again.

'It's getting quite dark. I think we should have a little light.' Blake watched him cross the room, envying him his self-control. He was, obviously, as concerned as Blake himself at this really terrible news, but none of the worry showed as he meticulously adjusted the lamp to throw a warm pool of light around the fireplace. Blake's own mind was in a turmoil. He could not envisage the country without the strong figure of Gorston at its head. Who could replace him? Who would be strong enough to take on such a job?

Steiner settled himself back in his chair. 'What is obvious, of course, is that we must make sure that none of his work is destroyed—that we maintain his breadth of vision, and ensure the country progresses as he himself has planned.' He leant forward, looking intently into Blake's face. 'You agree that these are the considerations we must put before our own personal sorrow?'

'But, of course, of course,' Blake replied hastily. 'It was just the shock. It takes some time to absorb. You're right. We must ensure that his life's work is continued—a perpetual monument to his greatness.' He fiddled with the empty glass, searching for a positive statement to make, feeling his inadequacy in achieving Steiner's wider grasp of the situation. There was no one who could take over from Gorston.

'That is why I invited you here tonight—to discuss the situation,' Steiner went on. 'It seemed perfectly clear to me that the only man capable of continuing Gorston's work as he himself would wish it to be continued is yourself.'

Blake stared in silence, utterly confused. He, replacing Gorston? His eyes were fixed on Steiner's lips, hoping, but not daring to hope, that he had heard correctly.

'Of course,' Steiner added easily, 'I know you never considered this possibility. Your loyalty to the president is as unquestioning and unquestionable as my own. But for the good of the country, we must consider these unhappy circumstances. And, my dear Blake, if you have one fault, it is that of excessive modesty.'

He had not misunderstood. Steiner *did* think that he was the man for the job. Blake saw himself walking across the cabinet room, taking the large chair at the head of the table while the ministers hurried to their lower places.

'Let me fill your glass.' Steiner was standing over him, solicitous, reassuring. Blake's little soul expanded as he gave the glass to his friend—the man who was feared by all the country—and sat back in the chair, stretching his legs in a glow of euphoria. To think, he had been considering refurnishing that stupid little house. He would soon be living in the presidential palace. He stopped his thoughts hastily. 'But, this won't be for some time. I mean, we must make sure that the president rests, takes greater care of his health. A man can live a considerable time with a severe heart condition if he takes good care of himself.' He was unaware of the transparency of his thoughts, as Steiner walked across to the window and looked out across the dark blue out-lines of the garden.

'But, of course. We must both pray that the day we have to implement our plans will be a very long way off. But, we must also be prepared. We owe it to the president.'

Steiner thus removed the guilt from Blake's exciting day dreams and he gave himself up to them completely. He would make a few changes—nothing very drastic. He had always thought it a pity that Gorston was totally opposed to state visits. The presidential palace was a superb setting for the entertaining of foreign heads of state. And, then, there would be the return visits. He could see himself being greeted on foreign tarmacs, the guard of honour drawn up for his inspection, the bands striking up the national anthem. He may have to alter the words slightly. At the moment, nearly every other word was 'Gorston'—not that he wanted to detract, in any way, from the greatness of the man, but it would not give the right impression to other governments if it appeared that the country was living on the glories of a dead man.

And he would never have to put up with petty officials pester-ing him. His ministers would protect him from that. His mind wandered petulantly over the phone calls that had ruined his day—until he had come here tonight, of course. Steiner's com-pany had immediately soothed his dignity. Although, he must admit, he had handled the whole affair with firmness—especially that doctor. The insolence of the man—phoning up a minister in his own home to complain about some trivial mix-up by some of his juniors. He looked across at the still man who had returned to his seat and was watching him, silently. He would show him how well he handled irritations. He swirled his brandy around his glass in an unconscious duplication of Steiner's manner.

'An amusing thing happened today,' he began. 'Although, I

must admit, I was rather annoyed at the time. Thorpe, he's one of my assistants, phoned me up with some ridiculous story about six women workers being mislaid. Well, of course, I told him— no one can mislay women workers, they're too large. But, then this doctor phoned. He really was an insolent man. I intend to do something about him. He claimed his whole training schedule had been disrupted because of the inefficiency of my depart-ment. Well, I mean to say, that is something I won't tolerate. That programme has proceeded with clock-work precision. It was only last week that I was able to tell the president that we had made up a whole week on the original scheduling. And then this trumped-up doctor accuses me of failure. So I said to him, "If, through the inefficiency of your own organization, you manage to lose the women workers you are supplied with, I suggest you contact the appropriate department and requisition six more. I will not have the education programme delayed because of your inability to train the technicians on time." That silenced him, I can tell you.'

Blake sat back, waiting for Steiner's approval of his handling of the whole matter. The silence drew out. Steiner was not responding to his anecdote.

'Cancel it.' The words cut across the room, cold, incisive, bleak.

Blake was bewildered. Steiner must have misheard what he had said. 'No, no, it can't be cancelled,' he blustered. 'I was talking about the training schedule for the education programme. We're using six women workers for the technicians to train on. We'll be starting the whole programme in about three weeks.' He looked at the figure opposite. There was an intensity of stillness that started a small worm of fear in the pit of Blake's stomach. His hands suddenly felt clammy, cold. He hurried on. 'It can't be cancelled. You see, Gorston is determined that I implement on schedule. I mean, I've been working non-stop for the last several months to meet the deadline. It was an almost impossible task, but I achieved it. Gorston was delighted.'

Steiner was still looking at him, not moving, silent. Blake's warm world had become a cold, frightening place and he did not understand why. The man opposite him, in whose company he had blossomed, had become a still, fearsome thing that contracted the muscles of his stomach and forced the sweet taste of fear up into his throat.

As the silence dragged on, Blake finally broke down. 'Yes, yes. Of course. You know best. I'll cancel the training programme, immediately.' He needed to get away from the heaviness of the room, back into the open air, away from this terrifying man. 'I'll return home and cancel it immediately. I'll get them out of bed, if necessary.'

Steiner rose and followed him to the door, his eyes and face, expressionless. As Blake stepped into the gentle, warm evening air, he turned, platitudes of courtesy on his dry lips, but Steiner interrupted him. 'We'll continue our discussion another time—soon.'

The words dried up in Blake's throat and he turned silently towards the gate, his hands trembling in their haste to open the car door and drive away from the man on the steps.

Twelve

Steiner closed the door behind the little man and walked slowly into his study. All his instincts told him that the disappearance of the six women was not a bureaucratic mix-up. It was too coincidental, coming, as it did, so soon after the publication of the paper.

He picked up the phone. 'Erling. Some women workers are missing from the central hospital—guinea pigs for the education programme. Get some men over there and then report back to me. Have there been any unusual occurrences over the past twenty-four hours that I don't know about?'

'Well, there's one, sir. I was discussing it with the civil crimes department a few moments ago. An ambulance was found abandoned by the river early this morning. It had been stolen from St Mary's Hospital, but there's no sign that it has been used in a crime.'

'I want a full report on that when you get back to me with the other information,' Steiner snapped.

So, it seemed the women were prepared to go further than just publish a paper. He sat in the chair, steepling his fingers in front of his face. He thought he had been dealing with a bunch of malcontents giving expression to their frustrations by scribbling some treasonable words on paper. But this was something different. And they had moved fast. The women had not been picked up until yesterday, and yet they had been removed from the hospital sometime last night. Steiner's thoughts flicked to Blake perched unhappily on his chair, twiddling his empty glass, and his fingers made an unconscious gesture of revulsion. Because of that imbecile, he had lost nearly twelve hours in tracking the women down. At least, he had been able to stop him making things worse by pulling in more. Any further orders in that direction would be given by him and only when they fitted in with his plans.

But where would she hide them? Steiner felt sure that it was one woman he was dealing with, someone who had organized a small band of women workers into an efficient unit, and also someone who had been able to withstand the brainwashing processes. Even more significantly, someone who had managed to break down the brainwashed responses in the other women and had enabled them to think for themselves again. It was going to be interesting getting inside her head, getting to know the way she thought, anticipating her next move.

He sat back, hand idly toying with the phone. Yes, he was going to enjoy it. And the fact that he was dealing with a Grey One would add to the enjoyment. He smiled slightly at the prospect—one of his own creations trying to rebel against him. It was almost like one of his roses refusing to bloom. Yes, he was going to enjoy the hunt. And then he would have the exquisite pleasure of the capture.

He pressed the button on the phone again. First, he must get to know her. 'Erling, I want the file on the newspaper investigation over here, immediately.'

Steiner walked into the dining-room, the clutter of the meal lying abandoned on the table, and poured himself another brandy before going out into the shadowy garden. The vivid colours of the flowers had been replaced with the dark blue of a summer's night, relieved only by the pool of light that spilt from the open doors as he slowly walked the paths and lawns cupping the bulbous glass in his hands. Suddenly headlights swung across the lawns, and he hastened towards the car, taking the file from the driver without saying a word, before walking back into the study. The report was thorough—interviews, surveillances, laboratory tests, investigations. There was nothing in it that Steiner did not already know, but this time he was not looking for facts. He was trying to get to know the mind that had organized the operation.

She was thorough, giving a lot of attention to details—he admired that. He opened a copy of the newspaper and started to read, carefully. She may have written some of the articles and the style could reveal something more about her. The room slipped deeper into the quiet of the night as he read intently, pausing occasionally to make the odd note, referring back to previous pages, until he folded the paper and returned it meticulously to the file. There was a depth of thought to the articles, a logical turn to the arguments, but there was also a slight flamboyance about the style that did not quite fit in with the picture he was building of his prey. There was a hint of emotionalism that did not equate with the cool attention to detail that characterized her work.

He sat back and stared at the ceiling as he considered the apparent paradox. It was obvious she had let someone else write all the articles. He was fairly sure they had all been written by the same person, but not the person who had organized the women's moves. He wondered why. Why wouldn't someone put on paper what they had obviously spoken about, with conviction, many times? He pushed the intriguing thought away temporarily. The contents of the paper had told him something of more immediate importance. She was daring in her thoughts, in her ideas, and she also had a feeling for balance. She spoke of equality, redressing the balance, a united people, and the fact that Gorston's administration held the seeds of its own destruction. He steepled his fingers in the familiar gesture. Somehow she would use Gorston to hide the women. But how? His mind flicked over the Institutions created by the regime. Schools, would she use a school? No, the special schools were all boarding so would be occupied over the weekends. Churches? One of the articles had spelt out clearly the part the church had played in supporting Gorston and reinforcing his bizarre ideas. But the churches were locked at sunset and no Grey One had access to them. Besides, early morning services started at six-thirty. She could not risk having the women there then. He tapped his fingers together absently, absorbed in his thoughts. No, she would use somewhere more obviously representational of Gorston, somewhere that was completely identified with him. He listed the appropriate buildings—palace, courts, parliamentary buildings, only to reject them all. He sat up suddenly, sure of his instinct. The People's Hall. She would hide the women in the People's Hall. It was empty, unused except by the workmen who did not work over the weekend, and most important of all, it was synonymous with Gorston—Gorston's gift to the people. He was right. He knew it. But, thanks to that idiot Blake, his men would be too late. She would have moved them to a more permanent hiding place by now. She would only have used the hall as a temporary measure. He hesitated. Maybe she still had not had time to find an alternative. It would not be easy to find somewhere else to hide six women.

Steiner picked up the phone, tapping his fingers impatiently. 'Erling, get men over to the People's Hall. Cover it completely. Search it for signs of those missing women. If they're not there, I want anything that gives an indication of recent occupation. *Anything.*'

His men might be in time, but Steiner doubted it. Still, he had got a lot closer to knowing her, and she may have left some more indications at the hall. He would soon work out where she planned to hide the women and where she planned to print the next edition of the paper. It was going to be an enjoyable few days. And then, when he knew her weaknesses, he would meet her. Face to face. He stirred slightly in the chair, a pleasurable excitement warming his cool body.

Thirteen

Sarah let herself in quickly through the small door, hurrying up the curving steps to where the women had been waiting since she had left them early that morning. She had been able to get the van she required without any bother, but had needed to wait till dusk before she risked moving them. She wondered if she was right in refusing to let Eli come with her. If they were stopped by one of the routine road checks, it might be better to try to get out of it by force. Despite her tension, Sarah grinned to herself at the thought of Eli launching herself at the unsuspecting policeman, her years of assiduous book-learning exploding in a flurry of judo kicks and shouts.

The women were tense and silent as she opened the door, the experience of the past twenty-four hours showing in their faces. 'We're moving out,' she said quickly. 'There's a van downstairs. Make sure you bring everything with you. Don't leave anything behind.'

'Where are we going?' Joan asked.

'They'll find us wherever we go.' The little woman started to sob quietly to herself.

Sarah looked at Joan and then at the other women. Why should they trust her to keep them safe from Steiner's men? They didn't know her. But they did know that Steiner was all-powerful. What did Sarah have to offer? Only a wild idea that Carl would not refuse her when she turned up on his doorstep with six women and asked him to hide them for her. Supposing he refused? She could not face that possibility. She had searched all day for an alternative solution, without success. She remembered his obvious distress when she had broken down at the river's edge. Surely he would want to help. And then she remembered his look of bewilderment and hurt when she had left him. Maybe he would not want to risk any further involvement.

Joan was packing away the remains of the food, moving quietly and efficiently around the small room, removing all traces of their occupation. 'This is Sarah,' she said to the others. 'If she's found us somewhere to go, it'll be safe.'

Sarah was thankful for Joan's swift understanding of the situation. There was no sign of their joint doubts in the confident smile they exchanged for a brief moment.

The women gathered in a small, silent group at the doorway as Sarah glanced briefly around the cold room before leading them back down the narrow stone stairs and out into the evening dusk. She had pulled the telephone repair van in tight to the trees, but its incongruous bulk still seemed to dominate the small driveway.

'Get in the back and lie under the tarpaulins,' she told them. 'We've about a twenty mile journey.' She started to climb into the driver's seat and then hesitated, looking back at the small door. She hurried back to it, locked it carefully and then picking up a piece of broken scaffolding from among the rubble, she prised the door open again with a sharp crack of splintering wood. She climbed quickly into the van, started up the engine and drove steadily into the mainstream of Sunday evening traffic.

'Where are we going?' Joan's voice asked, muffled by the tarpaulin.

Sarah hesitated. She still had not decided how to tell the women that she intended to ask a man for help and then leave them in his cottage. How would they react?

She moved smoothly through the gears, concentrating on getting the feel of the large vehicle. The only other experience she had had of driving was when Nesbitt insisted she drive him to appointments with his more important clients.

'Is it a secret?' Joan's face appeared almost at her feet, still partly hidden by the heavy tarpaulin. She was masking her tension with a quizzical smile and Sarah realized that she had sensed the insecurity in her and was offering help. She glanced back at the scattered tarpaulins, gauging the nearness of the other women. 'We're going to a cottage, about twenty miles out of town. I don't know exactly where it is, but I have a road map and have worked out how to get there.'

'Is it an empty cottage?'

Sarah stared fixedly out of the windscreen. 'No, it belongs to a man. He lives there.' She concentrated on the traffic until the silence forced her to look back at Joan, who was staring up at her, searching her face for answers, fear flickering again at the back of her eyes. 'No, Joan,' she went on. 'He's different. He isn't like the men we know.' She knew the trust that Joan would have in her and was banking on it. How could she expect the others to trust her too? She needed Joan's support to persuade them.

'You say he's different,' Joan repeated uncertainly, her voice seeking reassurance.

Sarah manoeuvred the heavy vehicle through the congested traffic. 'Yes. He isn't like a man. He sees people as they are and he lets others see him as he is. There's no pretence in him and he doesn't force pretence on others.'

So why had she run from him? Didn't she trust him enough to let him see her when she was weak? And yet she was prepared to trust him with these women, to let him know that she was somehow involved with resisting the establishment. He could hand them all over to the authorities. But she knew he would not.

'We're going to have a hard time persuading the others to stay there,' Joan said finally.

Sarah looked down at the partly-concealed face, accepting the gesture of trust. 'I know. I'm hoping he's got a barn or something that you can stay in. Then the others won't have to come in contact with him until they are ready.'

'Does he know when to expect us?'

For Sarah the panic stirred again. It was madness expecting him to take them all in. What would she say to him? 'The police are looking for these women because I abducted them from a hospital. Please will you hide them?' The whole thing was impossible. But there was nowhere else. She *had* to be able to persuade him.

'No,' she said stiffly.

They had left the city behind and the van felt conspicuous on the nearly empty road. If Joan had fully understood her last answer, she was not showing it. All conversation between them had lapsed as Sarah drove carefully, watching for the turning that would take them into the meandering lanes that led to the cottage. She had memorized the map that she had taken from the office earlier that morning when she had gone there to find out

Carl's address from the office files. No one had taken any interest in the van. Even the solitary police car had passed them without a glance, and there were only a few more miles to go. Her brain had gone blank. She had worried so much about what to say that her mind refused to think about the problem any more. Suddenly they were there. 'That must be it up ahead,' she said. It was now she had to persuade him.

She pulled the van on to the grass verge and glanced around the quiet lane. She had not seen any signs of people for the past two miles. 'Stay here and keep quiet. I won't be long.'

The lights were shining through the tiny cottage windows, rectangles of gold in the navy blue night. At least he was at home. And there was a barn—a large, old, solid building, tucked away to the side of the house. She would ask him to let the women stay there.

The little porch was filled with the perfume of honeysuckle as she knocked hesitatingly at the door. She knew, instantly, that he would not hear, but her second knock bounced back at her from the garden sounding too demanding and peremptory. The door opened and he stood framed in the sudden light, staring at her in amazement. 'Hillard.'

She looked at him, not knowing what to say, unable to frame any words to ask the important question.

'Come in,' he said, standing aside, gesturing her into the small hall and then hesitating. 'Will you come in?' Surprise still showed on his face as he returned her steady gaze, surprise and a questioning.

She pushed her hands deeper into her pockets and stepped inside the door.

'You look tired. We could go in by the fire,' he invited.

She shook her head, still groping for words. 'I—I've come to ask you—' Her voice petered out. He was looking at her, smiling gently, trying to make it easy for her.

'Well, go on. It can't be all that bad.'

She looked at his face, seeing the gentleness, waiting to see it replaced by rejection as she said the words. 'I have six women outside—in a van. They need somewhere to hide from the police. Can they hide in your barn?'

He looked at her in silence as the sound of her words hung around them, but she could not understand the expression on his face. 'And you? Are the police looking for you?' he said after a moment's pause.

'No.'

'Can't you tell me any more?'

She should not have come here. As she stood looking at this man, she realized she felt protective towards him, and the realization shocked her. Why should she feel protective towards any man, even one as different as this? Yet she did. She could not involve him in the women's struggle, endanger him with the police. She should have realized that before she brought the women here. Where could she take them now? She felt numb and heavy as she turned back to the door. 'I must go,' she mumbled.

She was almost through the door before he reacted and then he was standing in front of her, barring the way. 'Oh, no. Not this time. You ran away from me before and I let you. But tonight—tonight, you've driven six women down here to ask for my help and all you can still think of is running away from me. Why?' The anger in him reached out and touched her and she could feel the nearness of him. But it did not frighten her.

'I'm sorry. I shouldn't have come. I don't want you to risk getting into trouble with the police.'

'But you came,' he insisted.

What was it she had told Joan? There was no pretence in him and he did not impose pretence on others. It was true. She had no right to pretend to him. 'I didn't think I would care about your risks before I came,' she said, with effort.

'And you do now?'

She nodded. 'Now, please can I go.'

He did not move. 'And Saturday. Why did you leave on Saturday?'

Her mind turned away from the scene at the river. She did not want to confess to her panic then. The fear that she would be unable to replace the defences that she had lowered. He had no right to ask her such things. She looked up into the shadows of his face. 'I didn't want you to see the weakness in me.'

She could hear the night noises in the silence that lay between them; the faint rustlings of the night creatures as they played out their fatal games of run and catch; could see the deepening night hide outlines and horizons and give the illusion of safety.

'We'd better get the women in,' he said firmly.

'No. I will find somewhere else.' How easy it was to say the words, but where could she take them?

His voice was decisive as he cut across her words. 'You've told me about them. That gives me the choice. The decision is mine to make, so I suggest you get them out of the van.'

Relief swept over her. The women would be safe. Steiner's men would not find them here and as soon as the Rising was over they could go back to the city. 'Can they stay in the barn?' she asked.

'Why the barn? The cottage is small, but we can make enough room.'

He still did not understand the society he was living in. He could not see that, although he wore a man's body, he did not act like one and that it would take the women some time to accept that fact. 'They would prefer the barn. They will need time to see you as you are.' She looked at him apologetically. 'We all project our images, I'm afraid. However hard we try.'

He turned back into the hallway, his face still hidden in the shadows. 'I'd better leave you to get them in. I'll see what food I can rustle up.'

The women were stiff and tired as Sarah helped them from the van and led them towards the stone barn. She groped around the door for a light switch, risking the brightness, wanting to reassure them. They had been so patient, curbing their fears, trusting her to find them a safe place, and now she had to tell them where she had brought them. The barn was filled with the sweet, musty smell of hay that lay spilt in large piles across the floor, and she watched the women as they stretched themselves out in its softness, luxuriating in the relief of cramped muscles. She sat down with them, but paused for a moment before speaking.

'The owner will bring you food. You'll be quite safe here. The owner is a man.' She hurried on, ignoring the sudden expressions of alarm. 'Please, listen to me. We are fighting the establishment because they won't allow us to be ourselves. They insist that we are as they see us to be. They see us as mindless creatures, created either to work in a mindless way, or to serve and amuse men. They can't accept that we're anything else because they can't see us as anything else. We are fighting for the right of every individual to be what they are.' She looked closely at the women who were listening intently to her words. 'If you refuse to see this man as he is, you'll be doing exactly what we accuse society of doing. You'll be seeing the image and not the man himself. Believe me, he's different from all the men you've met. Maybe it's because he is from another culture. I don't know. But you must try to see him as he is and not as you expect him to be.'

Silence closed around her words for a short moment before the questions started.

'How do you know you can trust him?'

'Why should a man help us?'

The small, timid woman resumed her quiet sobbing. 'He could be contacting the police right now.'

Sarah got to her feet and turned to face the little group. 'I don't believe he will contact the police and I don't believe he will betray us in any way. I trust him. I can't give you any concrete reasons for that trust except that I believe he sees us as human beings. And I don't think of it as a man helping some women. I think of it as one human being helping other human beings in need of help.'

There was silence in the barn as Sarah looked anxiously from face to face.

'I believe Sarah's right,' a voice said. 'We are working towards the Rising so that we can build a society based on contact and understanding. We would be a pathetic lot if we weren't prepared to make a small move towards that contact now.'

Sarah looked gratefully at the dark-eyed woman and suddenly realized she did not even know the woman's name. They were all strangers to her and yet they had accepted her and her words, in the same way as she had accepted responsibility for their safety. 'He's getting you some food.' Sarah said. 'I'll see if it's ready.' She walked to the barn door, satisfied to leave the group to discuss their reactions among themselves. No one had spoken out against staying and she was sure they would cope with their new situation.

'Shall I come and help?' Joan asked, as perceptive as ever. They walked together towards the open door of the cottage and stepped inside. 'Mr Tolland,' Sarah said, introducing Carl. She nodded at Joan's look of surprise. 'Yes, the artist.'

He came down the narrow corridor, a loaf of bread in his hand, surprised at the sight of another woman with Hillard.

'Mr Tolland, this is Bartlett. We came to help.'

'It's a bit make-shift, I'm afraid,' he said, almost shyly. 'But the coffee's good and hot.'

They followed him into the large, bright kitchen and stopped in amazement at the sight of the clutter. He followed their gaze. 'Yes, it's a bit of a mess. I seem to do everything in here except paint and sleep.'

'No, it isn't that,' Sarah explained. 'It—do all these things belong to you?'

He looked around at the abandoned jumble: paintings, statuettes, books, mixed up with records, tape cassettes, casually rubbing noses with spice jars and piles of fruit. 'Yes.' He was hesitant, unsure of himself. 'I'm a bit of a magpie, I'm afraid.'

She wondered how he would manage. She had been so concerned about the women's reaction to him that she had not thought about his reactions to them. Would he be able to adjust to the women's barriers, to their reserve, their lingering doubts? Joan echoed her thoughts as they carried the food to the barn, together with the assortment of bedding Carl had gathered. 'Is he going to be able to cope with having us here? He seems very uneasy.'

'He's not used to the barriers we put up against men. I think he's used to women talking to him in the same way as they talk among themselves.'

'Do you really think it's like that in other countries? No false images and barriers between men and women?' Joan's voice was full of doubts.

Sarah felt an uncertainty that was almost a fear. 'I don't know. I used to think that once we changed this regime and implemented the educational system, it would be all right . . .' Her voice trailed off as she mentally tried to identify the vague, disquieting hints that had appeared in Carl's attitude to the women. He had not been concerned when she had told him of the attitudes of society that had given rise to the present situation. It was almost as if he could see no injustice in the restrictions on job opportunities for women. It was only when the injustices became more twisted and extreme did he become upset by them.

'But now you're not sure?' Joan's voice cut in on her thoughts. 'Are you saying that the Rising won't change the basic problem? That it will only remove the more blatant injustices?' She was looking at her with a new anxiety as they pushed open the barn door, but conversation between them ceased in the activities of handing out food and coffee, and sorting out the sleeping arrangements. The women became more relaxed and with the relaxation came the need for sleep. Sarah sat in the corner of the barn as they finished their meal and the few desultory conversations gradually gave way to silence as the women settled into the warm hay to sleep.

'How are you getting the van back?' Joan sat next to her, speaking softly to avoid disturbing the drowsy women.

'One of the women uses it during the day,' Sarah answered. 'I have to meet her near the depot at about half past six. There shouldn't be much risk.' She was very tired. This was the second night without sleep and tomorrow night the paper had to be printed. 'Did you alert the women about printing on Monday night?'

'Yes,' Joan said, 'but surely you're not still planning to print tomorrow? Steiner's men will be swarming all over the place, looking for us.'

'I know. But the longer we leave it, the greater the risk that he'll find the press.' Sarah looked enviously at the sleeping figures, vaguely visible in the gloom of the barn.

Joan was concerned, persistent. 'But, Sarah, you can't hide the paper among the women now. Steiner's men will be searching all the hostels. Besides, you can't go another night without sleep. You look dead beat.'

'I'll be all right. I can work out what to do about the paper tomorrow.' She got stiffly to her feet. 'You'd better get some sleep yourself. You can't have slept much last night.' Looking down at Joan's pale face, she suddenly realized that she would not see her again before the Rising. The chances were that she would never see her again. The realization brought the day very close. The climax of seven years of her life was only a short time away and panic rose in her. She needed more time; she was too tired; she needed to be stronger. She desperately wanted to postpone the date but knew that it was impossible.

'Sarah.' Joan's hand reached urgently for her. 'Did you mean what you said outside? That you were uncertain about being able to change things?'

A kaleidoscope of words tumbled over in Sarah's head as she thought of all the books she had read, written by men of all centuries, and remembered some of their words. 'Man is the hunter; woman his game.' 'Man to command; woman to obey.' She pushed the confusion away and tried to smile at the tense face looking up at her. 'It was just the tiredness talking. I don't believe that we'll change everything straight away. I think it'll be a long struggle, but we'll get there eventually.' She was thankful for the darkness that hid her face from Joan's eyes. 'I'd better go. I must talk to Mr Tolland. I owe him some sort of explanation.'

She bent down and tentatively touched Joan's hair with her finger tips. 'What colour is it?'

The emotion of the moment held both women in silence, both locked in their own confusion of thoughts, before Joan made an effort to pull them back to the present. She smiled up at Sarah. 'Nothing special. Just a sort of dark brown.' She reached out and touched Sarah's cheek. 'Take care.'

The door of the cottage was still slightly ajar as Sarah walked across the silent garden, held in the knowledge that she had walked away from someone very close to her for possibly the last time. She could see the dim outline of Carl as he stood in the open doorway, and she walked quietly up to him, standing silent, looking into his face.

'I was watching for you,' he said. 'I didn't know when you'd be going.'

'I owe you some explanation. You must have a lot of questions.'

He stood aside in an unspoken invitation and, after only a slight hesitation, she walked inside, letting him show her the way into a long, low-ceilinged room. The massive open fireplace dominated the enclosed space, the flickering flames from the large logs throwing animated shadows over the walls and timber ceiling, reflecting back from the shine on the red tiled floor. She saw the deep-seated armchairs pulled into the glow of the fire and longed to sink into their comfort and sleep.

'You look cold and tired.' He gestured her to one of the welcoming chairs and she took the offered coffee, sipping the hot liquid as she watched him, waiting for the questions to begin. He was looking at her intently and she could see the confusion in his face; not knowing what questions to ask first. She wanted to answer him but she would not tell him about the Rising. She would have to be careful; any of his questions would, inevitably, lead to that subject. Maybe he would concentrate on the immediate queries about the women and not ask about her involvement in it; why it was she who had driven them here asking for help.

He sat on the arm of the chair opposite her and she again realized that his nearness, even in a confined space, did not upset her. 'Why are the police looking for those women?' he asked finally.

She looked down into her cup, wondering how he would react to the latest horror of this society. She chose her words with care. 'Gorston is going to introduce what he calls his education programme. He has realized that the national intelligence average has been dropping over the last twenty-five years and he intends to raise it by selective breeding from the top ten per cent of the population. These women were taken in to be used for training the technicians.' She could see from his face that he did not understand—or, if he did, he did not want to look at it.

'What do you mean, training the technicians? And these women are all Gre—'

'Grey Ones.' Sarah finished it for him. 'It's all right. We are accustomed to the name.'

He was embarrassed by his slip and went on hurriedly. 'I was told that women workers never married, so why are these women involved in this—breeding programme?'

His question had taken them full circle. She was back at the river, trying to tell him about the selection at the age of ten. This time, she did not close her eyes, but kept them on his face, watching his emotions change and fluctuate, preventing her mind from conjuring up the memories that had swept over her before. 'The women workers are selected at the age of ten on the result of an intelligence test. The top fifteen per cent of female children are then sent to special schools and trained to become women workers. They never marry or have children. Part of their training is that they no longer see themselves as women, in the accepted use of the word. It is this that has caused the gradual decline in the national average intelligence. We estimate that it isn't very great at this stage but it will be an accelerating process and Gorston plans to reverse it. The health department has been collecting voluntary male donors for the past several months and the programme is due to start in the next few weeks.'

'Donors? Then this is artificial insemination?'

'Yes.'

'And the women, are they volunteers?'

'No.'

He stood up suddenly and walked over to the fire, staring into the flames, his body tense. She could see the suppressed anger in him as he turned towards her, his voice hard. 'What you are telling me is that women workers are going to be used in some sort of breeding scheme, without their consent, and that those women—' he pointed in the direction of the barn, his arm stiff with tension '—those women were going to be used to train the technicians so that they could get their bloody technique right?'

'Yes.'

He became very still as he looked into her face. 'How many technicians?'

'We don't know exactly. We estimate about three hundred.'

He continued staring at her, his face expressionless, until his anger exploded, startling her with its suddenness. 'For God's sake, what's wrong with you? You sit there and calmly tell me these horrors, without any emotion, without any involvement.' He was pacing around the room, his anger and frustration clamouring for outlet. 'Don't you care? Do you all just sit and let these things happen?'

His anger did not frighten her, but his accusations hurt. She realized that she wanted to defend herself, to tell him of the constant hurt and anger inside herself—the anger that started years ago as a small, helpless child in the special school; rebelling against the untruths that they forced her to say and accept about herself, withstanding the beatings, endlessly, until she was forced to repeat those hateful words, while still telling herself that they were untrue. She wanted to tell him of the hurt she felt when she looked at the women and saw the potential that had been destroyed; when she saw them trying to know themselves, unsure, distrusting, because what they saw inside themselves was not what society told them was there, unable to accept that they knew themselves better than anyone else until, slowly, she had been able to reinforce their self-knowledge and they had, at last, been able to say, 'This is me.'

She saw the accusations still in his face, waiting to be refuted. 'The women are here—not in the hospital,' she said quietly.

The anger disappeared as quickly as it had come and he sat back in the chair. 'Of course, I'm sorry.' He stared into the fire as she sat watching him. 'But they will take another six women. Hiding these hasn't solved anything.'

He had arrived there. If she could not channel his thoughts in another direction, he would soon make the assumption that the women were planning something else. Her thoughts wandered back to Steiner. Was he making the same assumption? She tried to think into the man's mind, trying to see the women as he saw them. No, he would not make that jump, at least, not yet. He was too firmly fixed in his own images of the women. He would not be able to conceive that they could make a strong, concerted effort. But Carl could. He did not see them as mindless robots, although his inability to see past their expressionless exteriors might delay the jump.

'No, I know,' she answered. 'We don't usually indulge in hasty actions.'

He looked at her sharply, looking for mockery on her face, but she just returned his look calmly. 'Did you get them out of the hospital?' he asked.

'I helped.'

'Then the police will be looking for you, as well. You can't go back to the city.'

'No, the police don't know who got them out. I'm quite safe.'

'But they'll be searching. They'll find out how the women got out, and then they'll be after the people who organized it.' A thought suddenly struck him. 'How *did* you get them out?'

'It wasn't difficult. One Grey One looks the same as the next.' She used the term deliberately, as she smiled at him for the first time that night. 'If you act as a bureaucrat in a bureaucracy, everyone acts automatically.' She stretched across to the small table to put down the empty cup and he was immediately apologetic, remembering the neglected food he had prepared for her. She was too tired to object. The comfort of the armchair and the warmth of the room had made her tense muscles relax, as she fought to keep her eyes open. She took the food he offered. If she slept now, she would never wake up again by four.

He was watching her closely. 'You need sleep more than you need food,' he said.

She concentrated on the plate, willing herself to stay awake. 'No, I must leave shortly after four.'

'Then sleep now. I'll wake you.'

Her mind was sluggish, unable to concentrate on anything except the need to stay awake. 'No, I mustn't sleep now.' She was having difficulty in keeping her eyes open. Her body was too heavy from lack of sleep. She was vaguely aware of him taking the plate from her hand as she drifted into a comforting nothingness. Some little time later, she felt his nearness as he covered her with something warm, his hands brushing lightly across her face, and the feeling increased her sense of comfort. She could sleep here for ever.

'Hillard.'

She opened her eyes, slowly, disorientated, trying to remember her surroundings, and then looked directly into the blue eyes watching her with concern. He was offering her another cup of coffee. It was only a moment ago she had finished drinking the other one.

'It's nearly four,' he said.

So she hadn't dreamed it. She remembered drifting into sleep, the feel of his hands on her face, his comforting closeness, and stood up, suddenly disturbed by the memories. 'I must go.'

'Drink your coffee. There's time.'

The abrupt need to get out of the cottage grew. 'No,' she insisted, 'I must go now.'

'Are you running away from me, again?' He was smiling at her as she tried to understand the uncertainty inside her.

She was confused but did not know where the confusion was coming from. She needed to get away from him, but why? He did not threaten her; she did not fear him. She tried to fill the silence between them that seemed full of unspoken things that she did not understand. 'I haven't made arrangements to pay you for the food—for the women. They'll be here for about a fortnight, if that's all right.'

He was still smiling at her and she knew she was not hiding her uncertainty. 'Yes, that's all right,' he replied. 'And I think I can manage to afford the food.'

She stepped towards the door. 'Thank you for helping. I don't know where I'd have taken them if you had refused.'

'When will you be coming back?' His voice was serious now.

She looked at him, puzzled. She had not intended to come back here at all. She would have sent someone to take Joan back to the city on the morning of the Rising, and the rest of the women would have been taken back after things had settled. 'It's very difficult to get away. I don't have the use of the van very often.' She was unaware of the irony of her words.

'Then maybe we could meet at the river,' he offered. 'You'll want to know how the women are.'

He was standing between her and the door, and she wanted to leave. She did not want to commit herself to meeting him again. But why? He was the only person who had helped the women. He was right. Of course she would want to know how they were. 'I could meet you on Saturday. The same time as before.'

He nodded. 'And don't worry about them. They'll be quite safe here.'

She turned to the door. 'I must go.' Her body stiffened as she felt his hand on her arm and he took it away hurriedly.

'Hillard.' He handed her a large brown envelope. 'You will take care, won't you?'

She took the envelope silently and gestured towards the small leaded window turning a pale, silvery blue as the dawn started to creep across the sky. 'It's getting late.'

Fourteen

So, he had been right.

Steiner closed the interim report and gazed absently at the flowers in front of him. The women had been in the People's Hall. His men had noticed the forced entry and the hurried attempts at clearing away the signs of occupation. The women had been quite thorough, but his men had had little difficulty in finding the odd food remains on the floor. They had also found partial tracks of two heavy vehicles; one set definitely belonged to the stolen ambulance. No other heavy vehicle had been reported stolen as yet, but he was confident his men would track down the second vehicle without much delay. He was quite satisfied that he had formed an accurate picture of the whole operation. Two of them had stolen the ambulance, one disguised as a nurse. A third had hidden in the bushes of the hospital grounds to watch the success of the ploy and had then made her way to the People's Hall and forced the side door in preparation for the arrival of the others. Some small twigs and leaves had clung to her clothes as she pushed her way through the bushes and had dropped in the long gallery as she had searched for a suitable hiding place. That meant she was a stranger to the hall. Any of the women who worked there as cleaners would have known that no rooms led off the long gallery. He felt satisfaction that he had learned this much about the women. He still had a long way to go before he could reach out and touch her, but he had taken the first steps.

What were her motives? If he could work that out, he would be much nearer that delicious, exciting meeting. He pushed himself out of the chair and walked over to the window. It was going to be another hot, sunny day; the morning sun was already drying out the heavy dew. He opened the glass doors and stepped out into the luxuriant garden. The women were going to print another paper. Could Blake, in his random selection of guinea pigs, have chosen one of the women involved? He walked through the rose beds, gently touching the perfect blooms, stopping occasionally to bend and smell the perfume. Suppose one of Blake's women was involved in the subversive group—someone important to the printing of the paper, maybe. Then the women would need to get her back quickly. A shade of annoyance crossed his face as he noticed a brown, dead rose marring the perfection of a bush and he quickly walked back into the office, crossing straight to the phone on his desk.

'Erling, I want those six women thoroughly screened. Look for any point of contact between them; their associates, at work and at the hostels.'

He took a small pair of secateurs from the drawer and returned to the garden. His men would carry out the investigation and he would have the report in a few hours. But what other reason could she have for abducting the women? If only one was important to her, why take all six? To hide the fact that only one was important. But was that the only possible answer? He cut the dead rose from the branch and walked across the lawn to drop it carefully on a concealed compost heap, before picking up a stick and idly prodding the decaying matter. He had to consider the possibility that she wanted all six women. Why? He remembered the articles he had pored over for most of the night. She had talked about the 'dignity of the individual', 'the rights of each separate entity'. Suppose she actually believed what she had written. He had assumed she was playing on the emotions of stupid people to build herself up as some sort of minor leader, but it was always dangerous to make assumptions. Just supposing she actually believed what was in the paper.

Excitement stirred in him as he walked back to the roses. If he was right, if she had taken all six women because of her beliefs, she would have to do the same if another six women were taken.

He absently plucked a rose from the stem and held it to his face, seeing clearly what his next moves would be. He still did not know how the women had found out so quickly that the six had been taken, or how they knew where they were being held. His men had already checked everyone concerned with the selection and picking up of the women and they had all been cleared. He had made Blake check and recheck the whole procedure until he was satisfied that the leak was not in that area. However, it need not delay his plans. He would ensure that Blake picked up the next six women in exactly the same way, using the same personnel, the same vehicles, the same locations, and the same timing. He would duplicate the events of last Saturday and the chances were she would find out in exactly the same way as she did before. She would be forced into another rescue. Only this time he would be waiting. He looked at the rose in his hand, mildly surprised to find he was holding a bare stem, the petals scattered on the grass at his feet, and walked into the office.

'Erling, get me the Minister of Health.'

He would get Blake over here right away and make sure he did not mess this up with his blunderings. The idiot had been stammering with terror when he had gone over the pick-up operation with him, still not realizing the significance of what had happened. The mild enjoyment that Steiner had felt in watching him crumple last night had given way to a bored disinterest. Still, he was the perfect man for his future plans.

'I'm sorry, sir. The Minister is with the President.'

Steiner's face was completely still as he thought over the possibilities. The chances were it was a routine meeting, but the fool could still let slip about the delay to the training programme. He remembered the little man's terror as he had warned him not to discuss the matter with anyone. His terror would keep him quiet.

'Who are you speaking to?' he asked.

'One of his personal assistants, sir.'

'Put him on.' His voice took on the smooth tones he had used on Blake the previous night. 'Commissioner Steiner here. It is of importance that I contact the Minister immediately. Could you tell me when he went to see the President?' He listened impassively to the nervous voice, the only reaction showing in the slight tightening of his hand around the phone. 'And when did this happen?' The voice continued to crackle in his ear. 'Have my men been called in?' His voice was hard, cutting like ice across the hesitancy of the voice in his ear. He put the phone down and then picked it up again immediately. 'Erling, there's been an explosion down at the Board of Health's Central Supply Depot. Get men down there. I want full details of how it happened. And, get my car.'

His mind was in a turmoil as he walked through the outer office to the lift; his face a stiff, passionless mask hiding the torrent of emotions that filled his being. She had anticipated him. She had been studying his mind, as he had hers, and she had anticipated his thoughts. A surge of revulsion swept over him at the thought that she had been able to make contact with him in this way. She had known that he would set a trap for her, and she had removed his excuse for setting that trap. How could he force Blake to pull in more women for training purposes, when she had set back the whole programme for months by destroying the semen bank? If he could get to Blake before he saw Gorston, he could still force him to follow his plans. But even as he thought it he knew the chances were very slim. Once Gorston knew the extent of the damage to the bank, he would insist that all effort and manpower be concentrated in replacing the necessary sperm. Gorston had always considered the training of the technicians as a refinement to the scheme. And he was a man with little time for refinement.

Steiner got into the waiting car and gave terse instructions to the driver. How would Gorston take the news? This could precipitate his plans before he, Steiner, was ready. Cold, blind fury seized him as he thought of the woman who had done this thing. It had been diverting to find that one of his creations was trying to challenge him; an amusing intellectual exercise in tracking her down, with the exciting prospect of returning the erring flower to the fold. But now she was not challenging him. She was competing with him, and using the same methods. He would destroy her, slowly. Beginning with the mind that dared to compete with his, he would infiltrate and destroy it, bit by bit, until it was in pieces. And then he would rebuild it, very slowly, into a master's tool so that it would be unable to encompass anything except what he put there. Her whole, limited world would be of his creation, and she would move and jerk through that limited awareness as a puppet following the whim of the puppet-master.

The car stopped at the main doors of the presidential palace, bringing him out of his reverie. He sat, still and cold; no sign on the blank face of the inner turmoil he was pushing into the dark recesses.

'Minister Blake received your message, sir. He's waiting for you in the ante-chamber.' Steiner looked, unseeing, at the anonymous figure of the minor civil servant, hovering at the door of the car, holding it open with obsequious respect. 'His appointment with the President is in fifteen minutes, sir.'

Without a comment Steiner got out of the car and walked swiftly down the long, carpeted corridors to where Blake was waiting. At least he had got here before Blake had seen Gorston.

Blake was on his feet, facing the door as he entered. The small, plump hands travelled in blind, erratic movements as the little man tried to control his fear. 'Steiner, this is terrible. Have you heard?'

'How extensive is the damage?' Steiner's voice cut across the torrent of words that hesitated on Blake's lips.

'The whole place is destroyed,' Blake stammered. 'Everything ruined. Over five months work—gone—in a few seconds. It will delay the programme by months.'

'Have you spoken to Gorston yet?'

'On the phone, yes. I had to tell him immediately.'

'What did you tell him?'

Blake's earlier, all-consuming fear of Gorston was gradually being replaced by his more immediate fear of the cold man standing quietly across the room from him. 'Well, I had to tell him what happened. I told him that the semen bank had been destroyed in an explosion, that a gas cylinder had exploded in the corridor and the refrigeration rooms caught most of the blast.'

'Anything else?'

'I didn't mention the delay to the training scheme, if that's what you mean, but I told him that the whole programme would be put back by months.' Blake sat down heavily in the chair. 'He insists that the programme starts on its original date. I told him it was impossible, but he just insisted.' His voice was rising in a tide of panic. 'I can't do it. It can't be done.'

'Blake.' Steiner's cold voice silenced his protests. 'You will go in to Gorston and tell him you over-reacted to the news. That the damage isn't as extensive as you first thought, and that, with extra manpower, you will be able to meet the original date. That the programme will start in three weeks time.'

'But it can't be done, Steiner.'

'It can and will be done.' Steiner's voice brooked no argument. 'Some of my men will assist in the replacing of the banks. You will tell Gorston that, instead of starting the whole operation at once, you intend to implement a planned escalation, starting on a smaller scale, and building up to full through-put over a three-week period.'

A flicker of hope crossed Blake's face as the confidence of the man opposite him started to break down his own hopelessness. 'Do you really think it can be done?'

'Yes, with my help, it will be done.' The quiet assertion completed the process, and Blake jumped to his feet with relief.

'You're right, Steiner. How can I thank you? Of course it can be done. With extra manpower and starting on a small scale, we can begin in three weeks. How many men can you let me have?'

'As many as you need.' Steiner replied. 'I want you to continue with the training schedule. Everything must be done to speed things up.'

'Yes, of course.' Blake's face showed his bewilderment. 'But you told me to cancel it.'

'Circumstances have altered. You will arrange for another six women to be picked up next Saturday. They will be picked up in exactly the same way as they were before and taken to the same hospital. We'll discuss the details later.' He saw the blind acceptance in Blake's face and turned to go. 'By the way, there's no need to mention the training scheme to the President. We have a responsibility to shield him from as much pressure as possible and this morning's events must have put considerable strain on him. You know how much this whole programme means to him, so you have to reassure him completely that there will be no significant delay.'

'Of course, of course.'

Steiner looked briefly at Blake, now brimming with the excess of confidence that comes to the little man when responsibility is assumed by others, before turning to make his way back to the waiting car. Blake believed what he wanted to believe.

All men did. So he would convince Gorston that his education programme would continue with the minimum of delay. And Gorston, with his usually incisive mind clouded with his hatred of women and his driving need to see the implementation of his latest scheme, would also believe because he wanted to.

Six women, Steiner knew, would be picked up on Saturday, forcing her into another rescue attempt. He had the puppet strings back firmly in his hands and she was already following his instructions.

Fifteen

Sarah locked the front door of the offices and slipped the key into her pocket, relieved that the working day was over. She had no clear recollection of the details of the day. She had carried out the routine tasks in a haze of tiredness, feeling only a momentary awareness when the strange voice came over the desk phone to remind her of the events of the past twenty-four hours. Maybe she should cancel the printing of the paper tonight. Eli had already collected the articles from Joan's room by the time she had met her outside the Central Supply Depot and they were now safely tucked into the lining of her coat. It may be safer to delay the printing until she had slept. Her mind was foggy from lack of sleep and that was the time mistakes were made. Against that, any delay gave Steiner extra time to discover the hiding place of the press. What would he be concentrating on now—the printing of the paper, or the escape of the women, or the blowing up of the semen bank? She was sure of the answer even as she asked it. He would be following all the leads that she had been forced to present to him over the last two days. The picking up of the women had forced her to counteract Steiner's moves, giving him the initiative. She had tried to regain the initiative by blowing up the semen bank, but had she covered everything?

Sarah gradually became aware of a vague disquiet that pulled her out of her thoughts and back to the dry, dusty pavements. There appeared nothing unusual in the familiar walk back to the hostel. The office buildings held their habitual blind air of neglected importance, their worn façades still trying to remember the forgotten grandeur of their earlier life before the sound of typewriters drowned out the sounds of parties and merriment, before the small engineering firms ousted the horses and carriages from the ample mews. The few remaining hurrying figures were those she had seen over the past years; the rush-hour cars sped past with the same self-absorption. She turned into the road that led to the hostel, and suddenly realized that she was not the only figure hurrying against the mainstream of pedestrians.

The hostel sat in an oasis of barren concrete, surrounded by the decaying terraces of long-dead elegance, now converted to the servitude of commerce. At this time of the day she was one of a number of women to walk towards that area. Others were leaving the offices and making their ways towards their homes and hostels in other parts of the town. Was it her imagination? Had she seen a figure turn into the road after her? She stepped closer to the railings that guarded the basement areas of the buildings and deliberately stumbled, clutching the railings for support as she glanced back down the road. She was right. A man was walking, casually, up the road towards her. Nothing suspicious in his manner or dress, nothing except his presence there at this time of the day. She turned onto the expanse of concrete, glancing back to see the man walk purposefully past. She was letting her tiredness create delusions. He most probably had some late business at one of the offices further up the road.

Her room was stuffy from the heat of the day as she crossed over to open the window, dropping her coat on the bed after removing the articles that Joan had written. The slight breeze brought in the assorted smells of the city; the peculiar mixture of concrete and car fumes that is the city-dweller's substitute for the fragrance of the countryside. She could see the man, all purpose gone from his stride, before she hurriedly drew back and sat on the bed, tension again taking over her body. She had been right. He was following her. Why? Think. Her mind could not see the full picture. Tiredness narrowing her vision to isolated incidents. They must have left some trace of their identity. But, where? *Think.* Coolly, logically. Start with the paper.

Sarah got up and stood in the middle of the room, trying to

control her thoughts that wanted to flutter, aimlessly, over the events of the past few days. She walked across to the table where she had sat and planned when her plans were comforting theories and not frightening realities. Start with the paper. Her mind went over the details of the first printing and distribution. No, there was nothing there to lead Steiner to her. He would have to get to her through a chain of women and there had been no arrests today. She would have heard. So, it was either the rescue or the blowing up of the bank.

She stared steadily in front of her, seeing again Eli waiting for her as she drove the van down the deserted street; the silent walk to the rear of the building and Eli's grin as she pointed to the open window, no evident sign of it being forced. She could smell the peculiar mixture of polish and disinfectant that permeated the corridors as they carried the heavy cylinders and carefully positioned them at Eli's instructions. She remembered staring at the large, white refrigerators that held the semen, wondering at the amount of horror concealed behind their bland, anonymous exteriors. And then Eli was pulling her towards the door, nodding, satisfied, as the small glass phial gently hissed on top of one of the containers. And then the ease of the return journey. No one around on the deserted streets. And the wait, the endless wait for the explosion that would protect the women for a short time more. No. There was nothing there to lead Steiner to her. So, it was the rescue. Unless—She rested her head on her hands. She was tired. She was not thinking how Steiner worked. He would check out the six women who escaped, and he would check all their associates. That would include her because of her working connection with Joan. It was a routine surveillance. Anonymous, blanketing. Relief surged through her for a moment before she realized the implications of the constant scrutiny.

Sarah moved the few paces across the room and took the written articles from their hiding place. She would have to cancel the printing. Who else was being followed? All the women who lived in the same hostels, or worked in the same firms, as the six women. But who were they? She could not make a move of any sort until she knew. She walked back to the window, closing it in an excuse to look for the solitary man. He was still there, silently watching, almost blending into the background of the shadows of the next office block. She had to warn the others who were being watched.

She tapped softly on Stephanie's door before walking quickly into the duplication of her own room.

'Sarah,' Steph said. 'Are you all right? You look exhausted. And the women, are they safe?'

'Yes. They'll be safe. Did you hear about the semen bank?'

'So it was you!'

'Eli and I.'

Stephanie placed the inevitable cup of coffee in front of her and waited to hear the details.

'I'm being followed, Steph,' Sarah said quickly, hurrying on as she saw the look of alarm come in to the other woman's eyes. 'No, don't worry. It's only a routine thing—all the associates of the six. But I've got to warn the others. They may not have spotted the tails. Three of the women were in your chain. Do any of them lead back to you?'

There was no hesitation. 'No.'

'Well, you've got to get a warning through to their associates. And the other women—one was in Eli's chain. Her contacts will have to be warned.'

'I can see to that,' Steph assured her. 'But what about Joan's women?'

Sarah looked at Stephanie. A lot seemed to be falling on her lately and Sarah knew she was the least equipped to cope with the added stress. 'I was going to meet them tonight, but I can't now.' She made a sudden decision, leaning forward towards the little woman. 'Can you contact Ann tonight?'

'Yes, between nine and ten.'

'Right, meet her as close to nine as you can and give her these.' She handed her the small bundle of articles, creased from being hidden in her coat. 'There's a note there, telling her the situation and where she can meet Joan's replacement.' Sarah paused at the look of surprise on Stephanie's face and felt an irrational need to defend herself. 'She had to be replaced immediately. None of us can be allowed to be indispensable.'

Stephanie took the papers silently as Sarah continued. 'Tell her to discuss it with the other woman and check if any of the women involved in the printing are in any way connected with the six. If they are, they've got to be warned and must not take any further part in the printing operation. I want those who are clear to meet at the printing place tonight, as arranged.'

'But why? The paper isn't going out for another week.'

Tiredness made Sarah impatient and the irritation sounded clearly in her voice. 'I know that, Steph, but I want the press dismantled as soon as possible. The women know what to do. It's been planned for weeks.'

'Do you want Ann to help with the printing?' Steph asked.

Sarah hesitated, seeing the face of the woman at the post office, the woman she had made Joan's replacement. She hadn't even asked her name. She was capable and cool. Sarah remembered, again, how she had coped with the unknown woman handing her the message across the counter. 'No. Tell her to get the message to the women and then leave it to them. She'll need to arrange a meeting for tomorrow so that we get a report back on the printing.'

'And the papers? Where are we going to hide the papers?'

Sarah didn't want to think. She still hadn't thought how to hide them, but she knew she wouldn't be able to think clearly until she had some sleep. 'Tell them to leave them there until tomorrow night. I'll think of somewhere in the meantime.' She looked at Stephanie's questioning face and knew she was alarmed at what appeared to be rushed decisions. 'Don't worry, Steph. I'd planned to print tonight. The women are expecting me. Nothing has changed, except that I can't be there.' She rose slowly to her feet, the tiredness surging back now that the decisions had been made. She felt relieved that circumstances had forced her into inactivity. At least now she would be able to sleep.

'You'll be able to see him as you go out,' she explained as she walked to the door. 'He's about forty, dressed in a dark blue suit, medium height. He was standing next to the entrance of the next block when I saw him last—tucked into the shadows. He shouldn't have any interest in you.'

She walked slowly back to her room. All her actions seemed to have slowed. She crossed again to the window, this time to draw the curtains as if to shut out the intrusion of the watching man. The paper would be printed tonight and the press dismantled. Tomorrow she would decide where to hide the papers. She thought again of the man outside and wondered how long the surveillance would last. Would he still be watching her on Saturday? If so, she would not be able to meet Carl. She frowned in anticipated disappointment. Why should she feel disappointment? She was only meeting him to find out how the women were. She sat heavily on the side of the bed and remembered the atmosphere of the cottage; the haphazard jumble of the kitchen, the warmth and comfort of the living room, the flickering shadows from the log fire, and the half-dreamt feeling of contentment when his hands brushed her face. The envelope. She had forgotten about it in the tension of the morning. It was still where she had hidden it on returning from her early-morning meeting with Eli.

She got up and walked across to the bookshelves and took the envelope from behind a row of books, turning it over in her hand before finally tearing it open. Two versions of her face stared back at her from the sheets of paper. She looked intently at one, seeing the grey hair pulled tightly back from the face, the lips closed and set, the bone structure of the cheeks clearly defined, continuing up to the finely moulded eyebrows, and the eyes— She felt a shock run through her as she looked at the eyes. Wide, clear, grey, but completely expressionless. It was something more than a lack of expression—it was an emptiness. Was that how he saw her? Was that how everyone saw her? She stared again at the eyes and could not recognize them as her own. Why didn't they show something of what went on behind them? How could eyes hide all the uncertainties and doubts and reflect only emptiness? She could see nothing of herself in those blank eyes, and it frightened her. She covered the sketches quickly, not wanting to know how she looked to Carl, and hastily undressed, pulling on the coarse grey dressing-gown and gathering up towel and soap for the shower. The showers would be empty now, and then she would sleep. She hesitated at the door and looked back to where she had left the sketches, still seeing vividly the blank eyes. If that was how he saw her, she should be able to see it also. She picked them up in a sudden decision and walked over to the small mirror, looking intently at the sketch that had so disturbed her, and then at her reflection in the mirror. The same face looked back at her, but the eyes were questioning, searching. She tried to hold the feeling of blankness she felt during the day but the blankness skittered away before it reached her eyes. She put the sketch down in exasperation and looked at the other piece of paper. Her face again stared back at her, but this time it was alive. It had so much life in it that it took her breath away. The lips were smiling; the hair tumbling loose about her shoulders; and the eyes, gleaming with happiness and the sheer joy of living.

Why did he draw her like this? This wasn't her either. She looked back at her reflection. No, it wasn't her. He'd made her beautiful in the sketch and she could see none of it. Her hands went slowly up to the tight knot of hair, untwisting it, letting it fall around her shoulders. But her eyes stayed still and questioning. Her fingers coiled a thick strand as she suddenly remembered the confusion she had felt when he had woken her and she had realized that his brief nearness, with its feeling of comfort, had not been a dream. But the confusion was not comforting. She did not understand the feelings she had felt. A small flicker of fear, when there was nothing to be afraid of; an expectation, when she didn't know what to expect; a vague, tumbling sensation of excitement, when all she was doing was telling him she must be going. She remembered the feel of his hand on her arm and the rigidity that swept her body at his touch, and her hand went slowly to the place on her arm, as if to bring back the feel of him, into the room, now. She stood, a small, grey figure, surrounded by grey—from the rough grey dressing-gown to the colourless bleakness of the small room—trying to take another step away from her greyness but not understanding it because it did not reveal itself to logic.

She turned away from the mirror and lay on the bed, staring at the painted ceiling, her eyes tracing the familiar patterns of thin cracks as her mind strayed to a conversation she had had with Mary, years ago, shortly after she had first met the older woman. Sarah had only been working for about six months and the memories of the special school were still close and constantly alive. She burned with an anger that equalled Eli's and her hatred called out for her to destroy. It was then she had first started to dream about destroying Gorston. She had wanted to know all about him, all about the society that had given him power. She had wanted to know her enemy so that she could understand him better, so that she could pinpoint his weakness. Mary had been married with a child when Gorston came to power, and with the insensitivity of youth Sarah had asked why her husband and all the other husbands had let Gorston bring in his legislation. She remembered her anger when Mary started to make excuses for the men and her rejection of the phrases she couldn't understand. Until at last, Mary, realizing that there was no point of contact between them, had leant forward and placed her hand on Sarah's arm. She could remember the experience vividly, still see the look of sorrow and resignation on Mary's face, the feeling of incomprehension at the words.

'He has taken more away from you than you realize.'

Sarah had been angry, aware of her inner flight to retain her identity, defensive of her success in rejecting the years of conditioning in the schools. 'He has taken nothing away from me. He has taken away my freedom, but I am still free here,' she had replied, pointing vehemently to her head. 'I'm intact inside this shell. He's taken away the external things but I can survive inside without them.' She had spoken with the narrow, defensive arrogance of youth.

'Yes, child. He has. You have defeated him and kept your reason and your intellect intact, but he has taken from you your emotions. In the same way that he has left your body intact but has forced parts of it into obsolescence.'

Sarah had not wanted to understand the strange words. She had not wanted to concede any victory to the man who personified everything she hated in society. But, supposing Mary had been right? She had mentioned it again in the basement, the night she had told her about the torturing of the students. Was there a part of her that had been destroyed, or had it stayed hidden and safe, and was now struggling for expression?

She got off the bed and walked back to the mirror, her hair still hanging loose around her shoulders, the grey eyes looking back at her with questions she had to answer. She undid the fastenings of the coarse gown and let it slip to the floor as her hands went, slowly, to her arm where he had touched her. A small fear stirred in her stomach. Her hand slowly traced the line of her breasts as the grey eyes followed every movement. What had Mary said? Part of her body was obsolescent. Obsolescent breasts—no child would ever feed from them. Her movements suddenly froze and the fear became larger as she looked, intently, into the eyes, suddenly able to answer the questions in them. This was the part of her that Mary had said had been taken away from her; the confusion of emotions; the timid, tentative demands of her body; the unknown part of her that existed outside of her mind. Was that what Mary had meant, in the basement, when she said that sometimes the heart speaks louder than the head?

She turned abruptly away from the revealing mirror, hastily pulling the robe around her. She could not consider the possibility that her head would not always govern her actions. That was the way she had survived. It had protected her from Gorston's laws all these years; and protected her, and the women, from Steiner now. The heart was for more peaceful times—when the struggle had been won and society would not take advantage of the weaknesses of the heart to destroy the spirit.

Sixteen

Sarah glanced out of the window for the ten thousandth time. He was still there. He had followed her for days, inconspicuous, plodding, thorough. But now he was bored. She could sense it. It showed in his small restless movements that had gradually replaced the blind resignation to the long, cold waits that had typified the first few days of his surveillance. Sarah had kept rigidly to a routine each day, seeking to lull him into carelessness. If the surveillance was maintained for another forty-eight hours, she would have to lose him.

A small thrill of excitement ran through her at the thought. Seven years of planning and dreaming would be put to the test in just over forty-eight hours. Sarah's old fears re-asserted themselves. She had had no contact with the women, except Stephanie, since she first spotted the watching man, and she desperately wanted one last meeting before the Rising broke. The last five days had seemed endless as she had gone through her routine duties in the office and then followed her solitary route back to the hostel, always aware of the shadow behind her. She stood up with sudden purpose. She needed to keep busy, to become absorbed in mundane things—anything to prevent her from thinking. She would surprise Steph and cook her a meal. She would be back soon from her routine meeting with her group. But Sarah's mind refused to be turned from considering the next two days. Everything was organized and ready, as it had been for weeks. The last arrangements were the small radio station that Eli and her women were working on, and the distribution of the papers. She was not happy about the papers. The printing had gone through smoothly, as had the dismantling of the press, but the papers were still in the printing place. She had not been able to make any other arrangements about hiding them. With so many of the women tied down by Steiner's surveillance, and so many of the hostels being searched at random, she had not been able to distribute the papers among the women as she had originally planned. She went over again the chances of discovery. They should be safe enough, but she never intended to use the place except at night. And now the papers were still there, just a few feet away from the people who went there every day.

She walked deliberately to the small cupboard, determined to suppress the pointless fears. If she didn't occupy her mind, she would find herself in one of her blind, questioning moods when she doubted her plans and her right to lead the women into this Rising. She could not let that happen now. She was just reacting to the claustrophobia generated by the close surveillance for so many days. She glanced automatically at the window. Every time she saw the patient man, she felt Steiner's presence.

She took some tins from the cupboard and grinned wryly to herself. There was nothing here to impress Stephanie with her cooking prowess. She busied herself with the simple meal, glancing out of the window occasionally, watching for Stephanie's return, her eyes carefully avoiding the building that sheltered

Steiner's man. At last Stephanie was hurrying across the concrete, and she laid the table quickly, waiting for her friend to knock on the door.

'Sarah, I think there's something wrong.' Steph had walked into the room without knocking and was looking at Sarah anxiously, slightly out of breath. 'The public lavatory is locked.'

Sarah stared at her in alarm.

'One of my women noticed it about an hour ago and happened to mention it,' Steph went on. 'She didn't know the importance of it, of course.'

Why? It was never locked at this time of the day. The old woman who supervised it opened it at nine in the morning and stayed there all day until about ten at night.

'I've sent a couple of my women down there to try and find out what's happened. I'm meeting them at the corner shop in about fifteen minutes.'

'She could just be sick,' Sarah suggested.

'That's what I thought. If she was just off for the day, they wouldn't bother sending a replacement. Especially as it's Saturday. She's one of Joan's women, isn't she?'

Sarah nodded absently. Supposing the woman wasn't sick. Supposing Steiner had somehow tracked them down and the old woman was now at Headquarters under interrogation. If that was so, the whole Rising was destroyed. She could not consider that possibility yet. She must find out what had happened. 'Can you contact Ann or Eli quickly?' she asked.

'Well, I can contact Ann in about half an hour. But I've got to meet my women.'

Sarah stared out of the window at the man still lounging on the steps of the office block. She could not do a thing. She could only rely on the others finding out for her. 'Meet your women and, if they haven't found anything out, contact Ann as quickly as possible. Tell her to contact Joan's replacement to see if any of the women in the chain knows what's happened.'

Stephanie turned without a word, leaving Sarah in a torment of fear and frustration. If Steiner had found the papers, he would know about the Rising. She forced herself to think clearly. What would he do first? He would break the old woman and get information from her about the women in her group. He would pick them up, including Joan's replacement—God, she still didn't know her name—and that would lead him straight to the leaders. No. It would lead him to Ann and herself. They were the only links from Joan's chain of women to the leaders. But, Stephanie, Eli and Mary could not manage everything on their own. Besides, although the other women did not know the details of Monday morning, they knew everything else.

She walked impatiently around the room. She still was not thinking clearly. If Steiner had the paper, he knew about the Rising. He would know how many women were involved and would start making arrests; random, blanket arrests. But he had not. Word of arrests would have reached her. So he did not have the papers. Maybe her desperate clutching at hope was justified. Maybe the old woman *was* sick.

She crossed to the window in time to see Stephanie hurrying towards the hostel, carrying a bag of groceries, and turned to face the door, waiting for her to climb the stairs and come into the room. The fear was growing in her stomach and her breathing was tight, painful. 'Well?'

'She's dead. The old woman is dead.' Stephanie was fighting to control her breathing, breathless from tension.

The fear left Sarah as she took the shopping from Stephanie's arms and led her to the bed. 'Sit down and tell me. Gently.' She could feel the near panic in the trembling woman and felt the usual wish to protect her from such stress.

'One of the women started a conversation with a street cleaner.' Stephanie stopped, trying to still the small tremble in her voice, as Sarah reached across to touch her arm. 'There was an accident. This morning at about nine. The old woman was crossing the road to the lavatory when she was hit by a car. She was killed instantly. No one's been near the place since. It's been locked all day.'

So, Steiner did not know. Relief surged through Sarah as she walked over to the small stove, trying to hide her feelings from the shaken woman. Her hands moved automatically through the routine of coffee-making as she worked out the moves that would have to be made in the next few hours. A replacement supervisor would be moved in, and she had no way of knowing who she would be. The papers had to be removed from there, and quickly. She placed the cup in front of Stephanie. Eli, she needed Eli. They would have to get the papers out the same way as they had before. Only this time it was the middle of the day, and the lavatories were locked.

Seventeen

Steiner sat in his study, eyes staring unfocussed. A week had passed since the six women had disappeared from the hospital; nearly two since the paper was distributed; and he still did not have a lead on the women responsible. His men had searched dozens of hostels when the women were at work, and he had over fifty of them under constant surveillance, and still nothing had turned up. A stab of annoyance showed briefly as he thought of his conversation with Gorston. If he had been able to pick up another six women as he had planned, he would have trapped all the leaders by tonight. Gorston was obsessed with getting the programme back on schedule and no amount of reasoning on Steiner's part had persuaded him to let the training programme continue. As far as Gorston was concerned, no training was needed. So, for the moment, his puppet was still free to make her own moves.

Steiner re-opened the file in front of him, turning to the chemical report. The laboratories had found traces of a germicide on nearly all the papers. This should tell him something. But what? His men had checked all the usual sources of possible contamination, but he was missing something. It was only a matter of time for his investigations to give him the small extra clue he needed, but he didn't have the time. The women had announced they would publish again in two weeks, and the two weeks were up on Wednesday.

The phone buzzed discreetly on his desk. 'Yes.'

Erling's voice sounded in his ear. 'Something important has cropped up, sir.'

'I'll be right over.' His men had found something. Perhaps

the first crack in the women's defences. He slipped the file back into the briefcase, suddenly sure that he was very much closer to meeting the woman who had dared to challenge him.

He walked out into the hallway and stopped abruptly at the sight of the woman standing in the doorway of another room. His face was blank as he saw the look of apprehension on her face. Tall, slim, classically beautiful, wearing clothes that enhanced her poise and beauty, but very frightened of the man who stood looking at her, she seemed unable to break away from the encounter. The silence held for a moment longer before he turned away, a look of repugnance and anger on his face. He would have to do something about her carelessness. She had the run of the house, was free to entertain her circle of pathetic friends. The only thing he expected from her, no, demanded from her, was that she ensure he never had to come in contact with the compulsory children of their marriage; never had to see or hear her. He would have to remind her of their arrangement, but he did not even get any pleasure out of that any more. It bored him.

Erling was waiting for him as he walked into the outer office, following him into the bare room.

'We've had a report in from the central station, sir. There was a street accident, this morning, involving an old woman who supervised the women worker's public lavatory at the Green. A replacement woman was sent over and she reported that some refuse collectors were in the lavatories when she arrived. She claims to have noticed something suspicious about them and reported back to her superior.'

'Where is she now?'

'I've arranged for her to be brought here.'

'Any indication of what she saw?' Steiner's voice betrayed none of his excitement.

'No. She became frightened when the police started questioning her and gave very confused answers.'

'Let me know when she arrives. And, Erling, I want that place searched thoroughly.'

Of course, Steiner thought, the germicide. Public lavatories. He stood up quickly, walking across to the window, a subdued elation growing inside him. The crack he had been looking for had finally materialized. He looked back at the desk, seeing a Grey One standing in front of it. He would bring her here first. He would see how she confronted him when she knew she was helpless. When she knew, fully, what was in store for her. He wondered what her face would be like. Was she young? Maybe she was an older woman who still remembered what it was like before she became a Grey One. That would have helped her reject the processing. He had never been very satisfied with the crash programme that had been implemented when Gorston first passed the law. He had wanted to organize a system of refresher courses for the older women but the President had dismissed the idea as a waste of time and money. But would an older woman have retained the will and energy to challenge him? He thought back, again, to the articles in the paper. They were the thoughts of an idealist, an impractical dreamer.

'She's here, sir,' Erling said.

'Get Steadman to question her. I want to know everything that happened there. Everything she saw, what the women looked like, every thought that went through her head when they were there. And I want a report of the search as soon as it is in.'

'The preliminary report is just coming in, sir.'

'Bring it in as soon as it's off the machine.' Steiner's impatience was gathering although nothing showed on his impassive face as he walked through the glass doors into his garden.

'Sir?'

He took the piece of paper from Erling and glanced quickly down the page. So, they had printed there. Traces of a substance that appeared to be printer's ink—the labs could confirm—scratches in one of the cubicles, possibly indicating a heavy machine, and remnants of insulating material in the supervisor's office. They had not disguised the noise with more noise. They had insulated the whole machine. They must have printed at night when the place was locked. But the press, the printing press. Would they have risked leaving it there between print runs? They had obviously printed in the supervisor's room, so the scratches in the cubicle seemed to indicate that they had stored the press there. It took nerve. But with an 'out or order' sign on the door and the place only open to women workers who had been trained not to ask questions, the risk of discovery had not been very great. The press had now gone. That meant they had already printed. Three days. He only had three clear days before the date by which they had promised to distribute the next edition.

He sat on the garden bench in a small arbour of greenery, his hand idly plucking the leaves and throwing them on the ground around him. They had obviously intended to store the papers there until ready to distribute, but the accident to the old woman meant they had had to act in a hurry. Where would they store them now?

'Sir.' Erling stood in front of him. 'The woman, sir. She has given Steadman some information, but he thinks she knows more than she's telling.'

Steiner's irritation flared. Steadman was one of his best inter-rogators. Why couldn't he get the information out of a terrified old woman who had been processed to obey any command from a man?

'She's terrified, sir,' Erling went on. 'Steadman thinks she's more frightened of something else than she is of him.'

Steiner stood up and walked back into the office. A woman frightened of something other than Steadman? 'Send her in,' he said. 'I'll see her.'

She came into the room, supported by a uniformed police-man. An old woman in her seventies, blind fear on her wrinkled face, her thin, wispy hair straggling across her eyes, her coarsened hands held trembling to her sunken chest, the small angry burns showing vividly against the mottled skin.

'Your name?' he asked.

Her lips moved silently, the tendons in her thin neck working convulsively. That fool Steadman. He had pushed her too far. He would never get any information out of her in this state. He nodded slightly to the vacant chair and waited while the man helped her into it.

His voice was smooth and calm. 'It seems my men have fright-ened you considerably. I will deal with them.' He leant forward, looking directly into her face, compelling her to return the look. 'You've no need to be frightened of me. I told you, I will punish the men who ill-treated you.' He turned to the waiting policeman. 'Get some coffee in here. I'm sure you would like some coffee, wouldn't you—I'm afraid I didn't get your name.'

'Lawlor, sir.' The words were a whisper.

'Lawlor, fine. And, officer, bring back some medication for those burns.' He sat back in his chair and looked at the frightened woman opposite him. The violent trembling of her hands expressed her terror. He would have to move very carefully if he was to get any immediate information out of her. What did she fear more than the attentions of Steadman? He glanced at the sheet of paper in front of him with the information she had already given. The women had been carrying refuse sacks out of the supervisor's room when one of the sacks was dropped, spilling some of the contents on to the floor. She had caught sight of newspapers. The whole contents of the sack seemed to be newspapers, and she had seen a photograph on the front page.

He waited as she tried to drink some of the coffee, and then wrote a brief note for Erling, handing it to the man standing rigidly to attention. He wanted all the associates of the original supervisor brought in for questioning. She had been an old woman so she must have lived in one of the smaller hostels reserved for the over sixties, and working in that public lavatory all day until late at night, she could not have had many contacts outside of the hostel. How did an old woman like that get involved with a group of agitators? If only she had not been killed by that car.

Lawlor had finished the coffee and he indicated the small tube of ointment near her. 'Put some of that on. It will take the pain away until I can arrange for a doctor to attend to you.' He watched her closely as she did as she was told. The trembling had almost ceased. 'You were very quick to spot there was something wrong with those refuse collectors. Tell me. What made you suspicious in the first place?'

She made a few unsuccessful attempts to speak before the words finally came out in a hoarse whisper. 'Mr Shirer, he's my superior, had given me the keys to unlock the place, but when I got there I found it unlocked and the women collecting the rubbish.' His silence forced her to continue. 'Well, they told me the place was open when they got there, but I've been working on this job since I was sixty and I know the rubbish is never collected on a Saturday.' He nodded encouragingly. 'Then one of them dropped a sack. It seemed full of papers. Not used papers—new ones.'

'And you saw the papers clearly?' he asked.

The fear was rising in her again. He could see it in her eyes. 'Not very clearly.'

'But you saw a photograph?'

'Yes. Of a group of women. Five or six of them.'

The six women who had disappeared from the hospital. They were carrying the story of the rescue. She was very frightened now, Steadman was right. She had seen more than she had told him. Had she seen the headline above the picture? It most probably told of the artificial insemination programme. Surely she did not think it would affect her at her age?

He led her away from the subject that frightened her. 'What did the women look like? How many were there?'

Her relief was obvious. 'I only saw two, but there may have been another one in the van—the driver. The two I saw were in their late twenties, or early thirties. They were wearing refuse collectors' overalls.' She stopped, searching for more information to give him. 'There wasn't anything else I noticed about them.'

'No, of course not. It's very difficult to describe anything about the women workers. They all look alike, don't they?' He continued, smoothly, no change in his voice. 'And what did the headline above the picture say?'

Her reaction was instantaneous. Panic back in her face, trembling back in her body, 'I—I didn't see any headline, sir.'

So, he had been right. It was something to do with the headline. Something about artificial insemination? But, that would not terrify her like this. What was she frightened about? Something she thought would incriminate her in some way? But, she wasn't involved with the group or she wouldn't have reported her suspicions. Was it something about him? That could make sense. She would be frightened to tell him because of his possible reaction. He forced his voice to sound gentle, regretful.

'You're not telling me the truth, are you? You saw the headline but you don't want to tell me what it said. That is very foolish of you. Are you frightened of what my reaction will be? Come now, do I look a frightening man?'

The silence lengthened as he watched the uncertainty on her face. He was nearly there. She had started to consider telling him. A few more moments of silence and she would make the decision. He leant forward to rearrange the roses in front of him, handling the blossoms with gentle hands.

'It—' Her voice was almost inaudible, the sounds sticking in her throat. He waited.

'It—it was about the President.'

Not about him. Gorston. No wonder she was terrified. He kept his voice gentle. 'And what did it say about the President?'

She would not meet his eyes, her head buried on her chest, the old hands now trembling uncontrollably. 'It said—' He could see the pulse fluttering in her thin neck as she tried to get the words out. 'It said, Gorston's rule is ended.'

He had it. But he was not dealing with a group of malcontents printing treasonable rubbish. They were militants. That headline could only mean one thing. They intended to assassinate Gorston.

He looked with distaste at the old woman. 'Get her out,' he ordered coldly.

The policeman hesitated, unsure. 'Is she under arrest, sir? What do you want me to do with her?'

'I don't care what you do with her. Get her out.'

Gorston's rule is ended. Is ended. And the paper was due to come out in three days time. That meant the assassination attempt would be in the next three days, and he still did not have a direct lead to them.

'Erling, have you picked up those women from the hostel?'

'Yes, sir. They're on their way.'

'I want them questioned about the woman who was killed this morning. Find out if they know anything about her involvement with a subversive group.'

'Sir.' Erling's voice was uncertain on the phone. 'Two of the women are in their eighties and are bed-ridden.'

'Are you bringing them in?'

'Yes, sir. By ambulance.'

'Well, what's the problem?'

The phone went silent for a moment. 'Nothing, sir.'

'And, Erling, have we a report back from the refuse depot, yet?'

'Yes, sir,' Erling answered. 'The depot manager is sure that none of the lorries have been used today.'

Steiner glanced quickly through Steadman's report. The old woman was sure it was a genuine refuse lorry, describing the city coat of arms on the door. 'Bring him in. He may be lying. Try to shake his story. And get men on to the streets. Someone must have noticed a refuse lorry out on the roads on a Saturday. And, Erling, I want a copy of the President's schedule for the next three days.'

Eighteen

Damn it, why hadn't she come? Carl bounced the car down the rutted track, annoyed at the disappointment he felt, irritated with himself for waiting nearly an hour after he realized she was not coming. He had sensed the hesitancy in her at the cottage, but when she had eventually agreed, he was sure she would come. Why hadn't she? His presence disturbed her, he knew that. He could still feel that remarkable reaction when he had casually touched her arm. She had gone completely rigid. Was it fear, revulsion, what?

He turned the car on to the road that led back to the cottage, suddenly tired of having to try to communicate with the women. They had been at the cottage for almost a week and, with the exception of Bartlett, they still tried to avoid him, keeping to the barn most of the time. He had wanted to break down the barriers of fear and distrust but, on the few occasions he had spoken to one of the others, he had been met with the polite blankness that had shocked him so strongly when he had first met it in Hillard. It was ridiculous he still had to call her Hillard. He had asked Bartlett what her other name was and she had looked at him with those dark eyes that resembled Hillard's in their emptiness and said, 'She's just Hillard.' He did not believe her, as he did not believe that she was just called Bartlett. It was as if concealing their names was part of their protection from society, part of their anonymity behind which they led their private lives.

He had developed some sort of a relationship with Bartlett over the last week and for some reason felt freer about asking her questions than he did with Hillard. He remembered the conversation they had had when she was washing up the women's dishes and he had sensed that they had fallen into a companionable silence. 'Why do you always hide behind that blankness?' The question was spoken without any conscious awareness, an audible echo of his thoughts. She had looked at him and he thought he caught a gleam of amusement, deep in the blankness. 'How do you know we are hiding anything? The blankness may be all there is.'

He knew she had been mocking him and also knew that this was part of her defence. His thoughts went back to Hillard as she had sat at the river's edge, trying to control her reaction to the memories he had forced her to recall. Would he ever be able to persuade her that she did not need to defend herself against him?

He turned off the main road and on to the winding lane that led to the cottage, suddenly dreading the thought of another evening in that difficult atmosphere. The women were no trouble. Bartlett had fallen into a routine of preparing their food and clearing away after them, and on occasions had even prepared his meal as well. But it was the knowledge that six other human beings were that close to him and yet completely inaccessible. He needed company, uncomplicated, cheerful company.

He swung the car through the gates and felt surprise at the sight of three women waiting in the driveway.

'How is she?' Bartlett, as usual, had spoken for the others.

An irrational annoyance flickered through him. Concern for Hillard had, momentarily, overcome their aversion to him. Even as he thought it, he realized the childishness of his reaction and the knowledge increased his annoyance. 'She didn't come.' He walked past them into the cottage, not wanting to be asked for explanations he could not give. He would wash and change and get out for the evening. He needed a break. Besides, he thought wryly, the women would be more relaxed with him out of the way.

Bartlett was still waiting for him as he came out, car keys in hand. 'Did you say Hillard didn't meet you?'

'That's right.' He walked past her to the car, slightly regretting his churlish manner. 'I'm going out for the evening. Maybe the women would like to listen to the record player in the cottage. I'll be quite late. I'm thinking of going to the Opera House.'

He backed the car on to the quiet lane, the thought of the enjoyable evening ahead completely banishing his earlier ill-humour. He would have a meal at the same restaurant; the food and service had been excellent. He pulled a small card from his pocket as he negotiated the turning onto the main road, and read it again. It seemed to be a peculiar way of running a night club. The head waiter had said that, as he was a visitor, the card would remain valid for the next month. It must be a very popular place if they had to control their numbers by such a comprehensive ticket system.

He wound down the window of the car and settled back to enjoy the short journey into the city. He would have to make sure he got clearer instructions tonight. His thoughts went back to the scene that had erupted into the silence of the night when he had last looked for the Opera House, involving him, briefly, in the horror and pain of another human being, and he thought again of his revulsion when Hillard had told him why she was hiding the women. This was a sick society, headed by a sick man. But without the backing of the people, Gorston would not have lasted in power. What sick need in them did Gorston fulfil? Why should they try to dehumanize some of their most intelligent people just because they were female? And why this obsession with child-bearing? He had got that much information out of Bartlett. The women were either wives or workers. The wives were married at eighteen and then had to produce a child every other year for the rest of their fertile lives. Contraception was illegal, both according to their interpretation of God's law and man's. It was a male society, by men and for men. But even the men had restrictions. They had to marry at twenty and—a thought suddenly struck him. If the population was married by the age of twenty and the wives were perpetually pregnant, why was the nightclub so busy? Suppose it was some sort of teenage disco? That was the last thing he wanted to walk into. No, it couldn't be. The head waiter had known exactly what he had been looking for—pleasant sophisticated surroundings, with pleasant sophisticated company, preferably female, intelligent, attractive female company; good to look at, good to talk to, and then, maybe—His thoughts abruptly threw up a picture of large grey eyes, cautious and shielded, but with an occasional glimpse of the person behind them. No, he intended having an enjoyable, carefree night. He could not stand the tensions of the women and all they represented, without having a break from them—and that included Hillard.

The meal lived up to its remembered excellence, the waiters hovered with gratifying attention, the lush decor increased his feeling of well-being, and the head waiter commiserated with him for losing his way the last evening, painstakingly repeating the directions.

He drove attentively down the main street, before turning into the dimmer lights of the narrower rows of houses. It must have been here he had gone wrong. He slowed the car, counting the turnings, passing the rows of old, terraced houses before turning into the new housing estate he was in before. Maybe it was not the same one. They all looked alike. He followed the road through the estate and turned left into an even dimmer cul-de-sac. Was this it? He had carefully followed instructions. The sound of church music carried in the still, warm air, a choir of boy sopranos soaring and falling in cadences of beauty that can only be captured by the crystal clarity of the young male voice. He stopped the car, held by the beauty of the sound. There must be a church nearby, but he could see nothing in the dingy street except a row of empty houses, abandoned, derelict, facing a high blank wall. There was no traffic, no pedestrians, no sign of life, no sound except the exquisite choir; the old-fashioned street lamps throwing dim pools of light on to the deserted pavements, darkening the shadows by comparison with the feeble glow. He must be lost again.

He got out of the car and walked towards the sound of the singing. It seemed to be coming from behind the wall. There must be a doorway somewhere. He found the gates at the far end of the street, large, double gates leading to a car park half full of cars; two officious attendants bustled around with the self-assumed importance of minor officials the world over.

'No car? Then through the doorway over there, if you please, sir.'

'No. I'm sorry. I'm looking for the Opera House.'

The man was busy directing another car into a parking space, impatient with Carl for distracting him. 'That's right. As I said, that door there.' He walked around the car, intent on his loud and unnecessary instructions, leaving Carl annoyed and confused. This could not be the night club, unless the door led through to the front of the building. Maybe this was the back entrance from the car park.

'Ticket, please, sir.'

'I'm looking for the Opera House,' Carl explained.

The man gave him a cheerful grin. 'That's right, sir. Straight down the corridor. Have you got your ticket?'

Carl handed over the ticket, still hesitant, but the little man was already busy with other customers. This *must* be the back entrance. Most probably there was a parking problem in the main street and regulars came straight round to the car park. He stumbled in the dingy corridor, the dim lighting doing little to illuminate the way. One would have thought they would have brightened the place up a bit if customers used it as a regular entrance. What a peculiar place for a night club. The singing was clearer than ever now. It must be right next door to a church. He stumbled again, as he tripped on the unseen step at the end of the corridor and grabbed at the door handle to prevent himself from falling. His surge of annoyance died as he opened the door and saw the hall beneath him. It was large and high, a contrast of darkness and intricate patterns of light formed by the hundreds of candles carried by the singing choir boys. The gallery in which he found himself was lit only by the reflected light from below and he had difficulty in making out the shapes of the other men who lined the rails, watching intently the kaleidoscope of patterns, oblivious of their neighbours.

He must have taken the wrong turning. This was obviously a hall being used for a rehearsal of some important church service. He looked down again as the soprano voices pealed like triumphant bells, echoing around the walls. The slowly-walking choir boys, with lighted candles in their hands shining around their heads, gave the illusion of angelic beauty that matched the angelic sound. The splendour of the scene took his eyes away from the dirt and drabness of the hall and he leant on the rail, absorbed in the drama and beauty of the event.

'The priests will be here soon.' He heard the muttered whisper run along the line of men and recognized the final crescendo in the throbbing hymn of praise. He turned to the man next to him, deciding to ask where the night club was, but he stayed silent as he saw the intensity of the man's gaze. He was oblivious of everything except what was happening below. Carl could feel the tenseness, the expectancy, a deep excitement, and looked around for someone else to ask. He saw the same intense anticipation on all the shadowy faces. Suddenly he became aware of the breathing of the man next to him as it shortened, coming in rapid gasps, and he looked back to the hall below. The scene had not changed. The candles continued to make their changing patterns as the boys wove their way into an enormous triangle, and the singing soared out its triumphant message.

Carl looked back at the men around him and abruptly he wanted to leave, to get away from this mixture of beauty and—he did not know what. It was sick. There was something terribly wrong. The tension and expectancy in the air was almost a tangible thing and it closed in around him, stifling and suffocating. He looked back at the hall, still only seeing the spectacular lights, still only hearing the magnificent sacred music. But something else was going to happen. He knew it with an awful certainty, and he did not want to stay to find out what it was. He wanted to get out. He edged his way to the door, turning the handle quietly, feeling an irrational need to escape without drawing attention to himself. The door was locked. He turned the handle more forcefully, pushing hard against it. It was firm. He was locked in this mad place.

'How do I get out of this place?' he asked the nearest man, annoyance making his manner aggressive. His voice sounded loud in the intense silence of his immediate surroundings. The man ignored him and a stir of movement went through all the men, intent on the hall below. Carl followed their gaze and real-ized that the singing had died away as three robed men appeared at the apex of the triangle of light. They stood, motionless and resplendent in their ornate vestments, as the silence spread to every corner of the vast hall, and Carl found himself watching with the other men, waiting for the next scene in this bizarre production.

The silence lengthened until, at last, the robed figures turned and walked slowly on to the raised dais, burnt incense coiling lazily into the air from the swinging censers as the phalanx of candles separated into two halves, forming a corridor of darkness down the length of the flickering lights. A flurry of movement drew Carl's eye to the furthest end of the hall and he strained to see the figures making their way through the gloom.

God, it was a woman. He could see her face now, illuminated by the passive choir boys, eyes wide, mouth working but making no sound, limbs jerking in terror but having no effect on the slow progress as the two men on either side of her dragged her silently forward, before finally throwing her at the feet of the waiting priests.

Until the central robed figure stepped forward, the only sounds were broken only by the rasping breaths of the prostrate woman and the faint, metallic sounds of the steadily swinging censers.

'Brethren, let us pray.' He stood, magnificent in his priestly robes, arms stretched upwards in supplication, his voice deep and melodious. 'Oh, Lord, give us strength this night, that we may guide this woman from the path of iniquity; that, by our exhor-tations, we may bring her to see the evil of her ways; and, by her confession, she may bring her fellow women to a true state of repentance.'

'Confess.' The intense response echoed around the hall as every man stared at the scene below him.

Carl stepped away from the rail, searching for another way out. He had to get away. The melodious voice droned on at the edge of his consciousness as he made his way back to the door, desperately turning the handle, shaking the door, no longer con-cerned with concealment.

'Confess!' The response throbbed out again, the suppressed hysteria coming closer to the surface as he turned from the locked door and forced his way to the other end of the gallery. There must be another door. The men were unaware of him as he pushed past them.

'*Confess!*' The tension around him was swirling, clawing, surging to a crescendo as he finally reached the far end and found another door.

A scream tore through the hall, obliterating the chanted prayer, forcing Carl to look again at the scene beneath, as every nerve in his body responded to the sudden, sickening sound. She was naked, her clothes in torn, scattered heaps, blood oozing from the welt across her breasts. He watched, frozen, as the whip lifted slowly and he saw the animal terror in her face as her head was dragged up by the male hand entangled in her hair.

'*Confess!*' The hysterical sound enveloped him again, a profane response to the profane prayer, as the whip came down again and the scream bounced back from the walls.

'Yes, yes. I confess. I confess.' She was screaming, babbling, past comprehending what sounds were coming from her mouth as Carl stared at the handful of grey hair still twisted around the man's hand.

A sigh went up around him and he sensed a movement among the watching men, felt them pressing around him, jostling for position at the door he was still touching.

'I am unclean.'

The male voice sounded calm, emotionless. The female voice was tripping, slurring the words in despairing haste before the ever threatening whip.

'I am an abomination on the earth.'

'I am the vessel of iniquity.'

'My body carries the seeds of destruction for all men.'

'Only through pain and torment can I hope to win salvation.'

The press of men around Carl was increasing, pushing him harder against the door, until suddenly it opened and he was forced down a flight of steps by the throng of crowding men; stifled by the tension, sickened by the smell of lust that exuded from all around him; revulsion and horror gripping his body as he anticipated the ensuing scene. Suddenly he was out of the confines of the stairway and into the main hall, behind the robed, chanting figures; the choir boys, silently filing past, positioned the candles around the walls, illuminating the whole room with a subdued, flickering light. The woman was standing, held upright by her hair, eyes closed, softly moaning—and behind her, replacing the choir boys, he could see more women. He could see the terror in their faces as they huddled together, some staring fixedly at the men, others shielding their faces with their arms.

The priest raised his arms and the jostling men stilled into an expectant silence as the mellow voice sounded through the hall. 'And I heard another voice from Heaven saying, "Come out of her, my people, that ye be not partakers of her sins, and that ye receive not her plagues. For her sins have reached unto heaven, and God has remembered her iniquities. Reward her even as she has rewarded you, and double unto her double according to her works; in the cup which she hath filled, fill to her double."'

The men remained tense and still as the three robed figures slowly walked the length of the hall, passing the terrified women as if they did not exist. The flickering candles gleamed off the metallic threads of their ornate vestments in a display of incongruous splendour. The large double doors at the far end of the hall opened smoothly, and silently closed behind them. The tension remained in the hall for an interminable moment before the men suddenly erupted into a pushing, swearing mass; each fighting and struggling in their haste to reach the women; eyes glistening, lips working; mouthing profanities in their frenzy of lust. Carl turned away from the scene, a sweet sickness clinging in his throat, the muscles of his stomach contracting with horror, his mind trying to shut out the noise and smell of the hell around him. He had to get out. He had to walk through that nightmare and reach the doors at the far end of the room.

He turned again and started towards the centre of the heaving mass, noticing the lessening numbers of struggling bodies. The men were dragging the women off in ones and twos towards the row of small doors that lined the walls, the screams of terror rising in waves over the muffled sobs. He tried to keep his eyes to the ground; tried to keep out the faces that would personalize the horror, as he made his way through the mêlée. He was almost through when a sobbing woman was dragged to her feet directly in front of him, causing him to lose his balance in his desperate effort to avoid her. Suddenly, he was looking directly into a terrified face, pleading, entreating eyes, hands held in a vain protection over a swollen belly. Oh, God. She was pregnant. He put his hand out to her, lifting her from the floor, unaware of her feeble struggles. Where could he take her? He'd never get her out of the main doors. He pulled her towards one of the small doors, fumbling urgently with the knob before pushing her before him into a small, dimly-lit room and slamming the door shut behind them. This wasn't real. It wasn't happening. He leant back against the door.

After a moment, he reached across to the woman curled up in the corner, sobbing with harsh, dry gasps that turned to a small scream as he touched her. 'Please, don't. I'm not going to hurt you.' His words were not penetrating the veil of fear that shrouded her mind. He walked the few steps towards her, seeing her shrink still closer to the wall at the sound. 'Please listen to me. I'm not going to hurt you.' He was on his knees, tentatively touching her arm, trying to make her understand. 'I brought you in here to protect you. Do you hear?' He repeated the words slowly, willing her to understand and accept. 'I'm not going to hurt you.' He sat alongside her, his back against the wall, waiting for the harsh breathing to subside, hoping his stillness would calm her. How could he get her out? He listened for any sound from the hall outside the door but all was silent—too silent. Why couldn't he hear the sounds of the other men? He put his hand on the wall to push himself to his feet and the question was answered for him. The room was soundproofed. Suddenly the silence pressed in on him with greater persistence than the earlier noise, sinister and concealing.

'What do you want me to do?'

He barely caught the whispered words. 'Nothing. I want nothing from you. I just want to get you out of here.' She turned her head slowly and looked at him for the first time, and he could see the terror that lay, waiting to sweep over her again. 'I'm not going to hurt you, believe me,' he repeated. 'And, I want nothing from you. How do we get out of here?' She stared at him blankly. 'You want to get out, don't you? I need your help.' Her stare was unnerving him. She might be in a state of shock and unable to talk, but he needed her help in finding the way out of this nightmare.

'I can't get out.' Her words were barely audible.

'Yes you can. I'll help you. We'll get out of here together.'

'This is prison,' she whispered.

He was kneeling before her, looking into the dazed face. Did she know what she was saying? He put his hand slowly on to hers, touching her fingers very gently, desperately wanting to comfort her, to still the violent trembling that shook her whole body. 'I don't understand,' he said. 'This isn't a prison.' But what was it? The terror in the women made it quite clear that they were not here of their free wills. Then why were they here?

'Yes it is.' Her eyes were looking into his, frightened and bewildered; but the panic was subsiding. Her words confused him. She looked as if she knew what she was saying.

'I'm sorry,' he persisted. 'I still don't understand.'

He could see disbelief in her eyes. 'You really don't know where you are?' she asked.

The unreality was increasing. 'Listen to me. I'm a stranger in this country. I came here tonight because I was looking for a nightclub.' Her eyes were questioning. 'A nightclub. A place where you can drink, dance, find good company.' His words sounded trite and trivial. What would she know about such harmless pleasures? 'I want to get us out of here.'

She shook her head, trying to understand him. 'This is the Women's Detention Centre. I'm in on a four weeks sentence.'

'But—' He gestured towards the door, encompassing all the horror he had seen in a single movement.

'They come here three nights a week,' she said slowly. 'It's part of the punishment. They punish us for our crimes.'

He got to his feet and looked around the small room, seeing for the first time the mattress on the floor and the other objects stacked neatly on the shelves. 'But what have you done?'

'I—I stole a ring.' She turned her head away from him and then looked back as he made no comment. 'It wasn't a real ring.

I mean, it wasn't expensive or anything. I wouldn't steal a real ring.' Her voice dropped still lower. 'It was only a cheap ring, but it looked so pretty. I took it, and they caught me.'

'And you were brought here because of that?' He could not absorb what she was telling him.

'All the women who are arrested are sent to places like this.'

'But the men? Who are they?' His mind felt sluggish, unable to comprehend, unable to accept.

'They are just members of the public. Each man is allowed one ticket every three months. They come three times a week, but different women are brought out. Sometimes the women are too ill to be brought out for weeks. This was my first time. I shouldn't be out again for about a week.'

Carl put his arms up on the wall and rested his head on them. What could he do? The nightmare had closed in on him, shutting him in this tiny space with a pregnant woman telling him things that could not be. He looked back at her. He could not even help her. He could not get her out of this place. She would be all right for tonight, but what about next week? 'Isn't there anything I can do?' He was pleading with her, begging her to tell him how he could stop this horror.

'No. You've been very kind. You could go now. No one else will come for me tonight.'

She was telling him to go. The same as that other woman had told him to go. He remembered the woman lying bleeding on the concrete, her companion begging him to leave them. And he had. He had walked away from their misery, the same as he would walk away from this. It felt as if he did nothing but turn his back on people's torments. 'But do the authorities know what's going on? Isn't there someone I can see—the Minister of Justice maybe?' He knew it was a futile question and he read the answer in the bewildered look on her face.

'You'd better go now.'

She wanted him to leave. She was still afraid of him; still frightened that he would suddenly behave like all the other men she knew. He put out his hand to her again, unable to find any words to say. He hated himself for his helplessness and for the knowledge that he was going to walk away from her as he did the other woman. She was still crouched on the ground, pressed up against the wall, still wary although the deep terror had gone from her eyes. His hand dropped back to his side as he looked at her in silence, before turning abruptly and walking through the door into the deserted hall, then out into the squalid street, towards his car that would take him away from that place.

Nineteen

Carl drove rapidly through the emptying city streets, unable to shake off the horror of the last few hours, looking at every man he passed, wondering if they were visitors to that nightmare.

The women. In the shock of what had happened, he had forgotten the women. He had told Bartlett he was going to the Opera House. He suddenly knew with sickening certainty that they would not be there when he got back. And he also knew that if they were caught, they would end up in that terrible hall. He fretted impatiently at the intersection that led to the fast, straight road away from the city, swinging out, uncaring, in front of a dawdling car, pulling into the fast lane, foot hard down on the accelerator. Maybe they would not have left yet. Even as he thought it, he knew he was trying to fool himself. They would have left immediately after he did. Why hadn't they told him? Why didn't Hillard tell him? If she was prepared to trust the women's safety to him, he had a right to know what would happen to them if they were caught.

The road seemed endless, stretching out like a ghostly conveyor belt in the lights of his headlamps, as he waited impatiently for the small turning that led into the maze of lanes that would take him back to the cottage. He pushed the car hard through the tight bends, risking a chance encounter with other cars on the quiet, deserted lanes. He had to get back as quickly as possible.

The lights shone out through the small windows as he pulled the car savagely through the gates, hurrying towards the door, engine still running, lights beaming across the solitary garden. The cottage was empty. He turned towards the barn, banging open the heavy door, switching on the lights. It was empty. He turned back to the garden, suddenly drained of any impetus, and slowly walked towards the lights of the car. A figure broke from the shadows, running towards the open gates, and his body started to function again. He shouted, he did not know what, as he raced across the space between him and the gates. It was a woman. He caught up with her, reaching out, grabbing her arm, trying to say something that would reassure her. She erupted into a whirlwind of flailing arms and legs. He felt a savage kick on the shin a split second before he felt her nails rake down the side of his face, his hands instinctively reaching for her wrists, pulling them away. He jerked backwards as her teeth sank into his hand and he lost his balance, bringing both of them crashing down onto the rough gravel of the drive. He rolled, trying to get the weight of his body across her as she still struggled and fought. He lay across her, pinioning her arms to her sides, as he fought to regain his breath. It was Bartlett, now still and silent.

'Will you listen to me,' he shouted. 'I didn't know.' She did not move. He could feel the tension in her body, but it was an inner, shrinking tension. She had stopped fighting. He pulled her to her feet, still tightly holding her arms. 'Do you hear me? I didn't know what sort of a place it was.' He tried to look into the still face; tried to see reaction; and shook her slightly in his frustration. 'Oh, God, believe me. I didn't.' The anguish in his mind was clearly audible in his voice. He needed her to believe him. It would not wipe out the memory of that place but she *had* to believe him. 'I thought it was a nightclub—an ordinary nightclub. That's what I asked the head waiter for—and he sent me there.'

She stood still, not trying to break free from his grasp, not saying anything. Quite suddenly she glanced down at his hands still grasping her arms, then back into his face. 'You can let go of me now,' she said stiffly.

'No. Not until you say you believe me.'

'I believe you.' The words carried no conviction for him. He stood there uncertainly. 'You can let go of me now. I won't run. I believe you.'

He let go of her arms, still wary, still expecting a sudden move, but she stayed quite still. 'The women. Where are they?' he asked.

'They're in the forest.'

'Will they come back?'

'I'll talk to them,' she offered. 'They'll come back when I explain.'

He still could not accept her words. There was no sign of emotion, no anger, no resentment, nothing. She could be hiding lies behind that blank mask. 'I don't know if I can believe you,' he said. 'I can't see anything in your face.' He thought he saw a flicker of a smile touch the blankness for a moment but it was gone in an instant.

'If you'll help me find my glasses, I'll take you to them.'

They walked in silence down the dark lane, Carl keeping close to her, still dubious of her acceptance. The darkness wrapped around them as the curve of the lane cut off the lights of the cottage, and Bartlett became a dim, dark shadow at his side. She turned off suddenly down a narrow, rutted track, the trees closing in on either side, and he hurried the few steps to catch up with her. 'Where does this lead?' he asked.

'To the forest and the bog. Haven't you ever been down here?'

'And the women are down here?'

'Yes.'

He stumbled in a deep tractor track and grabbed, ineffectually, at the shadowy branches, trying to regain his balance. She had gone. He looked around desperately, searching for her shadow among the many others, but there was no sign of her. She had melted into the navy darkness without a sound. Anger and frustration flared in him. He should have known she was lying. Desperation made him ignore discretion. He had to find her. She couldn't be far away. He would have heard the noise of her pushing through the dry undergrowth. 'Bartlett.' His voice seemed to be swallowed up by the dense trees. 'Bartlett!'

'I'm here.' Her voice came from the side of the track, quite close. But he could see nothing. 'We can talk from here, Mr Tolland. And don't try to follow my voice. There's a barbed wire fence between us and you wouldn't see it in the dark. You'd only hurt yourself.'

Her words made him suddenly aware of the stinging on his face and he touched the long scratch and found it still slowly trickling blood. 'I won't move,' he promised. 'Just listen to me.' He continued hurriedly when she gave no response. 'I told you the truth. I thought that place was a nightclub.' The horror of it came back to him. 'For God's sake, do you think I'd have gone there if I'd known? It was like a nightmare—the screams, the women, and there was nothing I could do to help. I just had to walk away and leave her.' The pain was obvious in his voice but she remained silent. 'Listen, about ten days ago I went out for a meal and I asked the head waiter if he could recommend a good nightclub. He suggested the Opera House. I told you, I thought it was an ordinary nightclub.' He heard himself repeating his words in his need to convince her, the desperation growing at her continuing silence. 'Bartlett, you've got to believe me. There's nowhere else for you to hide. You'll be caught. You'll end up in that hell.' He heard a slight sound from the undergrowth and he called to her urgently, fearing she would disappear completely into the thick forest. 'Bartlett, wait. Hear me out. Bartlett, are you still there?'

'I'm here, Mr Tolland.' She was standing next to him on the path, appearing as quietly and suddenly as she had disappeared. 'I'll take you to the women.'

'You believe me?'

'Yes.'

'You said that before.'

'I needed time to think,' she said simply. 'When you told me you were going to the Opera House, I was shocked. It didn't seem to fit in with what I had known about you over the week. When you told me you didn't know what the place was, I needed time to decide whether that was feasible.'

Anger flared in him at her cool words. 'And now you've decided I was telling the truth?'

She looked at him calmly for a moment and the quick burst of anger died. 'I'm sorry, Mr Tolland. I had to be sure.'

The activities of the next few hours blotted the memories from his mind. It had been difficult persuading the women to trust him and come back, and he had felt a deep surprise when listening to Bartlett talk to them. It was as if he was listening to a different person, eloquent, persuasive, logical. He caught a glimpse, for the first time, of the agile mind behind the blank exterior. And the other women had come alive as he watched, forgotten by them all, and he wondered how they existed, hidden so effectively from everyone except themselves.

They were now settled in the barn and the pictures came flooding back into his mind as he sat in front of the open fire. He could not shut them out, could not keep his mind on anything else.

'That scratch needs seeing to.'

He had not heard Bartlett come back into the cottage. 'How can such a thing be allowed to happen?' he demanded. His thoughts would not even allow him to accept her gesture of concern. She moved towards the armchair opposite him, the first time she had ever sat in the same room as him.

'You must understand Gorston's society before you could understand that,' she said.

'But I can't understand the society. Hillard has told me bits of it but none of it makes sense.'

'You'd be better off getting her to tell you all of it. She understands how it happened better than I. I know what it's like now, but she has gone deeper than that. She has tried to work out why it happened, and what society could be like if we all learned to live together.'

He suddenly remembered Hillard's expression, the day at the river, as she turned to him, searching his face. 'Can life be that beautiful?' That was what she had seen in his paintings. Someone else's interpretation of her dreams and hopes. Why couldn't she have told him all about it then? He could see again the anguish on her face as she had struggled to tell him about the selection of the workers, and he answered his own question. 'No, I can't wait for Hillard to tell me. I need to know now.' He had to try to come to terms with what he had seen tonight. He could see Bartlett looking at him as if silently debating whether to tell him. 'Please, Bartlett.'

She sat upright in the comfortable armchair, a contained figure, cool and emotionless. 'Gorston came to power about thirty years ago,' she began. 'Hillard must have told you that.'

'Yes, and the fact that the economy was on the rocks at the time.'

'That's right. It had been shaky for years and the unemployment problem was growing. Because of the influence of the Church, there had always been a very high birth rate, much higher than the economy could cope with. The traditional solution had always been emigration. Then there was a worldwide recession and the supply of overseas jobs dried up, leaving a rapidly increasing unemployment problem. Due to the large families, a quarter of the population was under twenty-five, so, you can see, the unemployed were going to increase at an alarming rate over the next few years. And then the men started agitating.' She stopped and looked into the fire for a long moment before looking across at him. 'This is the part that is difficult to explain because you have to see it in terms of those times.' She sat forward slightly in the chair. 'The society that had developed over the centuries was repressive towards women. Not in the active way that we have now. It was more injustice by default. Men had always made the laws, shaped the economy, structured society, and they did all these things with men in mind. When they passed laws to protect property, it was men's property and they included women as men's property. When a woman left her husband, for any reason, and formed a relationship with another man, her husband could claim damages from the other man because he had "stolen" his property. This attitude applied to all aspects of the culture. Women had no legal rights as individuals, only as property of either fathers or husbands. The effect of this, of course, was that men accepted, as a fact, that women were some sort of inferior beings. Hillard believes that they had brainwashed themselves for so long into believing this, that it had become an automatic assumption.' She paused, staring again into the glowing fire. 'I find that hard to believe. I can't see how an intelligent person can have that amount of illogical prejudice and be unaware of it. Can you?'

Carl sat and looked at her, a sick apprehension growing inside him. She was describing something so very familiar.

'Anyway, it was against this background that the men started to agitate. They said women should not be allowed to work when men were unemployed. They should stay at home and have children and look after their husbands. They had no right to work. Some people, men and women, said that the main cause of the economic problems was the fact that the birth rate was too high. This country had always been an agricultural economy and therefore no real economic expansion was possible. Then, the Church stepped in and reinforced what the men were saying. She claimed that a woman's role was to produce children and love her husband; contraception was a grievous sin because all children were gifts from God. Then Gorston came on the scene and he agreed with the Church and the men. He promised them all the things they wanted—more jobs, a stable economy, and women would not be allowed to work. He must have had an electric personality. The people demanded he took control and made him a virtual dictator. There seems to have been a purge of some sort immediately after he assumed power, because all those who had spoken out about the birth rate being too high disappeared along with most of the intelligentsia of the time.'

Carl sat back in the chair and closed his eyes. It all sounded so familiar. He had seen newsreels where male workers were saying the very same things; he had listened to churchmen preaching that the 'woman's place is in the home'; and he had even taken part in conversations that ridiculed women with the subtle male assumption that they were, in some way, inferior to men, of less importance, easily disregarded as irrelevant, with no contribution to make outside the sex act. A picture of a beautiful, green-eyed girl came into his mind, and he remembered the last conversation they had had. He had thought it amusing that she wanted a job. With a face and figure like hers, any man would have been pleased to keep her. That was what he had said to her. She had screamed at him. 'I'm not anyone's pet poodle.' And he had laughed—in wonder at her beauty and in his sureness that the anger would evaporate once they got into bed. But she had left and he never did find out where she went.

Bartlett waited until he opened his eyes and then went on. 'After he was in power for a short time, he discovered the economy couldn't function properly without some women workers. Women had always been paid less than men and the employers wouldn't increase the rates for the jobs, and the men wouldn't work for such low wages. So he started his selection programme and his education scheme. Women were separated out at the age of ten, into future workers and future wives. Special schools were set up to teach them their roles in life and, always, they were taught that women were inferior and subservient to men. The boys were taught that women were evil beings whose main purpose was to destroy man by undermining his manhood and leading him away from God.'

He could see it. A frightening short step from what he had always accepted as a basic fact of life. The horror he still felt from his evening's experience made him look harshly at his own attitudes. It was true what Hillard had told Bartlett. He had just accepted the fact that, somehow, he was superior to women. That they were there for his amusement. He had not even been aware of the assumption until now. He had always considered himself a liberal, sophisticated man, and he had felt these things, as did all the men he knew. So, take the innate prejudice and reinforce it with an intense educational programme, place it in a society run by a religious fanatic, back it, at least in the beginning, by the Church, and combine it with the sexual repression that springs from twisted religious beliefs—and the Opera House is born, together with all the other horrors.

'But didn't anyone try to stop him?' he asked. 'What about the parents? The parents of the children who were taken away to the special schools? Surely they tried to stop him.'

'I told you,' she replied, 'this is a country of large families. It always has been. The vast majority of homes have too many mouths to feed. When the authorities came and told the parents that one or more of their children had been selected for free, special education because of her high intelligence, they didn't ask questions. They were delighted that their child was going to do so well. It was almost as good as if they were going into a seminary or convent. And that was also part of the cultural tradition. When they found out what the special training entailed—it was too late.'

He persisted. 'Well, all right. I accept that. But what about now? Isn't there anyone who tries to stop it now?'

'No. A few intellectuals agitate now and then, but mainly about the fact that the national average intelligence will drop because of the top fifteen per cent of women never having children, and because of the high incidence of children being born with genetic diseases due to the age of their mothers. But Steiner makes a few arrests and the protests die down.'

'Steiner?'

'He's the head of the secret police.'

A feeling of helplessness swept over Carl. Sitting in this comfortable room, watching Bartlett's expressionless face as she explained this sick society had made the whole thing seem unreal. But what about the women? Bartlett, the others, who had to try and exist. What about the women in the barn? And what about that desperate, terrified woman he left in the Opera House? He couldn't just sit here and do nothing.

'I've got to do something, Bartlett. I can't walk away as if I never saw any of it. There was a woman there tonight. She was pregnant—about seven months. She was there, Bartlett, and I had to walk away and leave her.' He jumped to his feet. 'I've got to do something!'

She watched him as he paced around the room, calm in the face of his frustration. 'What can you do?' she asked quietly.

He stopped and looked at her, desperation, anger, frustration chasing each other inside him. 'I don't know. I could burn the hell-hole down. And I could get out of the country and stir up world opinion; bring political pressure to bear.'

'All that takes time,' she pointed out. 'And what do you think would happen here if other countries were sufficiently interested to act? Hillard says that what drives Gorston is fear of women. Her arguments seem logical. If he was threatened like that, he would destroy us all before he submitted.'

His frustration turned against the calm, reasoning woman. 'Then what do you suggest? Are you content just to let this continue? Are you so steeped in Gorston's brainwashing that you are prepared to exist like this until he eventually dreams up another law that will kill you?'

She sat very still and looked at him for a long time as the anger boiled inside him. Finally she said, 'We are doing something about it.'

He knew her words held a frightening significance and he watched her intently as he sat back in the chair.

'I'll tell you about it because I want you to do something for me, and because you mustn't make any stupid move that could ruin our plans.' She paused, as if feeling for the right words. 'We have planned an uprising—very shortly. Nearly all the women workers are involved. That was how we were rescued so quickly from the hospital. Our network spreads throughout the whole city.'

'But, how? How have you got the arms? Who have you got helping you?' He was excited but confused too.

She looked at him, slightly puzzled. 'We've no one helping us.'

'But you can't take on the whole state on your own. You're all women.' His words hung in the air.

'Yes, we're all women. And we won't be using arms.'

His annoyance with himself over his last words made him want to prove the lunacy of the scheme. 'Are you mad? What can you expect to achieve without arms? What do you intend to do? Talk Gorston out of power?'

He thought he saw a slight flicker of anger in Bartlett's eyes as she stood up and faced him. 'There will be a rising—without the use of arms—without help from anyone. And we believe it will be successful.'

He got up and walked over to her. 'Look, I'm sorry if I used the wrong words, but if you move against Gorston without weapons, you can't possibly win. You will all be killed, or else spend the rest of your lives in that place I saw tonight.'

Her face had assumed its usual air of blankness and he cursed his clumsiness. She had shut him out again. 'We all know what will happen if we don't succeed and we have tried to plan for that also. I told you I wanted you to do something for me. I would like you to drive me to the city.'

'But, you can't go near the city. The police are looking for you.' What was wrong with the woman? Hillard had stuck her neck out to help get Bartlett out of that hospital and now she calmly wanted to go back, risking her skin and Hillard's.

'I must go there.' She was adamant. 'If you won't drive me, I shall walk. I have a map. That's why you caught me—I had to come back for it.'

He fought down a sudden urge to shake her. She was looking

at him again as if he didn't exist. 'But why do you have to go back? Can't I go for you?'

She looked at him silently for a moment, then said. 'I'm worried about Hillard. She didn't meet you today and she said she would. She may be in trouble.'

A fear gripped him and he suddenly realized how important Hillard had become to him. Bartlett had said that nearly all the women workers were involved in this crazy rising. Did that mean Hillard? He could not bring himself to ask the question directly. 'Do you mean about the rescue from the hospital? But she said they couldn't be traced.'

'No, I don't think it would be the rescue,' Bartlett answered.

'Then what?' The words he did not want answered sounded surprisingly in the room. 'She isn't involved in this rising of yours is she?'

She hesitated a long time, the blankness disappearing from her eyes as she looked at him intently. Then, 'She planned it.'

Twenty

'Stop at the next office block. I can cut through to the back of the hostel.'

Bartlett had told him about Hillard's clandestine way in and out of the hostel and intended to use it to reach Hillard's room. When she first told him, he refused to credit her words. The idea of these women climbing in and out of windows and generally indulging in similar cloak and dagger stuff struck him as ludicrous. He had been sure that she was mocking him for his slip he made in the cottage. Hillard had been right, he did not realize how much stupid prejudice he carried around inside him.

'Are you sure you can manage?' he asked. 'It seems a bit precarious to me. I still think I should go.'

She was more relaxed with him and intonations were creeping into her voice. He could hear the coldness as she cut across his protests. 'We've discussed that. You could end up in the wrong room.' She slipped quickly out of the car as Carl pulled into the kerb. The street was still and deserted, the lighting dim, and she rapidly disappeared into the shadows, leaving him alone in the street.

His fear for Hillard's safety had grown steadily on the drive through the city, as Bartlett explained more about her role in the planned Rising. Had she been arrested? Was that why she had not turned up for their meeting? Pictures of the Opera House came vividly into his mind. If Bartlett found her tonight, he would speak to her, persuade her that this Rising could not work, beg her to call it off until it was properly organized. But all that hinged on Bartlett finding her. She could have been arrested already. He sat, hunched over the wheel, staring down the deserted road. If she *had* been arrested, he would find some way of trying to rescue her.

'She's not in her room.' Bartlett had appeared, unseen and unheard, at the car window. 'It's all right, it doesn't necessarily mean bad news. I checked the room of another woman who's in the organization and she's out as well. They may be having a meeting.'

'Well, let's go there,' he suggested.

She hesitated. 'I'm not sure, but I thought I saw a man in front of the hostel. He'd be just around that bend. I'll cut through to the next road and you drive around the block. I'll meet you on the corner.'

He was beginning to recognize the small mannerisms that showed her tension and she was, obviously, more worried than her words implied. He said, 'Bartlett, do you really think she's at a meeting?'

'I don't know. She could be. It just seems a bit odd that she'd risk a meeting if she knew she was under surveillance.' She was impatient to get away, glancing repeatedly at the curve in the road that hid the suspected man. 'Look for him as you drive past,' she told him. 'I may have been mistaken.'

He drove off, glancing briefly in his driving mirror to see that she had again disappeared into the shadows as completely as if she had never been there. He held the car at a speed that would not attract attention and scanned the pavements and shadows as he passed. She was right. A man was standing, close in to the steps of the adjacent office block, complete with cup and thermos flask, his car pulled into the small parking area. Carl felt a slight relief. If Hillard was under surveillance, she could not have been arrested. The relief was short-lived. As he turned the car into the next road, his worry returned. If the authorities were watching her, they must suspect her. He slowed the car and Bartlett slid quickly on to the back seat.

'Yes, you're right,' he said. 'There's a man there—set up for the night, by the looks of things. Does Hillard always use the fire escape to get in and out at night?'

'Yes.'

'Maybe she doesn't know she's being watched. She could just have been damned lucky that he couldn't see the fire escape from where he's standing.'

Bartlett directed him through a series of turns before answering him. 'No, I'm pretty sure she'd have spotted him. That's what's worrying me. Something must have happened to make her risk calling a meeting.'

Carl mentally filled in the other alternative that Bartlett had carefully not mentioned. She had gone to another woman's room and found it empty as well. Hillard could have been arrested and the man watching the other woman. Hillard's arrest would cause the women to call a meeting whatever the risk. He tried to shake off the air of unreality that was threatening to engulf him by thinking back to the day when he had walked into Nesbitt's office looking for a job and had met a pair of grey eyes that had attracted, puzzled, even frightened him. Since then he had been dragged into a growing nightmare until now he was driving around like a criminal, helping a woman to climb in and out of windows, and talking about destroying a government.

'Stop here,' Bartlett said suddenly. 'I can walk the rest.'

She had stopped him at the corner of a road of derelict buildings, obviously a slum clearance area as some of the buildings had already been demolished. She cut across his thoughts. 'A car is too noticeable up there. It's better for you to stay here. If anyone comes, you can pretend you're having trouble with the engine.'

He knew it was pointless arguing with her and as she turned to go he whispered urgently after her, 'Bartlett, if Hillard's there, I'd like to see her.'

She looked at him for a moment before nodding her head. 'I'll tell her. I shouldn't be long.'

He tried to watch her as she walked quickly up the desolate road but she rapidly disappeared from view. Would she find Hillard? His moods were swinging wildly between fear for Hillard and exasperation with her wild plans. How could the women possibly expect to win a confrontation with Gorston if they weren't prepared to fight? Bartlett had refused to tell him anything more about their plans, although he had tried desperately to get some indication of what they were. She would not even tell him when the Rising was scheduled. He had to speak to Hillard and persuade her that she was throwing her life away, and the lives of the other women involved. She could not have thought this thing through clearly at all. It was odd. The impression he had formed, from the little he knew of her, was of a logical, clear-thinking person—not the sort of person who would allow pressures to force her into a hasty move. He thought of the unimaginable aspects of the society that he had discovered over the past few hours and tried to imagine how he would react to such pressures. There must come a time when any move would be better than continuing to submit. Maybe the women had reached that stage. He repeated the word—women. It was peculiar. The image that came into his mind now at that word was completely different from the image that had always accompanied it before. For the first time, he realized, he had acknowledged the fact that they were revolutionaries. 'Women' everywhere else meant—He stopped his train of thought. He was doing it again. He was using the word 'woman' as an adjective, not as a noun. What was it Hillard had said? Everyone projects their own images, however hard they try.

'You wanted to see me.' It was as if his thoughts had conjured her up. Relief surged through him as he saw her standing at the driver's window, hands pushed deep into her pockets. She seemed even thinner than she had the last time he had seen her and he felt a sudden urge to put his arms around her and take her away from all the danger. The relief showed clearly in his voice. 'Bartlett and I—we thought you had been arrested.'

'She told me.' Her face was emotionless and her body still as she looked at him through the open window.

'Could we talk?' he asked, suddenly very hesitant. Why was it, when he thought of her, he always saw her face as alive and open to him and then, when he saw the hidden reality, his shock and uncertainty was all the greater?

'For a short time,' she conceded. 'I have to get back.'

Should he ask her to get into the car? She had already said she could not get into an enclosed space with any man. But since then she had come into the cottage. And besides, it was not safe for her to just stand on the pavement like that. 'In the car?'

She got into the back without hesitation, and as he watched her sitting there he suddenly did not know where to start, what to say.

'Bartlett told me you went to the Opera House,' she said finally.

'I thought it was a nightclub.' The nightmare came to life again as he remembered the woman he had dragged into the small room, trying to get her away from the confusion of curses and the crush of turbulent bodies.

'Try not to think about it,' Hillard's voice broke in. 'It will be stopped soon.'

Was she trying to comfort him? He looked at her in surprise, searching for a trace of irony. It was ridiculous. She was the one in danger, the one who suffered from the injustices of this society. 'Bartlett told me about the Rising,' he said. 'I understand you're opposed to an open fight. . . .'

'No,' Hillard interrupted. 'It will be an open fight. We are just opposed to killing.'

He started to protest, to voice all his fears for her and the women, his certainty that a bloodless rising was doomed to failure, and she cut across his words. 'Bartlett told me about your views, but we disagree with you.' There was no animosity, no resentment in her voice, only a calm self-assurance. 'We have planned this very carefully, over a long period of time. We believe that if we impose our wishes by force, we will have to continue implementing them by force. We will be building another society that survives by the strong terrorizing the weak. We believe there is a better way. It will take longer, but we have learned patience. We are not interested in replacing one rule of terror with another. We are only interested in achieving a society where everyone is equal. Equal in freedom, equal in opportunities, equal in the chance for happiness and fulfilment.'

'But that's Utopia. You'll never achieve that.'

'We intend to try. Up to now, men have tried to solve all the problems with male solutions, and the prime male solution is force, physical force. It was your solution. You still can't see any other. Strength has more faces than one and we intend to use another face.'

He looked at her for a long moment. She had lowered her defences slightly and he could see the strength of her belief in her words, her conviction in what she had told him. He would not be able to shake her, but he had to try.

'Changing a society by peaceful means only works in a democracy,' he said. 'This is a dictatorship. Built on fear and complete lack of concern for human life. The only way you can win is to be stronger than them. You have got to fight them and destroy them, or they will destroy you. They will kill you.'

'Everything you said is true,' she admitted. 'We will fight them and we will destroy them. But we won't use your weapons. And if we fail, we will be killed, as you said. But that is a risk that must be taken, whatever the weapons we use.'

He thought of the man waiting in the shadows outside the hostel. 'But they are suspicious of you already. There's a man watching your hostel.'

Nothing he said seemed to shake her. 'It's just a routine surveillance and they're getting bored with it. I can lose him when I need to.'

He turned around fully in the seat, impatient. 'This isn't a game you are playing.' The pitch of his voice was rising. 'You are fighting a dictatorship. A regime kept in power by its secret police, a regime that is completely ruthless. Do you realize that you are not only risking your own life, but the lives of all the other women?' Anger was growing in him, fuelled by his concern for the still, grey woman sitting silently watching him with eyes that revealed nothing but looked as if they saw all. 'And they're not squeamish. I'd have thought you would have realized that. It won't be a nice, clean, tidy death. They're too sick for that. It will be hell.' He should not have said that. She must have considered what would happen to her and the other women if they were caught. She must know far better than he.

'We all know what will happen to us if we're caught or if we fail,' she said, as if in echo of his thoughts. 'I have tried to provide enough poison for all the women who want to use it in the event of capture. We should be able to achieve a "nice, clean, tidy death".'

He stared at her, too shocked to speak. How could she sit there and tell him, in that cool, remote voice, that she had arranged for dozens, maybe hundreds of women to take their own lives? Suddenly he felt an immediacy about the Rising. Up to now it had seemed as if he were trying to persuade her out of an intellectual stand, but now her calm statement had pitched him out of the world of theory and into the nightmare of reality. He knew with absolute certainty that the women would rise, as she had planned. There was nothing he could do to prevent her. And, when their plans did not succeed, the women would kill themselves rather than be captured. Hillard would kill herself.

He felt as if he was being sucked deeper into a black dream, that he was spiralling helplessly downwards to the inevitable void where she killed herself. He knew how important she was to him; how much he wanted to take her away from this grey world and show her how good life could be; and he knew he could not tell her any of this. She had already broken any small contact between them, as if she had already relegated him to the past. He had to know when the Rising was going to be, but he dreaded the knowledge. He suddenly felt that it was very close. 'When?' The silence stretched between them.

'The day after tomorrow.'

He closed his eyes as if shutting out the sight of her would invalidate her words, his former feeling of helplessness swirling around him. 'Is there anything I can do to help?' he asked.

'No.' She shook her head. 'All the plans are ready. Steiner knows a women's organization exists but he doesn't know the size of it or what we plan to do. As long as we keep him from finding out over the next forty-eight hours, we will be all right.'

'Is that why you're being watched? Does he suspect you have anything to do with it?'

'No,' she assured him. 'It's just a routine surveillance of every-one connected with any of the women who were rescued. Bart-lett and I work in the same place.' She opened the door of the car. 'I must go.'

He felt she was walking out of his life, that he would not see her again, and he could think of nothing to say to detain her. She was standing on the pavement and he still had not spoken. 'Hillard.' She bent down to the window. 'The women at the Opera House—are they kept there all the time?'

'No, they live in a block at the other end of the street. They bring them up in the evenings.' She paused and looked at him intently. 'Try not to think about it. Things will be different soon.' She turned again to leave.

'Hillard. I don't know your proper name.'

Her hands were back in her pockets, shoulders slightly hunched as she stared down at her feet, and then looked back into his face. She gave a slight shrug and he thought he saw a shadow of regret on her face. 'I'm just Hillard,' she said.

He watched her turn and walk down the derelict street.

Carl wanted to leave the desolate place, to get away from the emptiness and destruction. It reminded him too much of the rubble left after a battle; the broken buildings gaping; the scat-tered glass and stones. But for the women hidden somewhere in the ruins, he felt sure the greater destruction was still in the future. Bartlett appeared with her usual suddenness and got silently into the car. He let out the clutch and aimed for the main road back to the cottage, neither saying a word. Hillard had walked out of his life. He knew he would not see her again. Sometime on Tuesday she would swallow the poison to avoid being captured and there was nothing he could do to stop it. He felt a sudden resentment that it was Bartlett sitting in the back of the car. He wanted it to be Hillard. He glanced in the driving mirror, catching sight of her face, illuminated briefly by a passing street lamp, and pushed the thought from his mind. He could see the strain and suddenly realized what she must be feeling. She had helped plan this Rising for a long time and now she had to walk away from the women, her friends, and leave them to face the dangers without her. He thought over everything Hillard had said. He still did not believe they had a chance, but she did. If only she had told him what they planned to do. There must be something he could do to help. He thought of the watching man. Whatever she said, she must be under some degree of suspicion. What had she told him? As long as they could prevent Steiner from finding out their plans during the next forty-eight hours, they would be all right. He tried to sort out the meagre information he did have. 'Bartlett, how does Steiner know a women's organization exists?' His voice sounded loud, breaking the heavy silence.

'We printed a paper,' she told him. 'And, of course, there was the rescue from the hospital. And then a couple of the women blew up the sperm bank to delay the education programme.'

No wonder Hillard had avoided answering him when he said that rescuing the women had not solved anything. She must have known then that the bank was being blown up. 'But does Steiner have proof that the women were responsible for all that?' he asked. 'Or is he just assuming it?'

He had caught her attention. She had come out of her private thoughts and was looking at him with interest. 'Well he obviously doesn't know who was responsible or he'd have made arrests. But it's obvious it's the women. No one else is sufficiently interested in what's going on to do anything about it.'

'But that means he still only suspects the women. Supposing something happened and he had proof that a man had done it? Where would that leave him then?' At last Carl knew what he was going to do—for his own sake as well as Hillard's.

He had Bartlett's complete attention now. She sat forward in the seat, trying to read his face in the dim light. 'Carl, what are you thinking?'

He concentrated on the white ribbon of road. 'Well, as I see it, Steiner is pretty close to Hillard, whether she'll admit it or not, and as you say Hillard is the leader of this Rising. If Steiner was tricked into thinking he was on the wrong track, he'd take some of the pressure off the women. That would give them a slightly better chance of success. Do you agree?'

'Yes.' Her voice sounded doubtful.

'So,' he kept his voice calm, matter-of-fact, '—I'm going to burn down the Opera House and make sure they know a man did it.'

'But—'

He interrupted her protests and grinned at her in the mirror. 'No, don't argue against it. I've got to do it for my own sake as well as the women's. And it is a perfectly logical action under the circumstances.' His grin widened. 'You women haven't got the monopoly on logic, y'know.'

Twenty-one

Carl parked the car a few streets away from the Opera House and carefully lifted the carrier bag off the back seat. The necks of the bottles were clearly visible, all distinctive shapes of well-known brands of spirits. To a casual passerby, he was on his way to a party and determined to make a night of it. The windows of the small terraced houses were open as he walked past, all trying vainly to draw in a breath of cool air from the heavy, sultry streets. The sounds of strangers' lives floated out towards him to reinforce his sense of unreality. His shirt was wet underneath his jacket, clinging between his shoulder blades as the heat swept over his body, making his hands slippery on the handles of the bag. It was going to rain. The heat and heaviness had built up steadily over the day, hanging over the concrete of the city long after the sun had set. The heat wave was going to end in a thunder storm. He shifted the bag to the other hand and looked up at the glowering sky with a small, ironic grimace of amusement. The gods were providing a suitable back-drop for the events of the next hour.

Bartlett had told him the Opera House opened at ten and he estimated the staff, if that was what they called themselves, would not be there much before nine-thirty. He could see again in his mind's eye the three men in their robes and the angelic-looking choir boys exposed to such depravity. When they arrived tonight they would find their hell in flames.

The street was deserted as he turned the corner and saw again the blind empty houses facing the threatening, concealing wall. He walked quickly to the double gates, his soft soled shoes making no sound on the neglected pavement. The gates were locked, as he expected, and he pulled a length of fine cord from his pocket, tying one end securely to the handles of the canvas bag. The other he knotted through his key ring and threw it high and looping over the spikes set along the top of the wall. His movements were quick and sure as he took the thin rope from around his waist and, holding both ends, threw it accurately at the foot-long spikes. It looped over and he pulled it taut as he glanced briefly around the barren street before climbing up the twenty-foot wall, his hands taking nearly all the weight as his feet scrabbled for the occasional foot hold. He perched precariously on the top, his feet between the lethal spikes, as he slowly pulled up the canvas bag on its slim line and lowered it to the other side. He pulled the double strand of rope up after it and slid quickly down into the deserted car park, leaning for a moment against the cool stones, fighting to control his breathing and the slight tremor in his body, a mixture of apprehension and excitement. The high walls of the enclosed space gave him an illusion of safety as he moved towards the row of grimy windows that faced him from across the expanse of concrete. They were the easiest way in. A sharp tap to break the glass and he would be in the long, dingy corridor. He would chance the noise of breaking glass.

The first large, slow drops of rain fell on his back as he squeezed his way between the jagged edges of broken glass and stepped into the narrow passageway. He moved quickly along the gallery with its memories of sweating, staring men, and down the stairs to the main hall. The beam from his torch picked out the dirty floor and the walls' stained wooden panelling, the row of neatly stacked candles that had illuminated the room. He stood in the centre of the empty hall for a long moment, aware of the smell of lingering incense and beeswax candles mingling with the smell of stale sweat, before moving rapidly across the floor, opening the doors, splashing the petrol from the whisky bottles over the timber-clad walls, trailing it back to the centre where he had stacked the large pile of candles. The fumes became more pungent in the airless place as he walked slowly back to the gallery, one unlit candle in his hand. He leant on the rail and looked down into the darkness that would soon be lighting up the night sky with its own destruction and imagined he could see again the three robed figures standing before the terrified woman. They should be burning along with their edifice, he thought. He took the last bottle from the bag and, leaning far out over the rail, he let the petrol trickle down the wall towards the darkness. His movements had slowed, had become more deliberate as the climax of his efforts came nearer. He lit the solitary candle and held it high for a moment, taking a last look at the place, and then slowly and deliberately he held it to the thin stream of petrol. It caught with a small flickering of blue flame and he watched, fascinated, as the blueness ran rapidly down the wall, licking and darting, growing stronger and surer, until it widened and ran, straight and true, for the centre of the room. He did not wait any longer, turning back into the corridor, towards the broken window, as a sudden roar sounded behind him and the whole area lit up, as by an angry sun. He pushed urgently between the broken glass, unaware of the jagged points that tore his jacket and skin, and raced across the concrete towards the hanging, waiting rope. It was stiff from the rain that poured down with summer intensity and cut into his hands as he pulled himself up, his feet scrabbling even more ineffectually to get a hold on the wet stones. His hair was soaked in seconds as he dimly registered the pale pink trickle down the back of his hand where the rain dramatized the small cut from the broken glass. He was almost at the top of the wall before he heard the voices on the other side: urgent, shouting, authoritative. He hung there for an eternal moment, listening to them and the sound of vehicles, as the blaze behind him grew in intensity, flames already bursting from the shattered windows. He dropped back to the ground, desperately searching for another exit, seeing only the surrounding walls and the burning building. The intense heat reached out to him as he stood indecisive in the pouring rain. He had wanted the authorities to know a man had burned down the Opera House and had intended to make sure he was seen, briefly, running from the area. Being captured was not part of his plan. The large gates were being unlocked as he ran across to the far end of the car park, climbing hurriedly on to some disused fuel stores and up on to the top of the side wall. He saw one of the gates beginning to open as he jumped desperately into another enclosed concrete area, a replica of the one he had just left.

His heart was pounding as he leaned back against the wall, the shock of landing from that height still shooting up his legs with sharp, jabbing pains. His heart sank as he looked around the yard. The same high walls around him on three sides, and an identical high building forming the square. He pushed himself away from the wall and hurried towards the small green door set in the corner of the building. Inside, the corridor was empty, a duplicate in grime with the blazing corridor he had left behind him, and he paused to rub vigorously at his legs in an attempt to make them function efficiently again.

The silence closed around him against the background roar of the fire and the dimly heard bells of the fire engines. The place seemed empty. He crept quietly down the corridor away from the burning building, past the row of identical doors, all closed and giving no sign of occupancy. The corridor widened in to a hall-way, stairs leading to the upper floors, another passage leading towards the back of the building. There should be a way out at the back.

A sudden clatter of footsteps sounded on the wooden stairs as two uniformed figures appeared, hurrying down the steps in front of him, engrossed in each other and their obvious excite-ment about the fire. Carl instinctively turned to run back down the corridor and then stopped, determined to bluff. He stood erect and assumed an easy air of authority. 'Hurry along,' he commanded. 'The fire is gaining.'

The men became aware of him for the first time and increased their pace with only a brief glance at the dishevelled figure, their years of training causing them to respond blindly to the voice of authority. He watched them turn the corner, seeing the neat brown uniforms and the leather holsters snugly holding the guns. He must be in a police station. He stood there trying to control his thoughts, fighting the panic that was beginning to grip him. He must be in the guards quarters, the men who guarded the women. Bartlett had said something about the guards being close by, but he had assumed they were in the same building as the women, at the far end of the street.

He could not go back; there was no escape that way. And he could not follow the men down the corridor. He started cautiously up the stairs, listening for sounds of movement from the floor above him, when he heard the eruption of activity in the corridor below. Running feet; shouted commands. He turned sharply, in time to catch a brief glimpse of running figures before he went down in a flurry of fists and arms. The step caught him across the small of the back as he jolted down on to it and he saw the butt of a gun coming towards his face, coming closer, filling his awareness as he watched, until the sight of it disappeared in a silent explosion of light inside his head.

He could taste the vomit in his mouth. Pains shot through his head, searing, jagged pains, in a rhythmical, nauseating pattern; absorbing all his interest and concentration; blotting out any knowledge of his surroundings; any consciousness of any other part of his body. Slowly, unwillingly, he became aware of the hard floor underneath his hip, the coldness of concrete beneath his hand and the pains in the rest of his body that laid increasing claim on his attention. He opened his eyes cautiously, anticipating the crescendo of pain the light would bring, but he was in almost total darkness. He lay there, eyes adjusting to the dim light, trying to remember where he was. Fire, breaking glass, men fighting, punching, a gun coming towards his face, slowly, slowly. He tried to get up, memories flooding back, and his mind swam in a fresh wave of nausea. They had captured him.

He pulled himself across the floor and leant against the wall, feeling gently over his bruised body, searching for signs of serious injury, wincing as his probing fingers reached his ribs and the thigh muscles of his left leg. There was nothing broken. He felt his head and his hand came away wet and sticky as he became aware of the same stickiness on his throat and neck. The sluggish flow had collected across his neck as he lay on the floor. He sat there, trying to clear his thoughts, trying to grasp existence outside the four walls of the tiny cell. His jacket had gone so they must have his papers. They knew who he was. What did Bartlett say? Something about her leaving the cottage on Tuesday morning? Was it Tuesday? He did not even know how long he had been there. He pulled his mind back to the moment he was captured. He had to think clearly. He had burned the Opera House on

Monday night. His mind did not want to concentrate, repeating each thought like a drunken man, as he forced himself to remember, to follow the sequence of events. It must still be Monday night, or early Tuesday morning. His head was still oozing blood in a slow trickle. That was where the gun had hit him. Would they go to the cottage tonight? There was no immediate reason for them to do that. They had captured him. Why send men tonight? No, they would send them in the morning. But what time was Bartlett leaving? And what of the other women? His mind kept slipping. He could not concentrate. The other women were not leaving. They would still be there when the police arrived, even if Bartlett had gone. And they all knew about the Rising. They would be forced to tell about the Rising.

The alluring blackness was closing over him again and he did not want to fight it any more. What had Hillard said? She had told him when the Rising was going to start but he could not remember. He could see her face clearly, looking at him with her large, grey eyes, smiling, happy. Until the darkness carried her away.

The clattering of heavy keys in the lock woke him from an uneasy sleep, the feel of the men's hands on his arms, dragging him to his feet, chasing away the last traces of welcome unconsciousness. A quick anger surged as they pulled him towards the door, no word spoken, no indication that he was anything other than an inanimate object. He jerked himself free of the proprietorial hands. 'Where are we going?' he demanded. The words sounded thick and blurred in his ears.

'Well, haven't we got a tough one.' The guard's voice was mocking, too loud and too close to his ear, but the note of grudging admiration still showed. 'After the going-over you got last night, you shouldn't be interested in where we're going.'

Carl concentrated on the cream-painted walls, long, endless. Keeping them upright in his vision was the only way of knowing if he was still painfully walking or slowly sinking to the floor. He lifted his feet carefully, unable to judge the position of the ground as it tilted and swayed like the deck of a small boat.

'In here,' one of them said roughly.

He stumbled helplessly through the door, blinded by the sudden light, his head sending screaming pains throughout his consciousness that continued after the beam was directed away from him and focused back on the bare wooden table. He felt hands guiding him towards the chair as he tried to see the man sitting in the shadows at the edge of the brilliant pool of light.

'Mr Tolland, we need a few answers from you.' The voice was brisk, efficient and completely impersonal. 'I'm afraid my men were over-enthusiastic last night, or we would have dealt with the matter already.'

Carl watched the well-groomed hands poised over the sheet of blank paper, the crisp shirt cuff disappearing beneath the uniform sleeve. The scene had been meticulously set. He could see nothing of the man opposite him except for his hands. Resentment flared, overriding the sick fear and the throbbing pains. If they thought he was going to be cowed by their theatricals, they were damn well mistaken. He leant forward suddenly, reaching for the lamp and swinging the beam to shine directly on to the concealed man. Middle-aged, grey hair, clean-shaven and well scrubbed; the anonymous face of a million civil servants. Carl forced down the gasp of pain as rough hands pulled him back in the chair. 'I always like to see who I'm talking to,' he said, the calmness of his voice surprising him. He felt satisfaction at the brief look of confusion on the man's face, before it disappeared back into the darkness.

'Mr Tolland.' He had regained his composure rapidly, but an edge of anger was in the impersonal voice. 'We are here to get a few matters sorted out. We need to know the names of your associates and your reasons for trying to destroy the women's detention centre. Shall we start with the names first.' The pen hovered expectantly in the pool of light. 'Come, Mr Tolland, I can't wait all day.'

Fear was holding Carl in its vice again as he tried to make his thoughts coherent. What time was it? Oh God. He had wanted to help the women, to try and take some of the pressure and suspicion off them and instead he had jeopardized the whole Rising. He had no illusions about his ability to withstand their interrogation methods. The most he could hope for was to hold out as long as possible. 'I'm sorry. I must refuse to answer your questions until I have a solicitor present.' Again he felt surprise at his voice.

The fingers tightened on the pen. 'Mr Tolland, you obviously don't appreciate your position. Last night you attempted to destroy the women's detention centre. We want the names of your accomplices and we want them now. We have no time for the niceties. There will be no solicitor and you will oblige me by answering the question.' The voice was as impersonal as ever, carrying more menace in its disinterest than it ever could by open threats.

'I don't know what you mean by "accomplices",' Carl answered. 'As you know, I've only recently returned to this country and I was sickened by what I saw at what you call your "Opera House". It was an abomination and had to be destroyed. I didn't need accomplices to tell me that it was the product of a sick society. I could see that for myself.'

The shadows moved and the man's face came into the circle of light, self-confident, bored, emotionless. 'You're lying, Mr Tolland. But no matter. We are efficient in these matters. Perhaps a small demonstration of our efficiency?' He nodded briefly to the two guards and pressed a button on the desk in front of him.

Carl felt his arms being twisted behind his back and struggled instinctively as the ropes cut into his wrists, tying them securely to the chair. His tongue felt thick and dry. How long could he stand torture? He tried to push his knowledge of the women far down into the darkness of his mind, to forget he had ever met them. 'I've told you the truth.' He fought to keep his voice under control. 'I went to the Opera House by mistake, a few nights ago. It was a sickening experience and I decided to do something about it.' He could hear footsteps coming along the corridor, stopping at the door.

'Still not good enough, Mr Tolland. The names, if you please.'

There was a short knock on the door and he heard the slight movement as it opened. He had to make them believe he was on his own. He braced himself, not knowing what to expect as he sensed a movement behind him and then saw the two guards come briefly into his line of vision. He saw the interrogator getting slowly to his feet, his face still hidden in the shadows.

'Now your gun as well, please, inspector.'

It was a woman's voice. Carl looked, fascinated, as the hands, shaking slightly, placed the revolver on the table. He felt the ropes slacken from around his wrists. A woman stepped into the pool of light. 'Are you badly hurt?' Concerned blue eyes looked into his. She was a Grey One, but the colour of her hair was no deception. The lines on her face and the texture of her skin told him she was elderly. 'Come on. We'll clean you up a bit.'

He stared at her blankly, dimly aware of the three men, arms high in the air, walking silently from the room followed by more women.

'It's all right,' she said. 'We're locking them up with the others.'

'And who are you?' Could Hillard have sent her? But she didn't know he was here. What the hell was a kindly-looking, elderly woman doing in police headquarters calmly telling him that she had locked up all the policemen?

'Hillard told me about you, last night,' she explained.

'But, she didn't kn—'

'No, not about you blowing up the Opera House. She told us you were hiding the women. And then when I came on duty this morning, I found out you were in the cells awaiting interrogation.' She helped him to his feet, gently persistent, and led him to a small adjoining room ominously equipped as a laboratory. 'I'll clean that cut. It looks quite deep.'

'But, what are you doing here?' he asked, bewildered.

Her hands moved gently and surely over his head, removing the caked blood, cleaning away the matted hair. 'Hillard told you about today?' Her eyes looked searchingly into his face.

'Yes. But I wasn't sure if it was today. I lost track of time.'

'We work here—cleaners, typists, telephonists.'

He tried to turn his head to look at her fully. 'Then this is part of it? It's started now?'

'No. This was supposed to be an ordinary working day for us—until this afternoon—but we had to stop them torturing you.' She stood back, satisfied with her work, as another woman placed a cup of coffee in his hand. 'It really needs stitches but it will have to do for now, I'm afraid. How is the rest of you?'

'Sore, just sore.' He winced as her fingers probed at his side. 'What are we going to do now? If this wasn't planned, what do we do?'

'I think you've got a couple of broken ribs. I'd better put some strapping on you.'

He stirred restlessly in the chair as the other woman started to ease off the torn shirt, anxious lest this premature move of theirs could wreck the whole plan. 'Listen,' he insisted, 'if the Rising isn't going to start until this afternoon, how are we going to cope with the situation until then?'

She was busy with the bandages. 'The first part of the Rising starts at ten this morning. It only involves a few. The rest of us just wait until three o'clock to see if we have to make a move. We have got to make sure the authorities don't know what's happened here until we get that signal.'

The fear started to rise in him again. 'Hillard is one of the few, isn't she?'

'Yes,' the woman answered.

'What's the time?' His voice was urgent. Hillard would be making her move shortly, and the police would be picking up the women at the cottage. 'Do you know if the police have been sent to my cottage?'

'It's eight-thirty.' He could see the deep trouble in her eyes that belied the calmness of her voice and actions. 'And the squad car had left by the time we found out about you. There's nothing we can do to get it back. We've tried.'

He pushed himself painfully out of the chair. 'Get them on the radio,' he told her. 'Call them back. I'll do it if you need a man's voice.'

'No, it isn't that. They're just not answering their call. The radio operator is still trying.'

'And what will they do with the women after they catch them?'

'Normally they would bring them in here for processing,' she answered. 'But there are standing orders at the moment— any Grey One arrested must be taken straight to headquarters. The men will just report in to here to say they have found some women and then take them directly to Steiner. Our only hope is that when they report in we can persuade them to call in here on their way to headquarters. That should be any time during the next half-hour or so—if we don't raise them on the radio before then.'

She was right, Carl thought. They had done all they could. They would just have to wait and hope. 'Do you know what time Bartlett was going to be picked up?' he asked.

'Eight-thirty. About now. But I wouldn't be surprised if Hillard didn't pick her up a bit earlier.'

He felt cold as he faced her. 'Hillard is picking her up?' She nodded silently. Oh God, what a mess. He had sent the police straight there in time to arrest Hillard. She would walk right into it. And if she was arrested, she would kill herself. So would Bartlett. Did all the women there have poison? His mind threw up a vivid picture of the peaceful garden, ablaze with flowers, silent except for the hum of the eternally working bees, and the women—

He felt her hand on his arm. 'We've got to get organized. We've got to prevent the authorities from finding out what's happened here this morning. It's possible, but we need your help.' She walked to the door. 'Are you feeling well enough to cope?'

The pain in his side had eased considerably, thanks to the strapping, but his head still throbbed with a dull, monotonous ache. She led him into the main office where about twelve other women were waiting. They were all Grey Ones, all dressed in the grey, shapeless clothes, their hair dyed the inevitable grey. But their eyes were alive. An excitement rippled in the room and the buzz of low, animated conversation continued as he walked. His companion took control as she made her way to the centre of the room and turned to address the women. 'Now, we have to make everyone believe that this place is running normally, at least for the next few hours. All the day-shift police are in the cells and there are no scheduled callers this morning. That only leaves any possible unscheduled callers and the phone calls.'

'Could we report a fault on the switch?' one of the others suggested.

'No, they'd send over repair men.'

Carl looked at the women in the room. They were behaving as if they were discussing some minor domestic crisis instead of an act of treason that could have them all tortured, or dead, in the next few hours. He interrupted, impatiently. 'Look, you said you needed my help. That means you've got a plan.'

'Yes,' the leader said, as calm and matter-of-fact as ever. 'A male voice will be very useful. If anyone phones and asks for a particular officer, we'll say he's engaged and transfer the call to you. Between us here,' her gesture took in all the women in the room, 'we know all the information you'll need.'

Her plan was as impractical as the whole Rising. They would never get away with it. The elderly woman turned to face him and he was struck even more forcibly by the incongruity of her appearance. She looked as if she should be walking her grandchildren in the park, not talking about revolution. It was almost as if she read his thoughts and her voice was gentle, as was everything about her. 'It may not be a very good plan, Mr Tolland, but it's the best we can do. If we are discovered within the next three hours, it could destroy the whole Rising. It's a bluff that's got to work.' He looked around at the women again and felt the hopelessness of their situation. They believed in Hillard's Rising. They believed they would win. He could see it in their eyes that showed the first sign of animation he had ever seen in the expressions of the women workers. If Hillard had done nothing else, she had brought the women to life for a short time, and he would have to help make that time as long as possible. Besides, he had got them into this mess.

'All right,' he said, 'we'll give it a try. You'd better start briefing me.'

The switchboard rang, as if challenging his words, and he started towards it instinctively, not knowing what he intended doing and colliding with a young, slim woman who was also reaching towards it. 'Are you the operator?' he asked.

She nodded, eyes wide, body tense, hands moving swiftly over the machine. But her voice sounded cool, efficient. 'Good morning. Men's detention centre.'

The silence in the room was almost tangible as they froze into immobility, staring at the machine. 'One moment, please. His line is engaged.' She flicked up the switch and looked at the small group surrounding her. 'It's police headquarters for Inspector Brady.'

'Is that the one who was questioning me?' Carl said. She nodded. He could hear the man's voice in his head, cool, impersonal, but could he make the same sounds come out of his mouth? 'We've got to try it sometime,' he decided.

The elderly woman was at his elbow. 'Take it on the desk phone.'

He nodded at the waiting telephonist and managed to grin at the women. 'Yes, Brady here.'

The loudspeaker on the desk sounded out the metallic voice. 'Good morning, inspector. My name is Berlitz. What sort of a shape is that watchman fellow in? The one from the refuse vehicle department.'

A woman pushed forward in front of Carl's line of vision and shook her head, scribbling rapidly on a piece of paper, 'Not good.'

'Well,' Carl answered carefully, 'he's not quite a hundred per cent.' His eyes were fixed on the woman, watching her reactions to his words as she nodded emphatically. 'Why?'

'Commissioner Steiner is satisfied with his story so he can be released. I suggest, though, that you keep him for a few days if he isn't feeling up to scratch.'

Carl read the note in front of his face: 'Authorization—written.' 'Right,' he said. 'We'll keep him until Thursday. You can post the authorization over.'

'Fine. It will be in the post today.'

The line went dead and they stared at each other in silence for a long moment before erupting into a wild display of elation. They had done it. The women clustered around Carl, talking, congratulating, smiling, and he felt himself being swept up in their enthusiasm. He had fooled the fellow from headquarters. Maybe they could get away with it for a few hours.

Then the excitement drained out of him and he turned away so the women could not see his face. Realistically, he knew that the Rising did not have a hope. All he could do was delay the inevitable. Hillard was most probably dead and these women would die sometime soon. The pain rose in him. *Hillard dead.* Why oh why did these women have to make this futile gesture? Why hadn't she listened to him? He could have got her out of the country somehow. He could have taken her somewhere where she could have come alive. He could have shown her the beauty she had searched for. But could he? He remembered the large grey eyes as they had recognized in him the faults she was fighting in others. Oh, not as extreme, not twisted and magnified, but she had seen the same blind assumption in him that women were in some way inferior. No, he could not have shown her the beauty she was looking for, but they could have looked for it together. A sense of loss and endless emptiness filled him and he needed to get away from these happy, confident, doomed women for just a moment.

He felt the touch of a hand on his arm and turned to see the elderly woman gesturing him towards the door. She turned to face him in the quiet of the corridor. 'I must go now,' she said. 'There's something I must do.'

He suddenly felt a stillness, a slowing of time, an importance in her words that belied their simplicity. It was the look on her face that made him realize that her words covered a matter of great importance.

'Where? Where must you go?' he demanded.

She shook her head slightly, ignoring his question. 'You will stay here and help?'

'Of course. But what have you got to do? Is it something to do with Hillard?' He knew immediately that his concern had betrayed him. The elderly woman looked at him with knowledge in her face.

'You care for her a great deal?' she asked gently.

It was a relief to tell someone. 'Yes. But she wasn't aware of it.'

She reached up and touched him, very softly, on the cheek. 'Hillard has survived this long because she is very careful. She may have picked Bartlett up earlier than planned.'

He refused the attempt at consolation, impatient at the triteness of the words. 'Why should she,' he snapped, 'if she arranged to pick her up at eight-thirty?' He was caught again by the tragedy in the woman's face. What was she hiding from him?

'She has something else to do at ten-thirty,' the woman said. 'She wouldn't want to be late for it.'

She turned from him to go and he felt a sudden need to help her, to share the knowledge that weighed so heavily on her. 'And you? Where do you have to go?'

She smiled, a small tight smile. 'I'm going to help Hillard. You're not the only one who cares for her.'

The smile and her acceptance of his feelings for Hillard formed a link between them. She would not tell him where she was going but—He looked at the woman who had prevented his torture, who had acted so quickly to save him and the Rising, and he reached out to take her hand. 'I don't know your name,' he said.

'Mary,' she answered softly. 'My name is Mary.'

Twenty-two

The breeze was fresh and cool as it blew across her face through the open window of the van. It was a good morning after the storm of the previous evening and Sarah felt strong as she drove the last few miles to the cottage. She would be back in the city by nine and inside the People's Hall by quarter past. She still had difficulty in realizing that today was the day she had planned for most of her adult life and she needed constantly to remind herself of the reality by touching the gun, heavy and uncomfortable, in her pocket. Her mind flicked over the last minute preparations that had gone so smoothly after the forced actions of the women's rescue and the destruction of the semen bank. The papers had been distributed to the runners and would be in the people's homes by mid-afternoon. Eli was already at their small radio station and her team of women were in position around the city. Stephanie's small group would be preparing the first aid centre. She looked around the peaceful countryside and prayed to some nameless source to prevent the need for Stephanie's services.

The cottage seemed deserted as she pulled the heavy van on to the grass verge. The drive was empty. Carl's car was not there and the curtains still blinkered the tiny windows. The peace and beauty of the spot struck her as she climbed down from the van. If she survived today, she would like to live in a spot very like this one. Her hand went up instinctively to the small patch of plaster fixed underneath her hairline, close to her ear.

'You're early,' Joan said, walking out to meet her, a mixture of tension and excitement showing on her face.

'Yes. There was a lot of activity in the city during the night so I moved the van out a bit earlier.'

'Have you heard anything about a fire at the Opera House?' Joan asked quickly.

Hillard looked at her in surprise, suddenly wondering as to the cause of her tension, and nodded silently.

'Did it burn?'

'Yes, completely. But what do you know about it?'

Joan was making no attempt to hide her concern. 'It was Carl. He left yesterday and isn't back yet.'

Hillard remembered their conversation as she got out of the car; him asking her if the women lived in the hall. She should have realized that he would not be able just to walk away from the Opera House and do nothing. But where was he now? If everything had gone well, he should have been back hours ago. The fire started at about nine o'clock—

She caught Joan's arm, pulling her towards the barn, realizing the implications of the news. 'Everybody out. Quickly. We've got to get out of here.' She turned and ran back to the van, turning it in the narrow lane so that it faced back towards the city. 'Hurry.'

The women were scrambling over the tailboard, pulling the tarpaulins over themselves as she let out the clutch and started the van back down the winding lane. 'If he's been captured, the police will search the cottage.' None of them spoke and her words hung in the enclosed space. *If he's been captured.* She felt a sickness in her throat and her hands were wet on the steering wheel. If he was captured. How much did he know about the Rising? What had she told him? He knew it was planned for today; he knew two of the leaders; that the organization spread throughout the women workers and some of the married women. Had he told them? They would have tortured him, and then everyone talks. The pictures Mary had painted for her came back into her mind and she could see him lying in the bare corridor, broken and twisted. She gave a small moan of pain at the thought of his torment, trying to banish the images and pull her mind back to the immediate urgencies.

'They may not have captured him. He may be hiding somewhere,' Joan said.

Hillard looked down into her face, desperately searching for a conviction in her eyes that would let her believe. 'Yes,' she answered. But she could not believe it.

'Is everything organized?'

She treated the facile question seriously, appreciating Joan's effort to break into her thoughts. 'Yes. Ann will be waiting for you when I drop you off. The others can make their way to Stephanie. They can stay there until it's over.'

'I still don't see why you can't come with us in the car.'

She became aware of the heavy weight in her pocket as she kept her voice deliberately cool. 'I've told you. There are a few things I want to check on.'

She changed gear to manoeuvre the heavy vehicle around a tight bend and saw the police car coming towards them. The two vehicles passed in a flash with no sign of interest from the uniformed figures. How many figures? She tried to retain the brief image. Two. Just two. The back seat was empty. They had captured him, but he had not told them about the women. They would have sent more vehicles, more men if they had known about the women. There was nothing she could do to help him until after three o'clock, and then it would most probably be too late. She glanced around at the other women. None of them could have seen the police car. She turned the van on to the main road and drove steadily towards the city. In less than two hours Gorston would be dead, and she would have killed him. She wondered again how she would feel if she managed to get out of the People's Hall alive. How would it feel to live, knowing that you had coldly killed another human being? But he had to die. The women had accepted her suggestion that he be imprisoned, but she knew they would never succeed if he was still alive. She glanced down sharply at Joan, lying wrapped in her own thoughts. Did she believe that he would be imprisoned? Or did she suspect what Sarah planned and was willing to relinquish the responsibility of knowing? 'Joan.' Her voice was casual. 'You've got your copy of the proposals?'

'Yes.'

They were entering the outskirts of the city and she would be able to drop the other women off soon. She turned to Joan again. 'Give me fifteen minutes after you get to the Town Hall and then start without me. I should be there shortly after you, but just in case I'm delayed—'

'But, they're your proposals,' Joan said.

Tension made her voice tight and angry. 'No they're not. They are the women's proposals. You know that as well as I do. You don't need to wait for me to start the negotiations. You know the routine.' She turned the van into the road that ran alongside the canal and called out softly to the hidden women. 'I'm dropping you off in a few minutes. Make your way to the first aid post—it isn't far—and tell Stephanie what's happened. Stay there until this afternoon, and let's hope you're not needed.' She pulled the van into a quiet turning. 'Right.'

She watched the women climb rapidly over the tailboard and start to disperse along the empty street as she accelerated away. 'What's the time?'

'Five to nine.'

The atmosphere was tense as each woman lived with her own thoughts and emotions. Sarah looked out at the streets and the hurrying pedestrians and wondered at the normality of it. She could see the women workers going to their places of work, their faces blank and emotionless as they automatically stepped aside for members of the rest of society to pass, no sign in their attitude or behaviour that this day was any different from all the others. And yet eighty three per cent of them were part of today's struggle. She caught sight of a few early-morning shoppers and wondered if any of them were part of today's history. Only a few of the married women had been recruited because of the difficulty in contacting them, but she knew that a lot of their most vital information had come from some of them—gleaned from the casual conversations of their husbands. She spoke her thoughts aloud. 'All those women.'

'Yes, I know.'

They had listened to her over the years and had agreed with her and today they were prepared to risk everything to claim their rights. And it all depended on the strength of a few women. She thought of all the women who had worked with her for this day, and would win, or lose, for all the others in the next few hours. They were all strong, all complementary, all determined.

'Sarah, have you got your capsule?'

'Yes.' Their thoughts were running parallel. If something,

anything, went wrong in the next two hours, the capsules were their only way out. She wondered what she would do if forced into that situation. It would be very easy to delay taking it, in the hopes of something turning up—and then maybe it would be too late. 'We're turning into the road,' she said, glancing down at the pale face of her friend. She smiled reassuringly. 'Tonight, we'll burn those clothes.'

Joan slid into the passenger seat, keeping low, and Sarah waited until the last moment before saying the words she had bitten back all the way up to the city. 'Joan, if the negotiations are successful and I'm still not there, get some people down to the men's detention centre as quickly as possible. Carl must be there.' She braked hard and reached across, opening the passenger door, forcing Joan to slip out quietly before she was able to say anything. She changed rapidly through the gears with only a brief glance in her driving mirror at the hurrying figure, and drove to the spot where she had planned to abandon the van, parking it among the clutter of a half-built office block. It should go unnoticed for several hours.

She turned on to the familiar route to the office that had been part of her life for four years and hurried up the steps to the front door, the keys already in her hand. Two minutes to unlock the offices, to delay any queries from the rest of the staff, and five minutes to walk to the People's Hall. She would be in the gallery in eight minutes. She moved automatically through the familiar building, briefly wondering what time Nesbitt would arrive at work. She would not be missed until then.

She clipped up the latch on the front door before pulling it closed behind her, then joined the other hurrying figures on the busy pavements. Her body seemed to move independently of her, carrying her through the early morning crowds. The last time she had walked this route from the office to the People's Hall was the day she had first seen Carl's paintings. She remembered her overwhelming panic as she had walked into the vastness of the entrance hall, her feelings of insignificance and helplessness. They were the emotions this society was built to instil in her and for a few moments she had believed them again. She had lost the certainty she had painfully built up over the years—the certainty that she was an individual, unique and separate, and not a piece of moulded uniformity. She had looked up at the soaring roof of Gorston's building and imagined herself standing in the distant gallery, and her insignificance, compared to the vastness of her surroundings, had taken away her confidence. But she was confident now, sure in her knowledge. She thought of Carl and the pain started inside her again. He had showed her that, despite all her efforts, she was an incomplete person. Despite all her struggle, society had destroyed a part of her that she had not even known existed. But she was aware of it now, and she was aware of the deep hurt in her as she thought of Carl at the detention centre, and the loneliness at the thought that she would not see him again. The large building loomed up ahead of her, flags flying, flowers and wreaths in abundance, and the inevitable giant face of Gorston looked down at her. Soon she would destroy him.

She walked unobtrusively through the tight knots of people already starting to gather for the gala occasion and turned in at a small, inconspicuous gate. The broken lock would have been repaired, but she had a copy of the replacement key, sent as a matter of course to Nesbitt. She unlocked the door and stood for a moment in the gloom as her eyes adjusted to the sudden absence of the sun. The coldness of the stone struck her, making her shiver violently. She must be more tense than she had realized, but she could feel no nerves churning in her stomach, only a steady calmness.

She started softly up the winding stone stairs, her hand on the rough coldness of the wall, her eyes now accustomed to the half-light. He would be here at ten-thirty; standing before the people, alone on the dais. His conceit never allowed him to share the first acclaim of the crowd with anyone. His ministers had to stay hidden, out of sight, until he magnanimously called them forward. Today he would be dead before he knew his ministers would not be coming.

She had reached the long gallery that overlooked the platform, the vast hall stretching beneath her, ornamented, beflagged, empty, waiting. She moved slowly along the stone balustrade, her eyes fixed on the bank of microphones set up in readiness for the speech he would never give, until she came to her selected spot that gave her the clearest view of the dais beneath. Her hand brushed against a soft object on the stone surface of the balustrade and she stopped, looking at the small piece of incongruous beauty. She picked it up slowly, and all time stopped. Holding it in the curve of her hands, the strong perfume of a perfect rose drifted around her.

'I see you have found my gift.'

He was behind her, close behind her, and she could not force herself to turn and look at him. How? What had gone wrong?

'It's Hillard, isn't it? I thought it would be.'

His voice was as smooth and chilling as she remembered. She had to turn and face him. Her mind could not grasp the full implications of his presence, only the isolated fact that he had captured her and she would be unable to kill Gorston. She put the rose back on to the stone balustrade and turned towards him, forcing her face to be expressionless, her eyes to conceal the fear that was climbing inside her.

'And now I think we should have the gun.'

She heard a small movement behind her. There were more men in the shadows.

'Don't try to do anything foolish,' he advised. 'My men would maim you severely before you could aim it.'

She could not see his face clearly in the gloom of the gallery but she could hear the suppressed excitement that ran around the edge of his voice. She took the gun slowly from her pocket, knowing she could not just hand it over in a token of abject defeat. She felt the weight of it in her hand for a moment, also knowing she would not use it, and looked back briefly at the empty dais beneath her before leaning out over the balustrade and dropping the gun into the dark depths below. The sound of it striking the stone floor echoed through the vastness.

'I didn't want you wasting your time here waiting for the President to come,' Steiner said. He was playing with her, as he had before. She had to make a stand against him, a futile stand perhaps. 'Such an unfortunate waste of effort,' he went on. 'I congratulate you. Your planning was first class. And all wasted because the President had a heart attack this morning.'

He was lying. It was part of his sick game. Suddenly, the fear left her and she felt a fierce hatred for the composed, taunting figure in the shadows. 'I don't believe you,' she said, the firmness of her voice surprising her, carrying none of the weakness that still clung to her body.

'Nevertheless, it's true. It was a severe one and the doctors do not expect him to live.' He made a small movement of his hand and she felt her arms being twisted behind her back, sharp stabbing pains running across her shoulders. 'We'll have our talk when I get back from the palace.' She forced herself to remain passive as he suddenly stepped close to her, scanning her face intently as if to read her thoughts. She thought she saw a slight hesitation as his gaze wandered briefly to the surrounding men and then returned to continue his scrutiny of her face. 'On second thoughts,' he went on, 'I think you should see the President. I think you deserve to see the man you planned to kill.'

His voice was smooth, emotionless, but she had seen the brief indecision. Was it true? Did he really mean to take her to see Gorston? Her mind started to race again, making her unconscious of the pain in her arms as the unseen men forced her forward, down the winding steps, following the trim, neat figure of Steiner. How much did he know? He had only mentioned her attempt to kill Gorston. Did he know about the plans to kidnap the ministers? It was possible that he did not know and had only missed the kidnap attempt on himself because he was already here, waiting for her. She should have killed him when she had the gun. There was a chance, a small chance, that the women had the ministers as planned, but with Steiner free, their plans could still be ruined. She should have killed him.

She stumbled through the small door into the brilliant sunlight. Steiner was standing at the door of a car, holding it open, gesturing her to get in, and she could feel the relentless pressure on her arms forcing her towards him. 'We'll pay a short visit to the Palace and then we can settle down for our talk,' he said smoothly.

His nearness in the enclosed space of the car sickened her. Her world had narrowed to imitation leather and wood veneer; the back of two male necks, one red and bulging over the tight uniform collar; the nearness of the man on the seat next to her; and the slight pull of the plaster concealed under her hair. If he was lying and the car turned towards police headquarters, she would swallow the capsule and be dead before they arrived. Strange, now that it was so close, she felt nothing.

The car swung smoothly across the wide bridge and up into the park that surrounded the palace. He was telling the truth—or was it still some kind of sick joke? They rolled to a stop outside the wide, imposing entrance and Steiner got out, waiting for her to join him. The fear tried to claim her again as he stepped close to her, looking carefully into her eyes, and she could see the coldness in him. 'I have looked forward to this meeting for a long time,' he whispered. 'We are going to get to know each other very well over the next few days.'

She fought down the panic, forcing her mind to think only of the next few moments. She still had the capsule.

He turned and walked through the large doors, past the saluting, and she followed, pushed along by the two policemen. There were only two of them. Surely there must be something she could do. But her mind would not work, absorbing only a confused impression of long, carpeted corridors as the small procession went deeper into the heart of the palace. Was he taking her to see Gorston? And if he was, what could she do? She stopped behind him at some double doors, vaguely aware of the deferential guards stepping back, then suddenly she was in a vast room. The carpet was thick and yielding under her feet, an enormous bed dominated the far end, and a figure, indistinct, obscured, lay beneath a transparent tent. Gorston. He had been telling her the truth.

The sound of whispering voices brought her back to awareness, and she turned to see an elderly man in obvious disagreement with Steiner. 'No,' the old man was insisting. 'As his doctor, I must forbid it. He is too weak.'

She strained to hear Steiner's reply, unable to make anything of the low, cool tones, but able to see the gradual lowering of the old man's resistance, until he eventually turned away with a defeated shrug, as Steiner walked towards the distant bed. He seemed to have forgotten her existence, intent only on the indistinct figure and the sheet of paper he held in his hand. She glanced quickly around; at the two silent figures behind her; at the few people scattered around the preposterous sick room.

Mary!

Sarah took a short, instinctive step towards the figure of a woman talking to the elderly doctor. Her back was turned to her and her reason told her that she must be mistaken. Mary could not be here—in Gorston's sick room. She stared intently at the familiar shape until the intensity of her gaze caused the elderly man to look across and catch her eye. The woman turned to follow his gaze and Sarah found herself looking into the face of the woman she had considered a friend for most of her adult life.

A coldness swept over her. Mary was at home here. She was not under arrest. Steiner had not even glanced in her direction as he hurried past towards the massive bed. Steiner, who had been waiting for her in the gallery. No, she could not think that. She tried to push the thought out of her mind. Mary had worked with them; planned and suffered with them. But she was here, in the palace, free, not a prisoner—and Steiner had been waiting in the gallery.

Sarah moved swiftly towards the elderly couple, uncaring of the reaction of her two guards. She had to know. She was aware of Mary's knuckles, showing white through the skin as she gripped the old doctor's arm, and the tenseness throughout her body as she stayed motionless at Sarah's approach. She was aware of the movement of the guards behind her and saw the doctor leave Mary's side to intercept them, but all these things were out of focus compared to her need to know.

'Why are you here?' she said, her voice sounded harsh and conviction grew as she saw the woman's eyes flinch at the sound. 'Steiner knew where I was.'

The words were an accusation but Mary's eyes took long seconds to register the fact.

'Sarah,' she whispered, but the uncertainty in her voice seemed to feed Sarah's own certainty.

'You betrayed us.'

Shock showed in the woman's eyes. 'Sarah—no.'

'Then what are you doing here?'

Both women were oblivious of the doctor who hovered anxiously at Mary's side.

'Believe me, Sarah, I came here to help—you and the women.'

'And how were you going to help?' she demanded. 'By asking a sick man to repent of his sins and make right all the wrongs he has done?' She saw the pain in Mary's eyes but her despair would not let her heed it.

The older woman's voice was calm when she eventually answered Sarah's outburst. 'I came here to prevent you killing Gorston.'

'And you sent Steiner to the People's Hall to arrest me. And the others—are they arrested as well? Did you tell Steiner everything about our plans?'

Mary glanced, instinctively, across the room to where Steiner bent over the sick man, a faint murmur of voices just audible. 'I've told Steiner nothing,' she promised. 'I'd never seen him until he came in with you. I waited with the other women until I saw them driving off with the ministers and then I came here to kill Gorston.'

Sarah stood silent, staring at the other woman, her hatred and anger dying inside her as she heard the words; confusion replacing them in her mind as she lost her grip on the events that seemed to be running away with her. 'You kill Gorston? Why? And why come here?'

'Dr Werner here knows me. We've known each other for a very long time. I waited in the grounds for Gorston's car to leave for the opening and I saw him fall as he was walking down the steps. A small group of men carried him back inside and I stayed in the bushes, not knowing what to do. Then I saw Dr Werner drive past me to a back entrance and I took a chance and called to him. He told me Gorston was most probably dying and he brought me in with him. Nobody questioned us.'

'But, why?' Sarah asked in bewilderment. She turned to the silent man, trying to understand the relationship between them. 'Why did you bring her in here?' She suddenly saw the same deep tragedy in his eyes as she had always seen in Mary's. Something very strong bound these two people, something she knew nothing about, something from the past.

She glanced over at the figure on the bed and saw Steiner guiding the feeble hand over the sheet of paper. 'Blake.' She heard

Steiner's voice very clearly as he repeated the word again for the dying man. 'Blake.' She sensed there was little time left and she turned back urgently to the silent couple. 'Mary, you must tell me,' she begged. 'Why did Dr Werner bring you in here? And why did you want to kill Gorston, instead of letting me do it?' She shook the woman's arm in exasperation. 'You've got to tell me.' She watched the silent conflict on the older woman's face, saw the deep sadness in her eyes; the same sadness she had seen in them in the basement by the light of the small, harsh bulb.

Mary nervously clasped her hands as she started to speak softly and rapidly, as if in haste to say at last the words that had been stored inside her for so long. 'There's a story about Gorston being a priest when he was a young man, and being seduced by some woman. This has always been the reason given for his bitter hatred of women.' Sarah nodded silently not wanting to break the flow of words. 'It isn't really true. Gorston was studying for the priesthood and then he met this woman and they fell in love. He came out of the seminary and they got married. They were very happy at first—and then a child was born. Gradually he began to change.'

Suddenly, Sarah knew what Mary was telling her and her hands went out instinctively to stop the woman's pain. 'You were his wife.' The words were barely audible through dry lips.

'Yes.'

A kaleidoscope of memories of Mary flashed through Sarah's head; the sadness always present; her agony at the tortures of the detention centre; the subtle barrier she always kept between herself and the other women. She felt responsible. She felt in some way part of Gorston's madness that had created all the misery.

'Is that why you wanted to kill him?' Sarah asked, her voice almost a whisper.

'I never wanted to kill him—the same as you never wanted to kill him.'

Sarah looked intently into the tired eyes. There was an even greater strength and understanding there than she had realized. 'True,' she said, 'I never wanted to take a life—but it had to be done.'

'And you felt you had to assume responsibility for it. You

thought no other had the strength to survive the act.' Sarah nodded, silent before the older woman's perception, as Mary touched her briefly on the arm. 'We all try to make it easier for those we love,' Mary went on, 'but that in itself is a kind of arrogance, I suppose. I also knew it had to be done and I felt *I* should assume responsibility for it—' the deep, perpetual sorrow showed clearly in her face '—in the same way I've always felt somehow responsible for the man he has become, the acts he has committed.'

'So, this was to be your atonement?' Sarah felt anger again. Anger at herself for doubting this woman and anger at Gorston. Not the impersonal anger she had always felt against the omnipotent dictator who had destroyed so many lives, but a hard, personal hatred against the man who had brought a lifetime of misery to the woman in front of her.

'I've finished my business here. We can now start our little talk.' Steiner was at her side, stiff and expressionless, and she looked at him uncomprehendingly as he turned casually to the old doctor. 'I suggest you see to your patient,' he said. 'I don't think he'll last much longer.'

Suddenly he no longer threatened her. Her fear of him died in her new anger at Gorston and she saw him for the first time as an individual; stripped of the army of subordinates that built his reign of terror for him; saw him as she had tried to see him that day in his office, as another human being evil, corrupt, but just one human being to fight and defeat. She glanced towards the large, draped bed at the far end of the monstrous room and knew she wanted to look into the face of the dying man—wanted to see what her mind already told her.

'I want to see him,' she said firmly.

Her wide grey eyes looked into Steiner's, seeing the thin smile and the suppressed excitement that skittered in the depths of his. He was supremely confident of his power over her but he remained—just a man.

'You still believe I am trying to trick you—that the figure in the bed isn't the President.' He paused for effect and then gave a small ironical bow. 'You are right. You should see him. You have earned that.'

She was vaguely aware of Werner protesting—insisting his patient must have rest—but her concentration was on Steiner as he brushed the old man's words aside and gestured her towards the bed. He wanted Gorston dead. Suddenly she knew it, knew the significance of the whispered conversation, and the name 'Blake'. Steiner had laid his own plans and it only needed Gorston's death to implement them—Gorston's death and the defeat of the women. But he believed the women were already defeated.

She walked across the room; seeing the hovering figure of the priest waiting with his prepared words of forgiveness and absolution; seeing Werner, with Mary at his side, hurry ahead of her to perform his small, ineffectual rituals at his patient's side: and sensing Steiner following her.

The bed was so large for the frail figure in it. All her adult life she had planned to destroy this man and she searched the white face, looking for something to recognize.

'Mr President.' The eyelids flickered in response to Steiner's smooth tones, but the eyes did not open.

'Mr President, we have identified the group who produced the newspaper. I have the leader under arrest.'

At last the eyes opened, groping towards the sound of the voice, trying to focus on Steiner's face. 'Good—very good.' The words were barely audible, the eyes still slightly out of focus. 'I knew it wouldn't take you long.' He was trying to struggle back to his former strength but the effort was useless.

'Mr President,' Steiner persisted. 'The plot was bigger than we originally thought. They planned to assassinate you.'

She saw the sudden widening of the eyes and knew Steiner was using her. He was using her to kill Gorston.

'I have the ringleader here, Mr President.'

Steiner pushed her in front of him, into the focus of the questioning eyes. She could see the lips working, with no words getting past them; could see the hand plucking at the covers—and suddenly all anger towards him died as she looked into the faded, frightened eyes. He had run his course. His reign of terror was over and soon he would be able to leave behind the private hell he had lived in for so long. She looked at the lined face, a parody of the posters, and felt no anger and no pity. His relevance had died before his body. She should waste no more time on him. He could not harm the women any more. The destruction would end today—if she was strong enough.

She glanced at Steiner and saw the intensity of his look as he watched the feeble movements of the man in the bed. He had forgotten her existence as he waited impatiently for his leader's death. He had used her, as he would use her again to get information about the women, but in the meantime she was unimportant.

She looked back at the bed, vaguely aware of Werner bending over the dying man, and remembered the tired, frightened eyes that had looked at her for a brief moment. Her image of Gorston had been completely destroyed when she had looked into those eyes. But she had started to lose the image when her anger had flared at Mary's personal suffering, and she had drawn strength from the act. But Steiner—he was locked into his image of her. Destroy his image and you would destroy Steiner. If his carefully manufactured puppet developed a wayward, unpredictable life of its own, he would not be able to adjust.

Suddenly she had a clear picture of Joan and Ann with the ministers. Of course, she should have realized it before. There was no doubt about the success of their negotiations. She had relied on the women's industrial strength, their ability to bring the whole economy to a standstill within minutes of the signal, but she had forgotten the psychological impact on the ministers when the images society had given them disintegrated and crumbled, leaving them nothing to relate to. A joyous confidence surged through her. Steiner was the only obstacle. He could still defeat them if he was free to track them down. He would learn about the missing ministers any time now and he would then get the information he wanted from her at police headquarters.

Her mind came back to her immediate surroundings and she looked across the bed into Mary's troubled eyes. Mary was frightened for her but Sarah no longer feared for herself. She knew what she had to do. She reached up into her hair, pulled the piece of plaster from its hiding place and dropped it quietly on to the carpet. That was not the solution now. It had to be a struggle between Steiner and herself—and she knew it was the logical outcome of all her planning.

She smiled gently at Mary. She would be safe. Steiner had ignored her completely, seeing only an anonymous Grey One assisting the old doctor. She turned to Steiner, her face expressionless again. 'I've seen enough,' she said.

Twenty-three

Marsham had his feelings under control again and could even see a glimmer of grim irony in his situation. The very first time he had agreed to use an official car and driver, with its risk of hidden microphones—and this had happened.

He had not given the driver a second glance as he had hurried from his house and got into the car on his way to the opening of the People's Hall. He had been too busy thinking of the boredom of yet another of Gorston's spectaculars to pay all that much attention as the car slowed at the end of his road. But his mood had abruptly altered at the sight of the Grey One who had slipped into the back of the car alongside him, a gun in her hand. He had started to protest but she had moved the gun very slightly and he had looked into her face. Suddenly the familiar inexpressive eyes of the women workers had become a frightening thing. He could not read her intentions, could not see any emotions in her look. He had sat in the corner of his seat, staring at her, waiting for the deafening sound and searing pain that seemed inevitable.

But the car turned smoothly into the cobbled yard of the Town Hall and stopped at a small side door. If she was going to kill him, she would have done it by now. But maybe they would kill him somewhere in the maze of alleyways that connected the numerous old buildings which made up the civic heart of the city. He forced himself to speak as she opened the door for him to get out, hearing the breathlessness in his voice that he was unable to control. 'Do you intend to kill me?'

The driver had joined the woman with a gun and the two pairs of eyes looked at him blankly. My God, he thought, they were like robots. He could feel no point of contact with them. Strange he should feel that now. He had never felt any point of contact with the women workers, but then there was never any need—they were anonymous creatures, trained to obey commands without thinking. Were these two just obeying orders? And whose orders? Steiner would not use women—he had his trained men for this sort of work. But who else?

He obeyed the unspoken command and turned to follow the driver of the car as she led the way through the small door, along corridors and up endless stairs, always aware of the woman behind him with the gun in her hand. Why didn't they say something?

The conviction was growing that they did not intend to kill him—not at this point, at least. Also, that they were acting on someone else's orders. His mind was working again now and the familiar processes calmed his knotted stomach. His thoughts brushed over each minister in turn, dismissing each possibility. No, none of the ministers was responsible for this. The Intellectuals then? Steiner had been pulling them in for his infernal interrogations and it was rumoured there had been quite a few deaths. Maybe a group of them had decided to hold him hostage. But why use women workers? None of it made sense.

His escort had stopped at a door and he became aware of the low hum of voices breaking the desolate stillness of the empty building. His mind was jumping to irrelevancies again as he wondered for the first time why the building was empty. Of course, Gorston's love of spectacle. Civil servants always had a holiday when Gorston mounted one of his public appearances. It ensured a suitably impressive crowd.

The sound of voices died away as the woman opened the door and gestured him to go in. He stared across at the suddenly silent group of men sitting at the far end of a large table. They were all here, all the ministers—sitting in a tight group at the far end of that shining table—their faces showing uncertainty, bewilderment, fear. He heard the door close behind him and realized the women had not followed him into the room. My God, they were sure of themselves.

The sight of Blake's face, white with uncontrolled terror, shining with perspiration, caused a sudden surge of anger inside him, his permanent contempt for the man giving him a focal point for his emotions. 'What the hell's going on here?' he demanded.

He strode across to the table, confronting the silent group, suddenly feeling his self-confidence return in the presence of his colleagues. He had the measure of these men; he knew them. They were showing varying degrees of tension and fear, but he had seen it in them before—many times—when they were in the presence of Gorston. The familiarity of their emotions gave him back his confidence.

'Martin, you tell me.' Marsham looked at his friend of many years and saw the tension in his face, but no fear. Thank God—no fear.

'Behind you, Marsham. Our hosts are behind you.' Martin managed a small smile at his own weakness as he pointed towards the large window behind Marsham's back. He turned and looked at the two figures standing in the sunlight that streamed in through the leaded window. Two women, Grey Ones, standing quietly, watching the men, saying nothing, showing nothing on their expressionless faces.

He turned abruptly back to Martin. 'But there are only two of them—and they're only women workers. Why are you staying here?'

'Mr Marsham, I'm glad you've arrived. We've been waiting for you.' The cool, assured voice cut across his words and he watched as the two women took their places at the table. 'If you'll take your seat, Mr Marsham, we can begin.'

He thought he saw a brief gleam of expression in the blank eyes behind the glasses, but it had gone before he could identify it and he turned, uncaring, to the men. 'Will one of you tell me what we're doing here?' he insisted again. 'And why you just sit like a pack of fools staring at these two women? They are only women workers—and there's only two of them. They're not even armed.'

'Mr Marsham.' The cool voice broke in on his words once more. 'Each minister was brought here by two armed women. Those women are outside the door, should we need them. However, if you would kindly take your seat, we will explain the reasons for bringing you here. When you have heard what we have to say, I am sure you won't want to precipitate any physical action.'

The voice unnerved him. It carried a sureness, a sense of command that belied the familiar blankness of the face. He looked at her hands, lying relaxed on the table, and glanced at the hands of the ministers as they moved nervously, reflecting the personalities of the different men. Woman worker or not, she was in command here—at least for the time being.

Marsham relaxed into the charm that had always been his chief defence and his main weapon for attack. He would hear what she had to say and then he would deal with the situation as it became clearer. He bowed, slightly, to the seated figure, his habitual disarming smile firmly in position now. 'Please forgive me,' he said smoothly. 'You understand, it was quite an experience—being brought here in that manner.' He sat in the chair before him, hands on the shining table top equalling her own in their relaxation.

She glanced briefly around the table, her eyes pausing for a moment on her companion who was calmly placing neat piles of paper on the table in front of her. 'Gentlemen,' she said finally, 'today brings an end to Gorston's rule.'

He was half expecting something of the sort, but the calm words shocked him. They should have sounded ridiculous, melodramatic—but they did not. They sounded factual. She had used them as a preamble to what she had to say—not as a statement in their own right. She had gone smoothly on, not pausing to judge the impact of her words. 'Our meeting here will decide what becomes of the country and the people living in it. We—that is the women workers—are determined that this country returns to a democracy; that social injustices be eliminated; that each and every citizen be equal—in law and in practice.'

Marsham remembered the articles in the newspaper. Utopia. They were looking for Utopia. Heady fantasies of dreamers—was that what all this was about? His confidence grew. He leaned forward slightly to interrupt her. 'I'm sorry—   you have the advantage of me. I don't know your name.'

'Bartlett,' she answered. 'My name is Bartlett. Why? Do you want to say something to me?'

The directness of the reply lost Marsham his advantage and he acknowledged the fact with a small ironic smile. 'Yes, I do,' he said. 'You stated that President Gorston is no longer in power. That is an easy statement to make—but can you back it up?'

'No, Mr Marsham, I cannot. Not at this time. Other things I can demonstrate for you, but I cannot give you proof of Gorston's fall from power until later in the morning.' She raised her hand as Marsham made to interrupt again and this time he was sure of the small smile that flickered across her face. 'That, Mr Marsham, is why the women are still outside the door with their guns—to ensure you stay here to hear what we have to say and to wait for the proof you have asked for.'

She turned her attention away from him and spoke to the group in general. 'We have here detailed plans for the restructuring of government; time schedules for the implementation of the new laws and the revoking of certain of the old. We have cost analysis of the change-over to the new educational system over the next three years—but I am wasting time. Accept, gentlemen, that we have prepared a detailed breakdown of the changes that have to be implemented over the next three years. Very briefly, the changes are these. Free elections will be held at the end of one year. In the interim, the government will appear to operate as it does now, although there will be a reshuffling of positions within the Cabinet. Each minister will be supported by a team of women who will help him implement the changes that his department is responsible for. The secret police will be disbanded over the next six months but in the meantime certain men will be removed from power today and placed in prison pending trials to be held after the free election. All discriminatory laws appertaining to women will be revoked within six months—certain rulings to be abolished as of today.'

'Bartlett, Bartlett,' Marsham broke in, his voice pitched at its most charming. 'How can you possibly expect us to take you seriously? You tell us Gorston has been deposed—but we have no proof of it. You demand we agree to all these changes—but you have given us no reason to even consider doing so—'

'Now you must forgive me, Mr Marsham,' she broke in. He could see no sign of mockery in her face. 'I haven't told you the alternative.' Again, she glanced around the table. 'If you do not agree to our conditions by three this afternoon, we will bring the country to a standstill. We are not the small band of women I'm sure you thought us to be. All the women workers are united—and a percentage of the married women as well. Women workers form eighty per cent of all retail store personnel, eighty-one per cent of bank personnel, forty per cent of all factory workers, they provide the labour for the public transport, the telephones, seventy per cent of hospital personnel are women. If you do not accept our demands by three this afternoon, all women workers will withdraw their labour. The country will be in chaos. No communications; no public transport; all banks and shops will close; government offices will be unable to function and hospitals will be unable to cope. To ensure the chaos is complete, all generating stations will be destroyed together with other strategic positions.'

There was a silence in the room as she broke off for a moment, her eyes passing over the faces of the silent men as if judging the effect of her words, before stopping at Marsham. It was as if she waited until he intended to speak and then she resumed smoothly, 'You see, gentlemen, the country will be brought to a complete standstill within a few hours.'

Marsham caught Martin's eye across the table and read his own acceptance of her words in them. She meant what she said. This was no bluff. It was true what she said about the women workers forming the major part of the workforce in all the important areas. But surely the women could not be that well marshalled. It would take an enormous organization and administration to control such a large group and co-ordinate their movements with such precision.

'Bartlett, are you trying to tell us that all the women workers are so organized that you can implement your threats at a moment's notice?' He forced his voice to carry the slightest hint of amused tolerance, hoping to bring some sort of reaction to the passive face. He could not relate to this woman; could not read any reaction to himself.

'We realised, of course, that you would need proof of what we say,' she went on, 'so we arranged a few demonstrations.' She lifted the telephone from the table in front of her and pushed it across to Marsham. 'Perhaps you would care to make a phone call to any part of the country.'

She had started to give him the proof he had demanded and suddenly, he did not want to put it to the test. His hand hovered over the phone as he still tried to read her face, then he picked it up in a sudden aggressive movement, dialling rapidly, pausing as an operator's voice cut in.

'I'm sorry, caller, what number do you want?' The voice was the usual cool, impersonal tone of all operators.

'I'm dialling a West Side number, operator,' he said harshly.

'I'm sorry, sir, all West Side numbers are out of order at the moment. We are doing our best to rectify the fault.'

He could feel the eyes of the other men watching him intently as he fought down the annoyance in his voice. 'All right, operator, would you get me the presidential palace instead then please.'

He knew the answer before it came. 'I'm sorry, sir. Those numbers are also affected.'

Bartlett's voice cut in. 'You will get the same reply to any number you wish to call, but you are at liberty to try others if you wish.'

She did not wait for an answer but walked across the room and switched on a television set. All eyes watched compulsively as the pictures came on the screen; the jostling crowds; the flags; the traffic jams of Gorston's latest spectacular production. It all seemed normal. What were they supposed to learn from that scene?

Bartlett picked up the phone and spoke briefly. 'Eli, we're ready.'

The screen suddenly went dark and then the blank eyes of a Grey One looked out at them from it. A Grey One had never before been seen on television. 'We interrupt this programme with a newsflash,' the woman said. 'It has just been announced from the palace that an announcement of national importance will be made at three o'clock this afternoon. We will be going over to the palace at that time to bring you the statement.' The blank face paused for a moment. 'We now return you to the coverage of the official opening of the People's Hall.'

The familiar scenes returned to the screen and Bartlett walked over and switched off the set. 'You see, we can black out the National Television Company at any time and transmit our own programmes—not entertainment programmes, I'm afraid, just news items. You will also note that the television cameras were still covering the crowds outside the People's Hall, although the official opening was scheduled for half an hour ago.' She nodded to the other woman who had sat silently throughout the whole proceedings. 'If you want further proof of our ability to enforce our threats, we can provide it. However, as we have a great deal to do before the deadline this afternoon, I suggest we consider the detailed proposals in those files.' The silent woman had quietly placed a file in front of each minister and returned to her place.

Marsham idly opened the file in front of him, vaguely registering his name printed neatly on the cover. They had given a certain amount of proof that they could carry out their threats. Certainly, if they could black out the television station like that, they would have no difficulty in contacting the women. He started to read automatically and gradually his attention was fixed on the contents of the file. Whoever had compiled these reports knew what they were doing. He could not speak for other departments, but the information, statistics and forecasts for his department were absolutely accurate and comprehensive. Where the hell did they get their information from? He stroked his hair in an habitual gesture. Of course, it was as she said. All the typists and general office staff were women workers. But now he had to accept that woman workers were not the anonymous robots everyone had considered them. They had carried out their work efficiently and all the time relayed the information back to some central body. My God. She had not overestimated their strength in the slightest.

He turned the pages rapidly to the proposed changes in government and legislation. He was satisfied that they were capable of carrying out all their threats—that they had the organization necessary. He now needed to see what they proposed.

'You're mad. You can't get away with this.' Blake's voice broke the silence and Marsham saw the sheen on the small man's forehead and the uncontrollable twitching of his hands. He was going to break completely. Blake was on his feet, his fear pushing him past all boundaries. 'Why are you even looking at those papers? They can't get away with it. Let them strike. What will it get them? Steiner will get them back to work. We will have been missed by now. Steiner's men will be here any minute and have these women under arrest.'

Marsham had not even noticed, but Blake was right, Steiner was not there, and unless the women had captured him, their rebellion would not last much longer. And God help the women then. He realized he felt regret. It was true, he had only had a chance to glance very briefly at the women's demands, but they did not seem all that preposterous. Some even coincided with his own plans. It would have suited him admirably for the women to overthrow Gorston. His mind was racing, subtly altering his plans, making use of today's events. The women were strong now—but it was the strength of desperation. They could not stay united for any length of time. Take away their identified enemy—Gorston—grant them some of their demands and their unity would crumble, leaving the country where it belonged, in his hands. Except for Steiner. He watched Bartlett's face intently, trying to detect any uncertainty.

'I'm sorry, Mr Blake,' she said, her voice as emotionless as ever. 'You mustn't rely on the chief of police to rescue you. He is also in our custody.'

Marsham felt relief. He only had to handle these women correctly and his plans would come to fruition.

Bartlett continued, 'I must emphasize, gentlemen, that if you do not agree to these demands and a statement by the next nominal head of state is not made at three o'clock announcing some of the immediate changes, the women will implement the actions described. Furthermore, if any of you are thinking that even if we take this action, we can be forced back to work by the secret police, without Steiner at their head, I must correct you in that also. The women are quite determined. If you force us into the action described, we will carry it through, whatever the consequences. If you try to answer us with force, you will destroy the country and we will die in our hundreds. We were prepared for that eventuality. Let me restate. If you force the women to leave their work this afternoon, they will never return. They will become a militant underground army and this country will be in a state of civil war.'

Blake collapsed in his chair, and the remaining men looked at each other in acceptance. They believed every word she had said.

Marsham returned to his brief scanning of the women's demands. They seemed to have thought of everything. Today their strength was supreme, but it would not last. The beauty of the situation was that he would use their strength today and their weakness tomorrow. They had even got rid of Steiner for him.

Twenty-four

Steiner stared, unseeing, out of the car window. He had badly underestimated Hillard and her group. First he had thought he was dealing with a bunch of malcontents who merely published treasonable rubbish, and then he had realized they planned to kill the president. Now he had discovered they had kidnapped the ministers. A cold anger gripped him. What did they hope to achieve? Did they really think they could get away with it? His fingers tapped impatiently and he quickly stilled the movement. He had sent Hillard ahead when he had received the message at the palace. She would be waiting for him at headquarters. He would find out where the ministers were being held and have all the women concerned in custody in a matter of hours. He would have to break her quickly. There would be plenty of time for the slow, permanent process after he had sorted out this whole affair and had Blake accepted as Gorston's successor. This was not the time for finesse.

Erling was on his feet, waiting for him in the outer office. 'She's in the main detention room, sir. Do you want her up here?'

'No. Take her to an interrogation cell and send Steadman there. Tell him not to start until I arrive.' He walked through into the bare, familiar office and sat at the desk, pulling a sheet of paper from his briefcase and opening it slowly as if to relish again the reading. It was there—with Gorston's signature. Blake would be the next president and would be all the more amenable to his control after he had rescued him today. Steiner's fingers made a slight, unconscious gesture of distaste. The fool. He could imagine him, terrified of the Grey Ones who held him captive. The man was frightened of everything. He locked the document away in the desk and walked to the lift. Speed was of the essence now. Blake had to be presented to the people as Gorston's successor within the next few hours.

The harsh light was reflected back from the white tiles that covered the walls and floor, and in the featureless room she seemed a small, insignificant figure. Steiner looked through the concealed observation window, noting the hands that lay at rest on her lap, the passivity of her pose, and wondered again how she had found the initiative and strength to lead the women into their mad acts.

'Have you spoken to her, yet?' he said to Steadman, standing at his side.

'No. I just let her sweat a bit.' Steadman towered over the precise figure of Steiner, large and muscular. 'How do you want it done?'

Steiner accepted his casual manner. Steadman was his best interrogator, with the skill and precision of a programmed machine. 'Quickly. I need the information within the next half-hour. And it's got to be the right information. I don't want her stalling for time.' He pressed a button on the console in front of him. 'Hillard.' His voice was cool and emotionless as it sounded, disembodied, around the small, antiseptic cell of light. 'We haven't time for our talk, now. It will have to wait until later. All I want to know from you is where the ministers are.' She had given no sign of hearing him, but he continued smoothly. 'You may think you can keep silent, but believe me, you won't. In a short time you will be begging me to listen to all the information you have about your little group. But I've no time for that now. I just want to know where the ministers are.'

He nodded briefly to Steadman and watched closely as the man quietly entered the small cell through a door directly behind the silent figure. He pressed the intercom button again. 'Look up, Hillard. I want to see your face.' She obediently lifted her face and he could see her eyes searching for him. But they were still blank. He could see no traces of emotion, no fear, no clue as to the personality that lay behind them. He watched as Steadman walked silently up to her and saw a brief flash of something in the grey eyes as the large man gripped her by the shoulders and whispered in her ear. She tried to turn and face him as he suddenly lifted her bodily from the chair and slammed her against the wall in a vicious, silent explosion of violence. His hands kept her upright as the impact with the wall forced the breath out of her body. Steadman's bulk almost hid her completely from view but Steiner could see one of the large hands move across behind her neck and the grey hair, loosed from its restraining knot, tumbling around her shoulders. He could see the small scalpel suddenly appear in the brown, muscular hand as it moved slowly, gently, down one of her arms, almost like a lover's caress, and the grey material parted and gaped to reveal the thin red line that quickly thickened into an urgent stream. Steadman stepped back from her and Steiner could see her, standing pressed against the wall, fingers stretched wide on the cold tiles, as the grey eyes followed Steadman and the red drops chased themselves from her fingers. Her face was a white mask and the fear was open, clamouring for expression in the watchful eyes. Steadman stepped towards her again and she suddenly broke her stillness, twisting underneath his grasp and running to the chair in the centre of the small room. Steiner watched the silent, macabre dance. Her defences were breaking. She was trying to fight back with the desperation of a trapped animal. He did not expect her to break immediately. He would have been suspicious of it if she did. Steadman moved casually towards her, dominating her with his bulk, easily stopping the arc of the chair as she swung it at him, plucking it from her grasp with one hand as he grabbed the long, loose hair with the other. Steiner heard the soft whisper as Steadman pulled her head close to his mouth before pushing her back into the chair with one easy movement.

Abruptly the fight went out of her body, as if in acceptance of its futility, and she sat, passive and still, as Steadman took the bloodied arm, stretching it out in a curiously gentle motion. The wound was clearly visible, running from just above the elbow, down the inside of the arm, to end at the wrist, red tributaries spreading out from the main stream. Her breath was coming in short, hard gasps as the grey eyes watched, fascinated, hypnotized, by the sight of the shining, slender scalpel coming down into the cut. The first scream came, short, bitten-off, harsh, as the probing blade buried its tip in red flesh above the elbow and her head jerked away, eyes tightly closed, as if to shut out the horror and pain. Steiner pushed the intercom button. 'Save yourself more pain, Hillard. Tell me. Where are the ministers?' He saw the grey eyes open wide at the sound of his voice.

'Hillard.' He barely caught the word, uncertain if he had heard correctly. Why should she repeat her own name?

The knife descended again with slow precision and her whole body jerked and strained away from the bloody arm as she tried to bite back the scream that eventually found voice as the probing point went deeper. Steiner waited for a few seconds, watching the small grey figure shuddering uncontrollably. Then he said, 'Hillard, Steadman is an artist. He knows exactly where to place that knife to give you the most pain. Come, why stand any more—tell me now. Where are the ministers?' He glanced at the clock set high on the cell wall. Steadman had only taken ten minutes and she was near to breaking. His voice sounded again around the white cell, bouncing off the shining walls. 'Look up, Hillard. High on the wall in front of you.' He saw, with satisfaction, the obedient lifting of the head. 'The clock, Hillard. Watch it. Every thirty seconds, that knife will probe into your arm, finding a nerve that sends screaming pain up to your brain. Watch the clock, Hillard. And then tell me where the ministers are.' He reached up and switched off the loudspeaker that enabled him to hear the sounds from the cell. Her eyes were fixed, with an awful concentration, on the clock. Her anticipation of the pain would break her more quickly than the pain itself and he found little enjoyment in the harsh screams that grated on his ears. He intensely disliked these crude sessions.

Steiner shifted his position slightly to get a better view of her face. He had not had time to study her since the arrest earlier that morning. She must be about thirty. One of the first to be fully processed. It would be interesting to find out how she had managed to resist the brainwashing. He looked into the grey eyes, clouded with pain, and thought back to his first meeting with her, when she had come to his office with that Nesbitt fellow. He had thought at the time that her eyes were quite remarkable;

very large and almost a translucent grey. What went on behind that blankness? She had been clever—feeding him clues that she knew he would look for. But she had underestimated him with that ploy of breaking the lock on the side door of the People's Hall. It was what had finally told him that it would be Hillard waiting in the long gallery. He had assumed that she was some- one who did not know the building, had no access to it, but when the old woman had told him about the newspaper headline, he had gone back over his reasoning, as he always did. Suddenly the dead leaves in the gallery held a new significance and he had to consider the possibility that the broken lock was a distraction. If it was, it could only mean that the woman had access to a key of the replacement lock. A check on all possible women with such access threw up only three names and as he had looked at the short list he had felt sure he would meet Hillard in the gallery.

Steiner always felt a deep satisfaction at the end of an investi- gation—and this one would be over in a matter of minutes. He glanced back at the clock and felt a shock of surprise. He had been lost in his thoughts for nearly ten minutes. Surely, she couldn't have—. He looked back at the silent scene as he reached up and switched on the loudspeaker. It was as if the last quarter of an hour had not existed and he checked the clock again to confirm the time. Her eyes were still fixed on the slowly moving hands, her hair clung damply to her face that was a white mask of pain. Why hadn't she broken? She was much stronger than he had expected. He turned the volume up high in time to hear Stead- man's quiet voice calmly counting out the seconds. 'Twenty- seven, twenty-eight—'

Her body suddenly went rigid and her head jerked around to stare into Steadman's face as a small uncontrolled moan cut across the relentless counting. Steiner watched. This was it. She was breaking. 'No, no. No more!'

The words were barely audible and he leaned forward to speak into the intercom. 'Hillard, where are the ministers?'

Steadman twisted her head so that she was facing the unseen Steiner and he could see the pale lips beginning to form the words, the eyes tightly shut.

'I can't hear you, Hillard,' he said.

'The town hall.' The voice was weak, defeated and Steiner felt a surge of triumph. She was finished. He had broken her.

'The town hall is a large complex. Where in the town hall?' he persisted.

She shook her head slightly and her free hand made vague, uncertain gestures in the air. 'I don't know.' She cringed back as Steadman laid the blade of the knife on her arm in silent warning and the soft words tumbled out. 'I don't know the buildings. I've only been there once—at night. I—I could take you there—but I don't know how to describe it.'

That would be even better. It would be fitting for the women to see their leader's act of betrayal. 'How many women are there?' Steiner asked.

'Two.' Her head would have slumped on to her chest but for the firm, restraining hand of Steadman under her chin.

'Two?' Steiner was incredulous. 'Two women to kidnap nine ministers?'

'Yes.' The information tumbled out of her in her haste. 'They have got guns but no ammunition. The ministers think they're armed!'

A bluff. Those idiot ministers—terrified of two Grey Ones—with not enough courage to challenge the threat of empty guns. The women's actions had no substance—all bluff. He would find out later what they hoped to achieve. He spoke into the intercom again. 'Steadman, get her cleaned up and bring her to reception in ten minutes. You've done a good job.' He pressed the button on the phone. 'Erling, I want my car and three others at the front in ten minutes.'

'Yes, sir,' came the answering voice. 'And do you want any extra men?'

Steiner glanced back at the small broken figure and thought of the other two women armed with their useless guns. He was confident again that none of them could ever break completely out of his control. 'No, Erling. Four men are quite sufficient!'

Twenty-five

The small cavalcade of cars moved discreetly through the crowds lining the roads that led to the People's Hall. They were still waiting for Gorston's appearance although Steiner could see signs of impatience in the restless movements and sensed the doubts in the ever-moving heads. He could get the ministers back to the hall in fifteen minutes and the announcement of Gorston's death and his dying nomination of Blake as his successor could be made from the ornate dais. Steiner had already made the arrangements for Blake's speech of acceptance to be written and delivered directly to the hall. His mind threw up the small, rotund figure of Blake, face ashen with fear from his recent ordeal, stumbling through the words. The performance would go down well with the crowd, who would attribute his emotion to grief over the beloved leader's death.

Steiner turned from the sight of the milling people to look intently at the white face next to him in the car. They had cleaned her up quite efficiently and the grey hair was again pulled back into its tight knot. She was staring straight ahead, no trace of the recent emotion showing on her face. The only evidence of her ordeal was the whiteness of the face and one hand carefully concealed in the pocket of her shapeless coat. Why had she started on this mad trail? She had achieved an amazing amount for a woman, but did she really believe she could have succeeded in her madness? He would start tomorrow, probing behind the blankness, discovering her aims and ambitions.

Unexpectedly and slowly, she turned her head and looked directly into his face for the first time, and he felt a shock as he met the calm gaze. The eyes disturbed him. They showed no memory of pain, or shock, or guilt at betraying her friends. They looked at him with the blankness of dead eyes, but he felt she was reading his mind. He broke the encounter with an abrupt turn of his head.

The car climbed the steep hill that led to the complex of the town hall. It was a good place to choose for holding the ministers, Steiner acknowledged, as they turned between the large stone pillars and drove into the huge cobbled courtyard. They were the only sign of life in the enclosed space and as the cars cut their engines a stillness brooded around them. Steiner got out of the car, giving low, curt orders to the four men gathered around him, before moving back and opening the car door with an exaggerated gesture of courtesy for Hillard to get out. In a few moments he would have the women and he could watch as they saw Hillard betray them.

She stood beside him, pale and silent, dwarfed by the men around her. 'Right, Hillard, lead the way,' he instructed. 'And don't try to shout a warning—it would only mean the women would get killed.' His feeling of triumph increased as she turned submissively, walking towards the far corner of the courtyard, leading them to a narrow passageway that skirted the main buildings and took them to the old, original buildings of the local government complex. She quietly opened the side door, flanked by refuse bins, and stepped into a long, narrow corridor. He stopped her with a touch of his hand and he felt a slight cringing in her at that touch. 'How far?' he asked.

She did not look at him, her eyes fixed straight ahead, her shoulders slumped, defeated. 'It's up a few floors and along some corridors. I can remember the way.' Her voice was dead, matching her eyes. She led the small procession of men along the echoing passage, moving surely up the flights of concrete steps, one hand still deep in her coat pocket as she carefully avoided brushing the walls with that arm. She stopped at the top of the second flight and stood facing down the long corridor—a replica of the previous two—and pointed towards a small archway. 'Through there. I think it's the third door down.'

Steiner nodded silently to the alert men and they quietly drew their revolvers. 'You won't need to use them,' he told them. 'She says the women's guns are useless and I'm inclined to believe her. If you do use them, make sure you don't kill the women. I want them alive.' He drew a small, neat Colt from his pocket and quietly slipped the safety catch before turning towards Hillard. 'You lead us quietly and make sure it's the right room.' She looked directly at him again and he saw the emptiness in those discon-certing eyes. She would not give them any trouble. All fight had gone from her in the small white cell.

'There are two rooms,' she said, her voice lifeless. 'One leads off from the other. They are in the inner room.'

He stepped back from her and she walked slowly down the corridor, turning under the archway and stopping outside a heavy, polished door. He listened as the men froze into stillness. There was no sound as he gestured to one of them to open the door. The silence of the building pressed in around them. The handle turned smoothly and the heavy door swung silently back as two of the men crowded noiselessly into the doorway. The room was empty. He turned to Hillard who pointed silently at the door opposite them before walking quickly across the room, throwing the door wide to give an instant glimpse of male figures as Steiner and his men raced across the room to catch up with her. She walked to the centre of the room and turned to face him as he came through the door, closely followed by his armed men. He faced the dark, lethal shape of a Stengun aimed directly at him by the woman at Hillard's side. His mind raced, throwing up images of Hillard in the glare of the lights, blood streaming from her arm and the broken, defeated voice telling him the women had no ammunition. He took a step towards them.

'No, Steiner. No further,' she commanded.

A shock ran through him at the sound of quiet authority in her voice and he glanced quickly back at his men behind him. It was a trap! His men stood, arms raised, looking with absolute disbelief at the half-dozen armed women who had come up behind them.

'Fools!' he shouted. 'There are no bullets in those guns!' The men still hesitated and he turned back to face Hillard, slowly rais-ing his pistol until it aimed directly at her. 'Do I have to shoot you to prove to my men your guns are useless?'

Two more women appeared at her side and she took a small step forward, isolating herself, challenging him. 'What makes you think they're useless?' she asked. Her eyes mocked him. 'Remember I also told you there were only two women here. If you care to count, there are twelve. I'm afraid if you pull that trigger, you'll never know if you hit me or not. Eli here has dreamed about killing you for years.'

Steiner's eyes went back to the big woman at her side and he recognized the easy familiarity in the way she held the gun. He looked at her hands, steady, cool, and the finger crooked around the trigger. He looked into her eyes, searching for fear or uncertainty, but all he saw was hatred.

'Steiner, don't start anything, please!' Blake's voice shrilled across the room. 'They mean it, Steiner. These other women only got here a short time ago and I heard them talking. That one with the Sten was talking about killing you! You'll get us all killed!' His voice climbed with rising hysteria.

A stillness seemed to settle on the room as he looked back into Hillard's face. He could see no trace of the broken Grey One who had led him to this room. The blankness had gone from her features and there was a subtle change in the way she held herself. She was not the same person. He looked into the grey eyes and she held his gaze, challenging him. There was no fear there, only a deep strength. And suddenly Steiner felt fear. He broke the contact with her and heard her voice, crisp, assertive.

'Take his gun, Eli.'

His mind refused to function properly as he allowed the gun to be taken from his hand. She had tricked him completely. Not only had she lied about the number of women and the ammunition, she had lied about her very being.

'That's right, Steiner.' It was as if she read his thoughts. She stepped close to him, holding him with those dominating eyes. 'It's finished.' Her voice was low, but he could not break away from those eyes. 'You couldn't win, Steiner, because you didn't know your enemy. You could only see anonymous, repressed beings that you called "women workers", with no initiative, no intelligence, no reasoning. But the only place they existed, Steiner, was in your head. And in every man's head. They had no reality. So you wasted your time and effort fighting your own images and you never once saw your real adversary. That is why they will agree to all our demands.' She gestured towards the silent men around the table who sat watching, listening intently, varying degrees of confusion and fear on their faces. 'They can't resist our demands because their images have been taken away from them and they can't cope with the replacements.' Her voice was hard, full of bitter contempt.

He tried to shake off the unreality. 'But you can't get away with this. My men will miss me shortly. Erling knows I'm here. There's only a handful of you. You can't take on the whole state.' He could hear his own voice, disjointed, confused.

'Don't try, Steiner.' The small, grey figure dominated the room, holding every eye; and again it was as if she could read his thoughts. 'You're still fighting *your* reality. But that's no good. *Your* reality doesn't exist. The women aren't what you've always thought them to be. And we're not just a handful. We are half the adult population. We have already proven to them—' her eyes flickered over the group of seated men '—that we can bring the whole economy to a standstill. We can stop all telephone communications, take over radio and television, bring seventy-five per cent of all businesses to a standstill. We can close the banks, stop all government departments from functioning, prevent any shops opening.' She smiled at him, an assured smile. 'We are the army that propped up your society without you even realizing it. It took us a long time to realize it ourselves because we believed your brainwashing. But that has now ended—along with Gorston and yourself.' She turned from him abruptly, looking across to one of the women at the table. 'What time is it, Joan?'

'Nearly noon.'

'I assume they know their position?' She did not even glance at the men she was referring to.

'Yes, they've accepted it. We are discussing the details of the proposals.'

She put her hand briefly on the big woman's arm. 'I'm glad you're quick on the uptake.' She grinned at her. 'I know Mary didn't know what I was talking about.' He could see the easy familiarity between them as the taller woman grinned back. 'What? After all the fights you and I have had about the "male solution"?' She suddenly became serious. 'I knew what you wanted me to do. I just couldn't work out how you'd get him here. Mary was convinced you were on your way to a torture chamber. We were giving you ten more minutes and then we were launching a raid on headquarters.'

'Eli, you idiot, you'd have ruined everything!' The tone was affectionate. The other women had joined them, concerned, anxious about Hillard. At least he had been right in one thing: she was the leader of the women. It showed in their attitudes and words. But leadership sat easily on her. He could see how she had brought the women to this day.

She broke from their concern, calm and reassuring. 'Come on—we've still got a lot of work to do. We have three hours to finalize our discussions.'

Steiner watched, fascinated, as she unconsciously took the seat at the head of the table. There was no trace of the Grey One he had studied, tracked and finally tortured. Hillard had taken over the discussions with easy authority and her words washed over him as he stood forgotten and ignored. He looked at the ministers. Even Blake, pale and nervous, had carefully avoided his eye since his outburst and was now nodding vehemently and pathetically in agreement with her words. He looked back at the woman called Eli, still holding the Sten but now nonchalant, relaxed, the weapon held casually in her hands, and realized she was the only one in the room looking at him, and she was mocking him. He could see it in her eyes. She stepped towards him, gesturing to the door.

'Come on—I'd better lock you up with the others.' She waited for him as he looked back at Hillard again before turning and walking through the door. In silence he retraced his steps of a short time ago. He still could not accept what had happened. He glanced at the woman by his side. She was dressed in grey and had grey hair, but there was no resemblance to the familiar Grey Ones he had created and fashioned over the years. A quiet chuckle startled him as she stopped, hand on the knob of a door. 'Sarah was right,' she said.

'Sarah?'

The amusement still sounded in her voice. 'You know her as Hillard. She always said violence was the male solution to a problem and they were expert at it. She said we'd be mad to use the same weapons. The only way to win was to use weapons men had no experience of. And she was right!'

Sarah. Her name was Sarah. He saw again the scene in the

white cell, her hair clinging wetly to her face as she whispered her name. No, not her name: his name for her. He was beginning to understand what she had said about images. 'And what weapons did she say you should use?' he asked weakly.

'Why, ourselves—the unknown quantity!'

She was laughing openly. No one had ever laughed at him. He fought to regain something—anything—in this nightmare. He pointed to the gun in her hand as she opened the door and gestured for him to go in. 'You had to resort to violence in the end,' he said.

'Oh this?' She propped the Sten casually against the wall as she held the door open. 'It hasn't got any bullets. The only guns that work are the ones we took from you and your men.'

Twenty-six

Sarah walked down the steps of the presidential palace, past the guards standing rigidly to attention, and out into the peaceful park that surrounded the official home of the country's leader.

It was done.

Gorston's ministers had accepted their proposals, and the broadcast had gone out at three, releasing all the waiting women from the need for open revolt and the inevitable blood-bath. She had been surprised at Marsham's attitude as the negotiations continued after Steiner had left the room. She had not expected him actively to encourage the others to accept the women's proposals. The memory of the room came to her with a crystal clarity that is found in dreams, every trivial detail registering but only serving to highlight the important ones, as if the senses were stimulated to strange heights. She had sat silently, listening to Marsham's easy flow of words, watching his arguments sway the few men still prepared to force the bloodshed, and she had wondered why. Eventually, with her new assurance, she had asked him. Asked him why, if he agreed with the women's demands and believed them to be just and reasonable, he had been content to serve Gorston without demur. And she had watched his reply, her ears accepting his words while she noted his gestures, his attitudes. And she remembered Stephanie telling her of the unrest among the men, and knew Marsham was responsible. He was using the women, seeing their strength as a temporary thing, an expedient to fulfil his own plans, a desperation, coalescing into a moment of power but without any stability. For a moment she had been afraid. Today had destroyed Gorston and his false images of women, and they had planned to replace him with Marsham until the free elections could be held. But Marsham had his own images—less extreme, far more subtle and consequently more dangerous. Subtle denigration could be gratefully accepted or even unnoticed after the deluge of Gorston's regime. She had listened in silence to Marsham's smooth words and glib compliments that, unknown to him, painted the picture of women he carried in his mind and then she had watched his eyes as she had leant forward and told them the name of the man that the women insisted would succeed Gorston. Blake. In that moment of contact, Marsham knew her, seeing her without the filters of his own images, and he accepted the unspoken challenge. She had checked his plans but his confidence was great. His conditioning told him the women would not stay united, that their strength was temporary, and Sarah knew the long, tedious struggle ahead would need an even greater strength than what had gone before.

She could see the lights of the city, springing pale into the half-light of the summer evening as she walked through the coolness of the trees, dim shapes of deer blending with the shadows as they grazed peacefully, undisturbed. Joan, Eli and the others would now be gathering at Stephanie's, preparing to talk the night away with their plans and their ideas, to go over again the events of the day. She had promised to join them, but first she needed to be alone; to absorb the changes in society today had brought, the changes in herself. She passed through the gates of the park and turned on to the road that ran along the river, past the law courts that had dealt out so much injustice over the years. It was all so normal, with no outward sign of what had been achieved today. Only the flags flying at half-mast and the dull, throbbing ache in her arm confirmed what had happened. Strange, she had not noticed the pain throughout the negotiations at the town hall, and through the long hours of discussions at the presidential palace that had followed. The new cabinet was formed—still all male, still safely acceptable to the people. But behind each minister there was now a team of women, implementing changes, removing injustices, re-structuring the educational system. In a year's time there would be a general election—the first for over thirty years. She had assumed that a few women would be elected, if only by other women, but now she knew the danger period for all their hopes was in this next twelve months. She had to hold the women together, make them see any new moulds that were being forced onto them, make them retain their sense of identity that they had struggled so long to find. If the women were strong, gradually, over the years, the imaginary barriers would disappear as the people learnt that primarily they were human beings, and that femaleness and maleness were the ingredients that brought the balance, comprised the whole.

She stopped on the wide, busy bridge, looking towards the vastness of the People's Hall dominating the city centre sky-line, then she turned to walk steadily towards it. So much of her was in that bleak mausoleum.

The posters and banners had gone. Only the flags remained, hanging lifeless, half-way down the poles. The large doors stood open, the contractors' van standing at the foot of the steps, the workmen dismantling the unused dais. She slipped quietly inside the vast hall and waited, curious, not knowing what emotions would fill her as she looked again at the soaring pillars and the distant, indistinct gallery. Sadness. Why sadness? It welled up inside her and broke out and engulfed her. A small sadness for such an awesome place. A private, inner sadness. She remembered the day she had stood here and feared; the day she had first seen Carl's paintings. She had heard what had happened at the men's detention centre, how he had been hurt and then had successfully bluffed the authorities until the announcement was made at three. But then he had left. The women did not know where he was. She realized, suddenly, she would have liked to share a moment of this day with him.

She walked across the wide floor, stepping over the tangle of dismantled microphone and loud-speaker cables, through to the inner hall. It was too dark. The weakening evening light could not show her the pictures of life that had helped her overcome her own weakness. She walked up to the wall, touching it gently, remembering the sweep of mountain and the wind bending the supple trees.

'I hoped you'd come here, eventually.'

He was standing beside her, the whiteness of the plaster on his forehead showing clearly in the dim light. 'I spent all afternoon trying to find you, trying to find out if you were still alive.' She could hear the tension and tiredness in his voice. 'I went up to your first-aid post and the woman there didn't have any news of you. Eventually she told me that you planned to move negotiations to the palace. The bloody idiots wouldn't let me in. Nobody seemed to know what was happening. So I came here. I thought—' His voice was suddenly hesitant. 'I thought, if you were all right, you might come too.'

She hardly registered his words as relief swept over her. He really was unhurt. She had not been able to accept fully the women's assurances that his injuries were not serious and now she just stood and stared at him, no words forming from the relief.

'Hillard, you are all right, aren't you?' he asked. 'I heard one rumour that Steiner had captured you.'

Her hand went instinctively to her arm. 'Yes,' she said finally. 'I'm all right. And Steiner is dead.'

'Steiner?'

'He killed himself.'

She remembered her feelings as Eli had come up to her as they were leaving the town hall, leading her away from the ministers, telling her he was dead. He was as neat and precise in death as he had been in life. She could not even recognize death in him as she looked at the still figure sitting in the chair and she had turned to Eli, disbelieving. 'Yes, he is, with that.' Her eyes had followed Eli's finger, pointing to the long, thin wire spike lying on the carpet, a few inches away from his dangling hand. Eli had shrugged wryly at her. 'He was an expert. He knew about such things. One of his men saw him at the last moment and tried to pull it away from him, but it was too late.'

She shook off the memories. She should have known that death would have been his solution.

'Hillard,' Carl broke in, 'let's get out of here. It's too dark. Besides, we'll be locked in if we stay much longer.'

She laughed softly and saw the surprise in him as he turned back to look at her. 'That wouldn't matter,' she explained. 'I've still got a key.'

She walked ahead of him, through the echoing halls and down the steps to the emptying pavements, turning to watch as he followed. His face was haggard and she saw the limp as he came down the steps. She stood still as he stepped close to her, searching her face.

'You did it,' he said.

A small flicker of fear and uncertainty came back for an instant and she pushed it firmly aside. 'Yes, but it's only the beginning. Today was the drama—the clap of thunder before the steady downpour.' She turned and started to walk up the street of deserted shops, towards the Green, back to the hostel, and he matched his steps to hers. 'Today, we had to destroy. Tomorrow, we start building.'

'And, you?' he asked. 'I suppose you go back to your planning, your endless, logical, careful planning.'

He was gently mocking her, but he was right. The quiet peace of the countryside with the flowers and birds could not be hers for a long time—not until after the struggle with Marsham, and all who thought like him.

She stopped suddenly as they walked down one side of the Green and stepped into the empty road. 'A woman died here,' she said. 'No, not by Steiner's men—just a road accident. She was killed by a car.' Sarah stood looking at the grey patch of road as if searching for some lasting trace of the small, personal tragedy. 'She was an old woman, one of us—she was always frightened—terrified of being caught. But her need to reclaim herself was even greater than her fear.' She stepped back on to the pavement and continued walking towards the hostel. 'Today, we only created the potential for freedom. Freedom itself is a longer struggle.'

'For men as well as women.'

She turned to face him, surprised at his words until she thought again of his murals in the People's Hall. 'I should have realized that you saw that as well,' she said.

They stopped on the bleak expanse of concrete that surrounded the hostel and she looked in surprise at the lights shining in every window and the sounds of talk and laughter and music. She turned to face him and her eyes had the familiar blankness that she used as her defence to hide the uncertainty in her. She could see the confusion in him as he tried to read her face.

'There you are. We've been waiting for you. Are you sure you're all right? I couldn't really believe the others when they said you were.' Stephanie had appeared behind her, giving full rein to her motherly feelings, bubbling over with happiness and concern. 'You look very pale,' she chatted on. 'I'm sure you're not all right. Come on up—food is ready. And I've got that present for you—remember, I promised it would be ready for the day of the Rising.'

Sarah threw up her hands in mock defence against the torrent of words and then leant forward impulsively to hug the smiling women. Dear Steph, she had already taken what today had given her—without hesitation and without fear.

'Steph,' Sarah said, 'this is Carl—'

'I know. We met at the first aid post.' She included him in her smile.

Sarah still hesitated for a moment, then made her decision. 'I was just going to ask him if he'd like to join us for a meal.' She laughed openly at the expressions that chased themselves across his face. 'I'd better introduce us. This is Stephanie and—' she held her hand out in the formal gesture of greeting '—I'm Sarah.'